The Will to Die

Joe Pulizzi

Published by Z Squared Media, 2020.

Z Squared Media, LLC
17040 Amber Drive, Suite 42
Cleveland, OH 44111

First edition March 2020
Published in the United States by Z Squared Media, LLC, Cleveland, Ohio.

For information on bringing the author to your next event, go to JoePulizzi.com/speaking. For discounts on bulk orders or information on special editions, send an email to info@zsquaredmedia.com.

ISBN (paperback): 978-0-9859576-7-4
ISBN (hard cover): 978-0-9859576-9-8
ISBN (ebook): 978-0-9859576-8-1
ISBN (audiobook): 978-0-9859576-6-7
Book cover and jacket design by Joseph Kalinowski. Web design by Michelle Martello.
02 03 04 05 06 08 09 10 12 14 20 24 26 42

For Pam

Prologue

Everything seemed to be in place. The desk was to Abe's right. How many meetings had he taken behind that old mahogany desk? Must have been thousands. He could see the legs of his desk chair and scanned down to the wheels that clung to the plastic roller mat, which was in dire need of replacement. The cracks in the mat were visible. It now made sense to Abe why the desk chair didn't glide from side to side the way it once did.

The lower half of the office door was open a crack, with the light from an exit sign shining in from the outside. That seemed normal. It was late. He was the only living person at the funeral home at this hour. The lone sound was a passing car every ten seconds or so driving on the main street, probably a few feet away from the adequately lit Pollitt Funeral Home sign.

Abe could see the lower pane of the office window and then looked down to where the drapes came in contact with the ground. He was in shock of how filthy the bottoms of the drapes were.

Abe shifted his eyes to his left and noticed a congregation of dust bunnies underneath the coffee table. He realized he'd never once in forty years looked under that table. He tried to sweep the dust particles away with his left hand, but nothing happened.

That's odd. Then he tried to blow them away, but he couldn't turn his head to make it happen. It was then Abe realized he was lying on the floor. How did he get here? He thought he knew but couldn't remember. He tried to turn over to push himself off the ground. Nothing happened.

Abe moved his eyes downward. Just above his chest he could see the tops of his shoes. Next to his right foot was his favorite coffee cup, but it was missing its handle. He could not remember the last time he used another cup while at the funeral home. He noticed some liquid forming a small pool next to the broken cup. His coffee?

He glanced left and then right. His arms were there, but he couldn't feel them. Abe recalled the many times his arms had fallen asleep during the middle of the night. It was a persistent problem for years, which became steadily worse after his wife died. There would be tingling and some pain, then full feeling would come back to his arms in minutes. This time, there was no tingling. His arms and feet were clearly attached, but they didn't belong to him.

He felt something. Like a current from inside his hands and arms, and from his feet and legs, flowing toward his chest. Thumping now. The beating was so loud he tried to cover his ears ... but he couldn't. Abe was blinking fast, but the picture went blurry. Water in his eyes? Water ... and stinging ... like sweat.

Then the current inside his body stopped, like someone turning off a switch. And the light in the room. It was going dim, then bright, as if God opened the morning shades. Too bright. Abe looked to the ceiling, staring and squinting at the small black dot above him, his last thought wondering if he did...enough.

Chapter 1 – The Proposal

B esides intermittent periods of sleep and steady drinking, the PopC account consumed my life for the past three weeks.

The proposal request was printed in bold, underlined and highlighted.

To: Will Pollitt, PT Marketing

Goal: PopC is seeking to become the leading worldwide beverage snack of choice for Generation Z. We are looking for a visionary campaign and a new marketing agency to match this mission.

I had to look up what exactly Generation Z was. I was just getting a handle on those pesky millennials. But Generation Z? What were they, like five to seven years old?

It turns out that Gen Z were those born between the mid-1990s and early 2010s, which means they have the buying power of a gnat. That said, they still make up about twenty-five percent of the US population. God help us all.

PopC, coming off a very successful initial stock offering that valued their beverage group at approximately four billion US dollars, had a new line of ingestible frozen liquids to market that tasted like variations of cotton candy. After beta testing in six cities, they were ready for the North American rollout.

As part of our marketing agency's pitch for PopC, my partner Robby and I took a drive out to Target and bought every variety they had—thirteen at that store. We found the other seven PopC flavors at GameStop, which apparently now sells sugary drinks and snacks to its teen gamers.

I tried six for myself, from blood orange passionfruit to strawberry orchid to fudge blister. They all pretty much tasted like those plastic popsicles that came in the forty-eight-pack rolls my mom bought back in the day at Pick-N-Pay. PopC's innovation was packaging the popsicles in six-pack cartons and including caffeine, which is important for the addiction process to take hold in the kiddos.

Although we never discussed it, the reason we received the call to participate is because Robby is half-black. Minority-owned business and all. When we launched the business together just over a decade ago, I wanted to lean into the minority-owned angle. My initial logo pitch was a clear rip-off of the *Soul Train* logo, and the business cards were jet-black. I even pushed Robby to purchase Don Cornelius bubble glasses.

I closed my laptop and headed out the door, turning around to take a good look at the PT Marketing sign above the window. Our cramped office sits between countless bars and restaurants in an area of Cleveland called West Park. Just down the street was Vito's, our favorite watering hole.

I took a left inside the bar, rubbing my hands for warmth as I entered. Even though it was May, spring hadn't yet come to northeast Ohio, and we were still getting hit with cool, Canadian winds.

The happy hour crowd was just arriving, and the air was thick with the smell of burnt chicken and French fry grease. I spotted Robby in our normal seat at the back right, a booth that rested against the original 1981 Namco version of Galaga. Since we liked to commandeer the arcade game during marketing brainstorming sessions, it was the perfect location to ward off incoming gamers.

Robby nodded as I slid into the booth. I pulled out an oatmeal cream pie from the inside of my jacket pocket and placed it on top of his yellow notepad. "Happy birthday, Thompson," I said.

Robby sighed and pushed the cream pie to the side. "Screw you, Pollitt." Although I could never remember Robby's real birthday, I never forgot May 10th. Growing up a diehard baseball fan, the other Robby Thompson was a serviceable second baseman for the San Francisco Giants during the '80s and '90s. In memorizing most of the statistics off the backs of my old baseball card collection, I knew that Robby Thompson was born on this date in 1962.

"You're looking pretty good for almost sixty," I said as I waved to Dell behind the bar for my usual, a shot of Tito's and a Tito's and tonic with lime. Tito's advertising says it doesn't give you a hangover, and although I generally woke up with a splitting headache, I kept trying nonetheless.

"Do you know anything besides useless information? You know, there's a Robbie Thompson that's a fairly well-known television writer, but you always opt for sports." Robby wiped the look of disgust off his face, ready to get down to business.

"So what's bothering you about tomorrow's pitch?" I asked. It wasn't rare for us to catch a drink at Vito's the day before a pitch, or any day for that matter, but Robby never brought his yellow notepad to mix with his bourbon.

"I've been reviewing the PopC marketing team through LinkedIn, Indeed, and a few other sites. The CMO is pretty traditional. Comes from Coca-Cola, but before they really immersed in social media. The VP of marketing cut her teeth at P&G in Cincinnati. From what I could find, she has a deep love affair with thirty-second TV spots." Robby shifted in his seat and took a drink. He set the drink down and looked at me, as serious as I've ever seen him. "I don't think they're going to go for our approach." He paused. "Why don't we shift thirty percent more budget to paid advertising and take a little risk off the table?"

Knowing the other four marketing agencies involved, their modus operandi was a collection of television ads, point-of-purchase displays, social media ads, and partnering with a YouTube influencer or two. If they felt frisky, they'd throw in Instagram. A predictable plan from older white men who, over their careers, have had the life sucked out of them through a wicked one-two punch of trying to meet the needs of their investors combined with the stress of hiding their own extramarital affairs. Mix in a little pot and a lot of alcohol, and voilà, one gut-wrenching marketing plan is born.

Dell, Vito's sole bartender, brought over my drinks. I took the shot, downed it, and then squeezed the lime into my Tito's and tonic. The pulp from the lime clung to the side of the glass. I cleared my throat and leaned in close to Robby. "I know part of us thinks we're in this because you're black, but the real reason is because we're the best at what we do. What we deliver is pure ... well, as pure as marketing can be. Do you think their Gen Z target wants to see more cheesy ads? The only reason our competition continues to push ads is because they can't market their way out of a paper bag. They've completely lost touch with today's consumer. So, no, I don't think we should alter our presentation tomorrow."

Robby sat back, as if contemplating his next move. He held two fingers up to get Dell's attention and waved them back and forth between the two of us. "Will, I think our work is done here," Robby said.

Without another word, we headed over to the machine behind the booth. I threw in two quarters, and Robby hit the two-player button.

IT WASN'T QUITE TEN p.m. when we left Vito's. I turned down the ride from Robby and walked the five blocks back to my West Park apartment. It was still chilly, but the wind lost its motivation and the walk was bearable.

The moon grinned at me as I pulled my phone out. Realizing the night was still young for a college student on a Thursday night, I texted my daughter.

Hey, Jess. What's the weather like in Happy Valley? After two years at Cuyahoga Community College in Cleveland, Jessica was accepted last fall into the Media and Journalism program at Penn State University. I helped her move in August but hadn't seen much of her since. I tried to text her every day. Simply put, she was my favorite person.

It took five seconds, and I already saw the text dots that showed she was responding. *Hey, Dad. U on a date tonight ;)?*

I coughed out a laugh. Her levity in the wake of the divorce and financial issues was a blessing. *Why, yes, how did you know? Jennifer Aniston says hi.*

Seriously dad you need to start dating.

She was right of course. *Going out tonight?*

Nope. I'm splicing together a video for my Future of Media class. It's due Monday. Plus, guess what Netflix released today?

I started to respond but she continued texting. *Princess Bride*!

Inconceivable.

I know, right?

Princess Bride was one of those movies that Jess and I would stop everything and watch together. While her friends had posters of Timberlake and Bieber on their bedroom walls, my twelve-year-old had not one but two posters of Inigo Montoya.

That's my girl. Need any help on your project? I was secretly hoping she did so we could FaceTime and discuss it. I hoped to put off sleep as long as possible. Since the divorce, the nights moved like glaciers.

I got it, Dad. Thanks. Love you.

You too. I followed it with some cute heart emoji thing that showed up as a suggestion from my iPhone.

The street outside my apartment was eerily still. No cars, no people, which seemed odd since I was in eyeshot of two restaurants. I breathed in the night air, turned, and opened my apartment door. The amount of mail scattered on the floor was overwhelming. I looked down at the envelopes and made a quick count—eleven. Not a record by any means, but definitely in the top ten. I bent over and swept the pieces into a stack with my hands.

Already sick to my stomach, I made my way to the living room couch. Thankfully the first letter was a coupon mailer and my tension eased. The second was a solicitation for house cleaning. Maybe today was my lucky day.

The luck was short-lived. The next five letters were from five different credit card companies. The first two were minimum payment bills where I'd already maxed out the balance. I had signed up for these and took the cash advance options so I could pay Jess's first semester at Penn State. The next three bills were about a year old and amounted to more than forty thousand dollars. I had opened those accounts to cover my gambling debts. The next handful of envelopes were all debt consolidation companies where I barely had enough each month to make the minimum payment. All in all, I owed about five hundred thousand dollars to a couple dozen establishments.

The last envelope in the stack was the one I was dreading. It was stamped in red with *Third and Final Notice.* I tore through the top of the envelope and walked to the kitchen counter, under a better light. The page contained words from top to bottom, but it was only the highlighted section that mattered. *If you don't pay at least 50% of this semester's full invoice by the end of this month, Jessica will no longer have access to her classes, her dormitory, or any other student area at Penn State University.*

I rushed to the bathroom and flipped the toilet seat up just in time, giving back everything I'd consumed at Vito's.

Chapter 2 – The Meeting

Robby pulled out front at 8:25 a.m., plenty of time to make our 9:30 meeting with PopC. Making my way down the steps, I could already see the two cups of Starbucks in the cup holders of Robby's car.

Always on the lookout for a bargain, Robby had purchased his dark gray 2014 Ford Edge at a police auction just a few months back, replacing his last automobile purchase from Craigslist. Apparently, someone was using the car to run meth back and forth across the Canadian border. When I didn't believe Robby's little story, he showed me the custom concealed panel below the rear seats, which happened to be just wide enough to fit a proper suitcase.

"What did I do to deserve this?" I said as I closed the passenger door, looking at the coffee.

"Absolutely nothing, but since I'm your only friend, I felt sorry for you."

"When did we become friends?" I said, taking the lid off the coffee, letting it cool.

The PopC beverage center was located on the east side of downtown Cleveland, about five minutes beyond where the Indians and Cavaliers play. We sat in silence as Robby drove by the old PT Marketing office just down the street from Progressive Field. We were forced to make some tough decisions to keep the business afloat over the past two years, which included moving the office from downtown to West Park. This was mostly my doing.

Robby made a left, then a right onto Superior Avenue. A few years ago this section of Cleveland, called Midtown, was abandoned warehouses mixed in between strip clubs and a few fast-food joints. Today, thanks in part to PopC coming to Cleveland, the block was reborn. The strip clubs became microbreweries while the Rally's, Subway, and KFC became Chipotle, Panera Bread, and Starbucks. The transformation was pretty startling and happened incredibly fast for any midsized city, especially Cleveland.

We pulled in the entry gate to what looked like a Coca-Cola Freestyle machine, except it was branded PopC. Instead of drink choices, there were two other options:

Are you here to take the PopC experience tour?

Are you here to visit a PopC employee?

Robby selected the second option.

Someone who sounded just a bit too happy welcomed us and asked us who we were there to see. "Hi, ... we're with PT Marketing. We have a meeting with the PopC marketing team," Robby said.

After a five-second silence, a different woman, this one a bit more adult-sounding responded. "Yes, hello, Mr. Pollitt and Mr. Thompson. Just park in one of the visitor's spots on the left and go to the front desk in the lobby."

Robby drove away from the gate. I asked, "Do you think there are two women working the phones or was the first one a recording?"

"I don't know," Robby said as he turned left into the visitor parking area, "but I wouldn't mind meeting the first one."

"Maybe it was the same person with a personality disorder."

"That's perfect," Robby said gliding into the parking spot. "Sounds like your next potential date. I'll make it happen."

The PopC reception area was a collision of colors. Orange and pink walls, a grape floor and a lime-green ceiling. Plasma screens lined the entry-way into the main reception area and repeatedly showed a young kid morphing into a PopC popsicle, then into a different kid, and back again. As we approached the front desk, each panel of the floor appeared to glow with a footprint aftereffect when we lifted our feet from one tile to the next. The whole experience was Willy Wonka meets Elon Musk. The music playing in the background sounded like gumdrops or maybe the theme music to the Candy Land board game.

"Will Pollitt and Robby Thompson here to meet AJ Davis and Sarah Arnold," I said, approaching the reception desk.

The receptionist behind the desk looked thirty-five but was trying hard for twenty-five. The skirt was a little too short and the makeup a little too visible. She gazed up with a fake smile, "Yes. Take a seat, gentlemen. We'll be with you in a few minutes."

"Thanks," I said, and Robby and I turned around and headed for the seating area. I took the long way around on the right and Robby went around the couches to the left of the waiting area. We spent a few minutes trying to see how much of the floor we could light up at one time.

I sat down in the chair farthest away from the receptionist's desk, while Robby found the couch two feet away from one of the plasma panels. While the reception area was busy when we arrived, Robby and I were the last to remain after everyone else scampered to their nine-thirty meetings.

Robby asked, "Fresh odds this morning?"

"I think four-to-one. Maybe three-to-one. You?"

"Three-to-one sounds right to me. Either way, we go to the mattresses on this." In the wake of such an important meeting, Robby's levity was not only refreshing but necessary.

My phone rang. I pulled it out of my pocket and hesitated. "My sister. She never calls me."

"You need to take it?" Robby asked.

"I'll text her that I'm running into a meeting and will call her after. I can't remember the last time she called me instead of texting."

"Maybe she butt-dialed you."

I sent the text to my sister, flipped the setting to vibrate, and slid the iPhone into my backpack.

"Mr. Pollitt, Mr. Thompson, they're ready to see you now." The sound seemed to come from the receptionist's area.

We headed for the receptionist, where two visitor badges, one pink and one butterscotch in color, waited in her outstretched hands. She led us down a long hall, with cubes lining the left, to a conference room.

The receptionist stepped aside and motioned for us to enter. As we did, two people stood up from their seats behind a large orange conference table. Formal handshakes and greetings ensued, and we sat down.

"Thanks for coming in today. We apologize for running a bit late," said AJ Davis. AJ looked to be in his early fifties. His bald head made him look like Mr. Clean. He was a day or two late with the whole-head shave, so you could clearly see his male-pattern baldness on display. The suit he wore was fitted, and his pocket square matched his shirt, which seemed odd since most executives matched the pocket square not with the shirt, but with the tie.

Sarah Arnold sat next to Davis, nodding her head. She wore some sort of Hillary Clinton navy pantsuit and was clearly trying to look plainer than she was. I immediately thought she looked like an older Tina Fey, but not much older, and in dire need of a makeover. After a few seconds, I decided she was doing it on purpose.

"Both Sarah and I were very impressed with your portfolio of clients, which is why you're here. We've checked out a few of your client references, and you passed with flying colors. As you know, I'm the chief marketing officer and Sarah is vice-president of marketing. We will jointly be making the final decision on who the agency of record will be for PopC this year, and hopefully for many years to come. We have our calendars open until eleven for your presentation."

Sarah looked back and forth at Robby and me. "Do you need to plug in to the projector?"

"Absolutely. Thanks," I said, pulling out the laptop from my bag. As I turned on the computer and plugged in the cord that ran to the PopC projector, I froze and looked at Robby. I could tell immediately that Robby knew the look I was giving him, most recently right before I told him I was getting a divorce and another time before I got sick at a Red Hot Chili Peppers concert.

Robby immediately turned to the PopC executives. "AJ, Sarah, do you mind if we take a minute to confer about something before we begin the presentation?"

AJ leaned back and nodded while Sarah blandly stated, "Sure, no problem." Both immediately picked up their phones and started typing.

Robby stood up, took me by the arm, and led me to the corner of the conference room, far enough away from the PopC team as not to be heard while whispering.

"What's up?" Robby said.

"It's the presentation. I can't believe I'm just realizing that we're going to present something so incredibly different than our competition, but in exactly the same way as them. What was I thinking doing a PowerPoint?"

"Well, if we aren't doing a PowerPoint, then what are we doing?"

"I have an idea. Do you trust me?"

Robby paused. "Well, of course I trust you, but ..." Robby paused again. "You realize how important this is for us."

Fact was, we needed this account. We'd lost a few accounts recently to New York firms, and getting PopC would start the healing process. But in the front of my mind was Jess's tuition. Just getting my half of the up-front retainer from PopC would keep Jess at Penn State for at least another semester.

Still huddled in the corner, I looked at Robby. "I say we ditch the PowerPoint. Let me go Knute Rockne." Knute Rockne was our code for a solo motivational pitch.

"Okay, man. I don't know, but if you're feeling the force that much. You be Jordan, and I'll be Pippen."

At that, we headed back to the center of the conference table. Robby moved his chair off to the right, giving me some much-needed additional room, while I rolled my chair to my left, just beyond the table.

I closed the laptop and placed it into my backpack. As I walked back over to the center of the conference table, Robby sat down. He was smiling, but I thought it was a nervous smile.

Don't screw this up. I remembered my eighth-grade basketball coach always saying that the best players in the world constantly keep the mental image that they are going to make the shot, not the negative. "Never say 'don't miss it,' Will. You should visualize yourself making the shot before you take it. Saying 'don't miss it' focuses your energy on missing the shot." I quickly looked back at Robby. *Don't screw this up. You can't afford to screw this up.*

There was a small wrinkle between the third and fourth button of my shirt. I pressed down with my index finger over and over again, but the wrinkle stayed. I looked up at the PopC marketing team, now standing directly in front of them, and moved my hands down, my fingertips just grazing the table.

"AJ, Sarah ..." I paused. "May I call you that?" Both nodded. "First of all, thank you for including us in this presentation round." I looked at my watch. It read 9:55. I felt nauseous. I told myself this was normal, but it's been happening more and more lately.

"You've given us over an hour for this presentation, but we are going to give some of that valuable time back to you. We've decided to go a different direction with this meeting. Our presentation will take half that." I could feel Robby staring through me, but I didn't dare look over at him. The presentation would actually take fewer than twenty minutes, but I like to set specific expectations and do just a bit better. It generally creates a positive impression for the audience.

"If our intelligence is correct, we are the last of the four agencies to present ... not including your incumbent agency, of course. If I had to guess, they each gave a dazzling presentation combining television advertising, point-of-purchase displays, social integration, influencer partnerships, and most likely some event sponsorship concepts, including the annual gamer convention in Vegas." I shot a look at Robby. We'd been doing pitches together for years and when the odds were less than fifty percent for us getting the gig, we always started with our guess of what the client had already been pitched. If we were even half right, it generally left the impression that the other agency's pitch was stale and obvious. And knowing the other agency owners in this case, we were probably dead-on. They lost their creative souls years ago.

AJ was leaning back in his chair, smiling, with his hands joined together. Sarah was expressionless. I could only imagine how difficult a first date with her would be.

"Now, if you were a big, consumer-facing company like a Proctor & Gamble or Coca-Cola, that would be a perfectly adequate strategy. It might even work to give you the three percent to five percent growth rate you'd be looking for. But the challenge is, you're PopC. You are one of the fastest-growing and most innovative companies in the consumer space, let alone the beverage space. Single-digit growth next year would send your stock reeling, and you both would be fired." A chief marketing officer lasts fewer than two years in the average company. Davis just celebrated his twentieth month with PopC. I knew he was thinking about his tenure and how long it would last. I wanted him to associate hiring the other agencies with getting fired.

"Well, our job at PT Marketing is to make you look like rock stars. That your specific names will be mentioned in the next investor conference call because the executive suite will recognize the PopC marketing team, and the underlying strategy, as a key reason for PopC's growth."

AJ was leaning forward. Sarah, on the other hand, hadn't shifted in her seat once. But if I could read women—and I definitely could not—I was sensing that she was enjoying what she was hearing. Perhaps dreaming of the recognition she most likely never received at the male-dominated marketing department at P&G.

That's where most agency professionals got it wrong. Most believed that pitching the best idea would win the client over. While that obviously helped, the ideas, and the pitch itself, are secondary. What you want is to get beyond any rational thinking possible and hit them emotionally. Make it personal. In my many years as a marketing professional, clients rarely made rational decisions when picking an agency or a campaign ... it was something small, yet personal, that tugged at the heartstrings.

I continued and turned toward Robby. "Could you pass me two of the reports we put together, please?"

At that, he stood, handed me two stacks of paper, then proceeded to sit back down in his chair. I placed the reports just beyond AJ and Sarah's grasp. I didn't want them to look at the documents until we were finished.

I took in a deep breath. Robby and I had put our hearts and souls into this. Regardless of my current mental state, I truly did believe this plan could and would transform PopC. I breathed out and tried not to focus on my churning stomach.

"The report before you includes a three-year strategy and tactical plan that will make PopC the dominant, go-to resource for your Generation Z target audience. PopC today offers a wide range of beverages and popsicles. In order to grow at a clip like the Facebooks and Amazons of the world, PopC can't just offer beverages. I'm sure you've been told as much by your CFO. Since this is the case, in anticipation of a growing and diversified product line, PopC cannot just interrupt its audience through advertising and influencer relationships. In other words, PopC needs to become *the* resource that delivers amazing and ongoing experiences to Gen Zers."

I cleared my throat, and then looked down at the documents. "In this brief, you'll find a detailed analysis of how PopC will grow the largest audience base in the Gen Z space. And there's more. We are confident that by the end of this three-year period, your marketing investment into this concept will not only break even in terms of expense-to-revenue but will also garner a direct profit from activities." I paused. "You heard that correctly. Your marketing spend will actually make direct profit. Red Bull has done it. LEGO has done it. And PopC will do it as well.

"Now, the *how* is the tricky part, but we've got that covered. Our analysts at PT Marketing have uncovered over twenty specific opportunities that no PopC competitor is currently considering. Note that I say 'currently.' Simply put, these opportunities are too good, and your competition is smart enough to figure them out at some point." The analysts at PT Marketing consisted of just Robby and myself, but I failed to mention that.

I looked over to Sarah. What was that look? Intrigue. She was anticipating more. I took one step back and gestured toward Robby. "Can you give the highlights of the plan?"

Robby stood, went over to a dry-erase board on his right, and picked up the marker. He began to outline the plan. He wrote on the board: *Movie, Daily News, PopC Event, Talent Agency, Music Label, Magazine, Blogs,* and *Social.* I caught Sarah looking at Robby's backside more than once. Maybe AJ was as well, but I couldn't be sure.

Robby said, "We've identified opportunities to purchase small media companies and celebrity influencer sites. We aren't looking to partner with these organizations. Our goal is to actually purchase them and ultimately own the content brand and the audience database. PT Marketing has already done the research, of course, keeping PopC anonymous in this process, and we have the purchase price range for half of these opportunities and how the terms would work."

Robby and I went on disclosing the rest of the plan. I wrapped up, looking at both AJ and Sarah. "If you want to be like every other consumer beverage company, then do not go with PT Marketing. But if you want to completely revolutionize the beverage industry, like you've transformed your waiting area out there, the plan you have in front of you is the answer."

I paused, feeling light-headed. Everything in my being told me to stop the presentation and get out as fast as possible. I took a deep breath.

Sarah asked a question about the process of purchasing an influencer site. While Robby was answering, I heard an incessant buzzing inside my backpack. I discreetly pulled out my phone and saw over twenty notifications, all of them from my sister. The first five were *CALL ME ASAP.* The sixth one made my heart skip a beat ... *DAD DIED.*

Robby must have noticed something, probably wondering why I was looking at my phone during such an important meeting. I didn't know what to say. I felt the blood draining from my extremities. My forehead was sweating. All I could do was lean over and show him the last text.

Robby cleared his throat and turned toward AJ and Sarah. "Now, I'm sure you have many questions. The report will answer most of them. Unfortunately, Mr. Pollitt and I have to attend to an urgent matter and need to leave." At that, both AJ and Sarah looked a bit perplexed but didn't question us.

Robby and I shook hands with the PopC team, dropped our pink and butterscotch badges at the reception area, and headed out the door toward Robby's car. I began opening the door and almost threw up whatever was left from yesterday's drinks next to Robby's tire.

I stumbled into the passenger's seat and Robby backed out of the PopC visitor's spot. He was on I-90 heading west toward the office two minutes later. As per custom after a marketing pitch, Robby had turned on "I Want It All" from Queen. I could hear it, but it seemed far away as I gazed at the billboards out the window. I was having trouble keeping my eyes open.

"You know, you rocked it in there," Robby said. "I had my doubts, but I actually think the shortened presentation and then leaving the report with them added a sense of mystery. They probably have no idea what hit them."

"Thanks," I said. "Raspberry Beret" by Prince started to play. It seemed like a split second, and we were out in front of my apartment. Robby killed the motor.

"Run inside and get your toiletries and a change of clothes. You'll probably need a suit. I'll wait here," Robby said.

"For what?" I said.

"I'm taking you to Sandusky. Do you think I'm going to let you drive like this?"

I paused, looking for the words to argue with him. Nothing came. Then I headed into the apartment and did exactly as he had told me. I came back to the car a few minutes later.

"Where to?" Robby said.

"Just head west on I-90. I'll call Denise and get the exact location."

Chapter 3 – The Funeral Home

Less than an hour's drive west of Cleveland, Sandusky was known for two things. First, Cedar Point, one of the greatest roller coaster parks ever created. At one point they boasted the most standing roller coasters in the world, but I think one of the Six Flags parks now holds that distinction. Second, Sandusky was the fictitious location for the movie *Tommy Boy* starring Chris Farley and David Spade. Callahan Auto Parts T-shirts are sold in most of the downtown stores. It's a small town at heart. The kind of city where everyone knows everyone else. If it has twenty thousand residents, I'd be surprised.

I had lived in Sandusky my entire life until going off to college. These days I get back just a few times a year, either to catch up with Denise or to stop at the funeral home to see my father, although the trips with my dad have been less frequent since my financial troubles. I got a strange feeling in the pit of my stomach when I realized this would be my last trip to see dad.

Yesterday's reminder of winter gave way to warmer winds and the kind of spring day people in northeast Ohio rave about. Rolling down the window, I could smell the scent of flowers blooming.

Robby merged onto the interstate while I called Denise to get a full update. She answered from the hospital. I could tell she was mad about me putting her off this morning, but she quickly ran through the details. Dad was found around six thirty this morning. Janet, the funeral home's long-time secretary, discovered him lying faceup next to his office desk during her morning rounds.

Against Janet's wishes, Dad was transported to Firelands Hospital a few miles away. She thought it was just "plain silly" that they were taking him to the hospital and would have to cart him right back to the funeral home to be embalmed. Apparently the EMTs who arrived on the scene were not prepared to determine the cause of death, even though heart attack or stroke was likely. Dad was well-known in Sandusky, and they probably wanted to put the pressure of determining how he died on the hospital pathologist.

"Are they performing an autopsy?" I asked.

"Yes, the pathologist has been in there with him for a while," Denise said. "The nurse said that Ohio law requires an autopsy when the person dies alone. Anyway, he should be done any moment, and Jack will take him back to the funeral home." Jack had been friends with Dad for over thirty years and has worked at the funeral home about that long. His presence at the hospital was not surprising.

"Will?"

"Yes, Denise."

"Hold on," she said. I could hear her walking, down the hospital corridor most likely. The background noise went quiet. "Will ... I don't think Dad died of natural causes."

"You mean as in he was killed? Or suicide?"

She paused. "No ...well, maybe. I don't know. It's just a gut feeling. He was acting strange this past week. Strange more than normal I mean. And now this happens."

Denise was never one for drama growing up. Her instincts were usually right, so I immediately took her concerns seriously. But right now I didn't know what to think. "I hear you. We're less than forty-five minutes out. Hospital or funeral home?"

"By then, we should be at the funeral home."

"Okay. See you in a few. Love you, sis."

As I ended the call, I realized that was the longest conversation I'd had with my sister in months. I made a mental note to rectify that in the future.

"GET OFF THAT CASKET!"

If my father told me once, he told me a thousand times.

It was challenging as a six-year-old to keep occupied in a funeral home. The embalming room was strictly off limits. That was where I really wanted to play. Even though I was curious beyond belief, I knew better than to stick my nose into those parts. But the rest of the facility was my domain.

The funeral home was an adapted two-family house built in the late eighteen hundreds. Its storage areas had storage areas. If I chose to hide somewhere, no one would find me.

But on occasion, I liked to be around people—even dead people.

Before a public visitation, the body would be moved from the embalming room into the purchased casket. Sometimes wood, mostly steel though. My favorite was copper. Copper was for rich people.

My dad's staff assisted in presenting the body just so once it was placed in the casket. Makeup? Check. Jewelry? Check. Hands folded properly? Check.

Flowers were placed around the body, and it was ready to receive visitors … including me.

I grew up in that funeral home, so generally no one paid any attention to what I was doing. I could walk from room to room without a "Hi, Will," or "How was your day, William?" A ghost in a funeral home, you could say.

There was always a kneeler next to the casket for people who wanted to say a few prayers. Before the rush of visitors, I would push a folding chair against the kneeler, giving me enough leverage to crawl up and sit on the unopened side of the casket without disturbing anything. I would look at the body and wonder what they were doing now. Maybe she would be looking down at her funeral from heaven. Maybe he was so preoccupied hanging out with Jesus that he didn't even realize he'd passed away. Or maybe they were in the other place. I tried not to think about that.

It always amazed me that just a day or two before, this body was alive. It had blood flowing through it. The body could talk and move around and communicate with others. Now, it was a makeup commercial. The older the person, the more makeup was caked on. If the person smoked or was really old, it would take an entire tub of face-colored pancake just to rub out a few of the creases.

But I took my job seriously. I was the first visitor for nearly every dead body that passed through Pollitt Funeral Home.

I don't even think my father cared that much. Heck, he spent his entire life looking and talking to dead bodies—he must have appreciated his son's curiosity about his work. But if someone saw me sitting on their loved one's casket, the words *full refund* could enter the conversation. My dad was an entrepreneur first, a funeral director second, so business relationships took precedence over his son's quirks.

"Will? You okay?" Robby said, his voice bringing me back to reality.

Robby stopped the car below the overhang leading into the funeral home. We sat there for a bit. I could hear the air conditioning kick on in the car. ELO was playing in the background.

"I'll follow up with PopC and see about next steps," Robby said. "Just take care of yourself and your family. I can come back and get you anytime."

"Thanks," I said. I grabbed my duffel bag and suit from the back seat, closed the door, and headed for the front doors of the funeral home, slinging the bag over my shoulder.

The realization hit me that over the forty years visiting this place, I had entered through the front only a handful of times. The oversized doors were protected by two tired white pillars, one on each side. The paint at the bottom of the right door was chipping, showing part rust and part red, presumably the previous color showing through. The black rug leading into the home was gray in the middle, where far too many people over the decades had wiped off their dirt before entering.

Inside was a waiting committee. As I walked in, Jack Miller was on my left. Outside of my father, Jack taught me the rest of the funeral business. Jack was tall, about six foot four. He'd always been a large man, but over the years he'd lost some weight, and now his size forty-eight jacket was one size too big.

I remembered the first time he showed me how to deliver flowers to a gravesite. Before processioning from the funeral home to the cemetery for burial, the family paid their final respects. This was generally the time when the spouse and the children let down their guards and emotions flowed. It was my least favorite part.

Once the family retreated to their cars, the rings, necklaces, and any other family heirlooms were removed from the deceased and placed in a box or bag for the family. The body was lowered through a series of cranks inside the casket, the casket was closed, and then more cranks sealed it from the outside elements. The casket was then moved to a rolling cart and pushed out to the hearse.

Then the race began. Back inside the funeral home, every flower basket and floral presentation was quickly removed and taken out to a back-seat-stripped Ford Econoline at the side entrance. I lost my breath the first time moving the flowers to the van with Jack.

"Why are we in such a hurry?" I remembered asking him.

"My boy," Jack said. "These flowers need to be present at the gravesite before the family arrives. If we don't beat the procession there and have these flowers positioned just so, there'll be hell to pay from your pop."

Once the flowers were in the van, Jack sped off, with me riding shotgun. The first time, I distinctly remember him blowing through three red lights on our way to the cemetery. Arriving at the gravesite, Jack and I placed the flowers around the funeral tent, which covered an open hole surrounded by what looked like AstroTurf. Jack seemed to be a tad more careful with flower placement compared to how quickly he'd thrown them into the back of the van, so I was equally as careful.

Two minutes after we were finished placing the flowers, the first limousine showed up with the family.

Now, as I approached Jack, he reached out his hand to me. We shook and he placed his other hand on top. I could feel his concern for me, with his thoughtful eyes and his caring Texan smile. We held the grip for five seconds, but Jack said nothing. He didn't need to. Even though he was close to seventy and looked every bit of those years, Jack was all there. Both the expression and the three-piece suit told me he was, even now, in work mode.

To my right sat Denise and my Uncle Dan, in two chairs facing the front doors. Dan rose, shook my hand, and pulled me in for a tight hug.

"I'm sorry, son," Dan said. "Abe was a truly great man. And a great friend."

Dan McGinty was my father's best friend for some forty-plus years. They first met while serving in Vietnam, and were assigned to the same Army unit. I always thought it odd that they both came from Sandusky, my father on the west side and Dan on the east side, and met for the first time while serving in battle. My father loved Dan like a brother. Only one time did they ever have a falling-out, and that was over a woman. What I cobbled together from all the stories was that both Abe and Dan met my mother, Laura, at the same time, and both fell for her. Laura, better known as Linnie, chose Abe, and after that, the boys didn't talk for about six months or so. I heard punches were thrown at one point, but none landed.

Dan was sixty-five, looking like fifty-five. He had always looked younger than my father. The only difference from the last time I saw Dan was a little gray hair showed through his full head of dark-brown hair.

"Thanks, Dan," I said.

I moved over to Denise and crouched in front of her. Her eyes were red and swollen. Her left hand was shaking and held a few used tissues. I pulled her head into my shoulder, and she let out a horrible sound of grief.

"I'm here," I said. "I'm sorry I couldn't be here sooner."

"It's fine," Denise said in between breaths. "It's going to be a tough couple days." She paused and murmured, "Too young. Too young."

Denise and I had always been close, but even more so after my mom died in a car accident about two years ago. While Denise was older than I by a few years, I'd generally taken the role of eldest child.

"He's with Mom now," I said. We paused for what seemed like minutes. "I take it Dad's here, since Jack is here."

"Yes," she said. "Sam has him in prep."

"All right," I said. "I'm going down to see him. I'll be right back."

"You want me to go with you?" Denise said.

"No. I'm good."

"Go easy on Sam," she said.

I just stared back at her. A look we'd shared a thousand times. She knew me too well.

THE EMBALMING ROOM was in the basement. On my way to the stairs I passed two visitation rooms, the office, and the lounge where visitors and family get coffee and snacks while they mourn and greet friends and family. I was surprised to see the Keurig machine sitting on the counter next to the sink. Dad loved his old percolator. I couldn't believe he gave it up.

The stairway was protected by a large hundred-year-old door with a sign that said *No Admittance*. It was one of those signs you can buy at any office supply store, but from 1960. As I opened the door, the smell of embalming solution was overwhelming. Ventilation is key in an embalming room, and Dad never spent the money on better indoor air quality.

The dark stairs led to a long hallway of halogen lights, which pointed to the meat locker. I started calling it the meat locker when I was about eight years old, after taking a tour of a butcher shop. Clearly different purposes, but both shops used the exact same four-inch stainless-steel door with a spring-loaded latch handle. But then again, why not? Both kept meat from going bad.

I couldn't see Sam yet, but I knew she was there. As strong as the smells of embalming fluid and death were, they were no match for Sam's perfume. I picked up the scent as soon as I entered the room.

Her back was turned to me, and I could see that she was looking down at my father. Sam was never skinny or overweight, always just right in my opinion, but she'd clearly lost weight. Her hair was definitely darker and a little shorter.

"Hi, Sam," I said.

She gasped as if I'd surprised her. Sam was the kind of person who was never frightened or surprised, so she must have been in deep thought. Sam learned everything she knew about the funeral business from my father, and I forgot how much of a blow this was to her as well.

She turned, took three quick steps forward, and hugged me. In that moment, I lost control, and the tears came. The combination of standing next to my dead father and feeling my ex-wife in my arms was simply too much to handle.

We held each other for what seemed like hours but was just a few seconds. I hadn't held her like that since a year before we were divorced. Before she found out about my gambling problem. And before all my lies to cover it up. That she was willing to hug me—let alone touch me—was a surprise. She backed away and looked into my eyes. "I'm so sorry, Will."

"I'm glad you're here. More than anything else, he would have wanted you to handle his death."

"I'll give you a moment alone with him."

"No, please stay here. But I'd like to have a look."

A white sheet was pulled over his naked body, only exposing the top of his chest, shoulders, and head. Dad, half-Sicilian and half-Irish, was lucky to reach five foot eight, but he looked like a child on the embalming table. I'd seen hundreds, maybe thousands, of dead bodies before, and every one of them looked dead to me ... except for today. He looked like he did when he used to fall asleep on the couch in front of the television. The only thing I wanted to do at this moment was wake him up and tell him there was a new *Law & Order* on the tube.

After a moment of silence, Sam interrupted my thoughts. "He came in about twenty minutes ago, and I started prep on him immediately." She pulled down the sheet to just below his navel. The chest had been cut open and sealed back up, looking like a large letter Y moving from the shoulder blades to his belly button. "I'm sure you heard the news about the autopsy. I almost forgot about the autopsy rule and dying alone until Denise prepared me for it."

"Did they give you any results on cause of death?"

She shook her head. "No, and I wouldn't expect anything for a couple of days. Jim McGinty is the coroner, but you probably knew that. Uncle Dan's brother's kid. Anyway, I chatted with him on the phone this morning, and he said they had a policeman shot and killed last night and that's taking most of their resources. And with your dad probably dying of natural causes, I wouldn't expect anything quickly. We didn't get the call to handle the policeman by the way. Traynor got it."

Dad competed with Traynor Funeral Home his entire life. It was the small-town version of Coke versus Pepsi. Pollitt was the largest funeral home in town until a few years ago.

I bent down to take a look at the autopsy incision. "It looks like they did half the work for you. I take it the major organs are gone?"

Sam nodded. "There are a few bits of organ in the abdomen I'll need to take care of, and of course I'll need to switch out the blood with the embalming solution." Sam paused. "Would you like me to wait to do the procedure?"

"No," I said. "Don't wait. I don't want to get in your way. Just give me a heads-up before you do the hair and makeup will you?"

Sam said nothing. She didn't have to. Out of anyone in the world, she knew best that I liked to be overinformed in matters like these.

I pulled up the sheet to just below his chin and took one long look at him. "I'll see you later, Pop," I said touching the side of his head. "I'm sorry I wasn't around more."

As I walked away, I paused, then turned around a few paces before the doorway. I wanted desperately to take Sam in my arms and hold her. There were so many things I wanted to tell her, but the words didn't come. So many regrets. So many mistakes to atone for.

I turned back and was about to head upstairs when she called, "Will, wait a second."

I turned around. "Yes?"

"This is going to be a rough couple of days. I'm here for you and for Jess. And I have some of my own issues to work out since I loved your father like my own, but this doesn't change anything between us. I've made some progress rebuilding my life without you, so let's get through this the best we can and then move on. I'm here to support the family through this situation, but that's it." She paused. "I just wanted to make that clear."

I never wanted the divorce. Sam pushed for it and I acquiesced. I honestly didn't have much of a choice.

I nodded and went to turn away. Then after a few seconds, she said, "Make sure you talk to Jess. I was going to call her, but this is something you should do."

"I'll call her when she's out of morning classes," I said.

I headed out the door and up the stairs, in desperate need of fresh air.

BACK UPSTAIRS I FOUND Denise in the lounge inserting a cup of breakfast blend into the Keurig. "Don't shut it off when you're done. If I don't have a cup of coffee right now, it's going to be something much stronger," I said.

"You see him?" Denise asked.

"Yes ... I haven't seen him look that calm since the Cavs won the title. Almost every memory I have of him is in a hurry to go somewhere or do something really important, and he certainly never looked calm."

"He looks good. I didn't realize how much weight he'd lost."

"Great, we can use a thinner casket and save a few bucks," I remarked.

"William!"

I backed off, putting my hands up. "Geez, sis, you sound like Mom. I'm just trying to bring a little levity to this very depressing situation."

Denise grabbed the cup of coffee from under the Keurig and opened a small container of half-and-half. "I know ... normally I wouldn't mind ..."

I approached Denise and held her hand. "Tell me more about Dad. Tell me why this is something more than a heart attack. How was he acting before all this?"

Denise peeked around the corner, presumably to check if anyone was within earshot. "I don't know, Will. When I got the call he passed this morning, that's all that I could think of—that Dad was acting strange this week. A few days ago he actually was talking to me about Mom. He *never* did that. He was also asking a lot about you."

"What did you tell him?"

"I told him that he should call you since you were too stubborn to initiate." She paused. "I don't have anything more to go on than that, but that he did two things this week that were new to his behavior, it just set off my alarm bells."

"Thanks for telling me. I'll look into everything." In growing up around dead people, I had heard dozens of stories about how nostalgic some people became just days before their death. What Denise experienced could be explained away pretty easily. That said, she's my sister and she made a career out of proving I was wrong growing up.

I grabbed a pod of robusta and inserted it into the Keurig while Denise sat down in the corner. She cleared her throat. "So, tell me, how was it seeing Sam? Had to be at least a year since you've seen her."

"No," I said. "I dropped Jess off at her house about two months ago when Jess's car broke down during spring break. We do text each other quite a bit, but now everything revolves around Jess."

"But you didn't talk to her then, did you?"

"Uh, no."

"So today was the first time you had a face-to-face conversation with her since ..." Denise waited for me to answer.

"Since the divorce," I admitted. "A little over two years ago."

"I'm sure you know the exact number of days, hours, and minutes since you last talked to her." Denise must not have liked the folding chair she was sitting in as she rose and moved two chairs down the line. "You know, we've never *really* talked about your divorce. What did you do?"

"How do you know it was me and not her?" I said.

"Everyone knows Sam is perfect. I'm sure you know of one or two things she's done wrong, but you won't find anyone else in the world who would say a bad thing about her. I was surprised she agreed to marry you."

"And how is Brenda these days?" I said sarcastically.

"You can be such a dick sometimes; you know that?" she said. Brenda broke off a six-year relationship with Denise a few months ago. I didn't know all the details, but apparently Brenda realized she wasn't gay after all. Or maybe she was bisexual or just didn't love Denise anymore.

"I'm sorry," I said. "Low blow." I turned away and walked toward the other side of the lounge. "Just go easy on me regarding Sam. It's still a struggle every morning to function like a normal person."

"So what happened?"

I looked down into my half-filled cup of coffee. The fluid was still moving counterclockwise from stirring in the packet of Equal. "You know how I've always loved casinos. Well, I found what I thought was a better one online. I took a few thousand and put it into a brokerage account. Then I turned that two thousand into about one million in six months of day-trading."

I looked up at Denise. "Remember that market downturn about four years back? I was playing the market to go back up. I started leveraging my bets using margin." Denise looked confused, so I explained. "Margin is where you borrow money from the brokerage company. Anyway, there was this one stock I was researching that looked too good to be true, the numbers lined up perfectly, a sure thing you could say—and before you know it, I was in the hole over five hundred thousand dollars. To make the margin call, I had to put a second mortgage on the house, sell my entire sports memorabilia collection, add a few credit cards. Needless to say, I kept all this from Sam."

As I was relaying all this to Denise, I could feel my heart pounding. The last time I had this feeling I was at confession with Father Patrick telling him the exact same story. "The whole time, trying to keep everything from Sam, it was like hiding a lover. When Sam found out, she was obviously furious."

"And that's why you two broke up?"

"No, Sam was pretty great about it, considering. We talked it through. I talked about getting help with my gambling problem. We discussed ways we could repay the debt and we could go on with our lives."

"Okay, then what?"

"About a month after she found out, I did it again. I don't even think it was anything about the money for her. It was that I lied, and she couldn't trust me, and she didn't know who I was. Frankly, I didn't know who I was. Anyway, I've been going to Gamblers Anonymous meetings since after the divorce. It's a struggle every day, but I'm in a better place now, minus all the debt. Unfortunately, I lost the love of my life in the process."

"Does Jess know?" Denise asked.

I exhaled. "She knows about the gambling problem, but she doesn't know the journey. Or how bad I'm in debt. Dad knew about the debt. Creditors were calling him to collect on my sins. Probably the reason we hadn't talked much over the past year."

Denise stood up and walked over to me. Then she wrapped her arms around me and pushed my head down into her shoulder. "Aren't the both of us just a pair of geniuses when it comes to relationships?" she said. "I'm so sorry you had to go through this, Will."

"And I'm sorry about you and Brenda."

We held each other in silence for a few seconds. Then Denise pushed away and remarked, "Damn, Uncle Dan wanted to see both of us ASAP. I forgot I was going to get you after my coffee was finished."

"Did he say why?"

"Something about the estate, but he wasn't very specific."

Chapter 4 – The Will

As Denise and I headed out into the main lobby, we spotted Uncle Dan sitting in Dad's office. He was ruffling through two odd stacks of papers. He looked up with a warm smile.

"There you both are," he said. Then he looked at me. "You okay, Will? Denise told me this could have been one amazing day for you with that morning presentation, then it all went to hell."

He motioned for the two of us to sit.

"I'll get right to it. You both know I served as your father's attorney since, well, after we toured together. He also made me the executor of his will and last testament. Now I like to play by the rules and all, and we will have a formal will reading at some point after the funeral, but there are a few things that need immediate attention with the funeral home." Uncle Dan pulled out an envelope with the flap hanging open from one of the stacks of papers. He singled out what looked a piece of tattered paper torn from a steno notebook. Bits of paper fell onto the desk as he unfolded the note. "As you can probably tell, your father handwrote this document. He gave it to me a few weeks ago, and I authenticated it."

It seemed odd Dan would have this with him so close to my father's death. "Why did he update it a few weeks ago?" I asked.

"Your father updated his will continuously. I would say he gave me a note like this twenty times over the years. This is just the most recent one." He looked at me and then looked down, scanning the paper. "The easiest thing to do is just read the damn thing, then we can discuss it. Is that okay with you, Denise?"

Denise nodded but said nothing.

"Okay, here goes," said Uncle Dan, clearing his throat.

Dan, this note overrides all the other notes I gave you as part of my last will and testament.

Denise, you've been a wonderful daughter, and I love you dearly. As I've told you many times, my only real regret was not spending enough time with you, especially in your formative years. I put work ahead of you. Over the past decade, I tried to make this up to you, but it always seemed I was running after something uncatchable. Anyway, regarding the house, you know how much I love that little house on the Sandusky Bay. I had it appraised about six months ago at $400,000. If you want to keep it, keep it. If you'd like to sell it, do that. Dan has a few contacts for the offers we've received over the years. I remember you always loving our walks and talks out on the dock, so I wanted you to have it. I just want you to be happy. Do what makes you happy. Find the joy in your life, Denise.

And William, I'm leaving you my sports memorabilia. I know you'll take care of it. If only I were a Yankees fan and not an Indians fan, they might actually be worth something. But whatever you do, take care of the Colavito card. Regarding the funeral home, I'm giving it to you, warts and all. I'm sure you knew this was coming. I actually thought about selling it a few years back when your mother passed, but then what the hell was I going to do, sit home and watch Law & Order? *So what does a kid in the prime of his life with marketing chops do with a declining funeral home? You know that the funeral business was all I ever knew. I was happy to share that with you for a few years during your summers off from college. Growing up you spent more than your fair share of time in this place, so you might know it better than anyone. I don't expect you to drop everything in life to take your pop's dead-people business. Hell, I don't know if you are happy to have it. I think you'd like it. It doesn't pay much though. Didn't used to be like that. Most people think funeral directors make a ton of money, because they drive around in limos all the time but, at least in my case the last few years, that's not true.*

Regardless, I would like you to make a choice. If you want to sell it, I already had the papers drawn up. Jack wants to buy it and always has. If you wish it, the deal is done. Just tell Dan that's what you want. It's a fair price. Dan agrees, and Jack has the funding. It might help with some of the issues you are going through.

The other choice would be to keep it, run it, and live the funeral business. Not for the rest of your life, but for at least one year. Take it and see what you can do 365/24/7. After that one-year period, you can do whatever you like—keep it, sell it, set up your own marijuana farm with it, whatever. I actually hear that's a pretty good business these days. William, Pollitt Funeral Home has a great history, but the last few years have been rough. When you see the numbers, you'll figure out why. Someone with vision can bring it back. I'm hopeful that vision can come from you. Take a good look at the numbers. Read between the lines.

Whatever you decide, know that I love you and am proud of you. Remember, no regrets.

Oh, and one more thing, William, don't sit on the caskets with bodies in them. At least not while customers are around.

All my love to both of you, Abraham Pollitt

Uncle Dan folded up the letter and put it back in the envelope. "That's all there is. Denise, we can deal with the house later, absolutely no issues there. But, boy, I needed you to know about this ASAP for obvious reasons." He got up and walked to the window. Looking out at the street, he said, "If I were you, I'd sleep on this. Maybe talk with Robby, then meet with me in the morning. Before you make any final decision, you need to see the books."

He turned back to us. "Do either of you have any questions?"

Denise was visibly crying. I, on the other hand, didn't feel anything. I looked over at Denise, then at Dan, and said, "I think we're good for now, Uncle Dan. Thanks for letting us know. Yes, let's meet in the morning. Here?"

"No, son. Let's meet at my office. I think that would be more appropriate. Say, nine o'clock?"

"Sure."

I walked out thinking that my father's passing may have just saved Jess's education.

AFTER TELLING JESS the unfortunate news that her grandfather passed away, I had a quiet dinner with Denise at the Cedars, an Italian joint just outside of the downtown area. She offered for me to stay at her place, but I didn't want to put her out, so I asked if it was okay if I stayed at Dad's house ... now her house. "That's silly, Will," she said. "You can stay wherever you want."

She dropped me back at the funeral home, and I picked up the Econoline to drive. *I guess this is mine now.* As soon as I opened the door, I smelled the fresh flowers from countless deliveries to the cemetery. Dad's place was five miles away from the funeral home, but the drive took me thirty minutes as I dealt with the remnants of traffic from Cedar Point enthusiasts.

Dad's street turned toward the Sandusky Bay right before the railroad tracks. The road used to be hard to navigate, with no streetlights, but tonight it was lit like a Christmas tree due to the new condominium complexes built in the last few years, one to the right of his house and one to the left. I didn't believe his last will and testament letter that the place was worth four hundred grand, but now I saw why.

I parked the van in front of the garage and entered through the back door. The smell of Dad's cologne mixed with must hit me immediately. I went through the back porch and into the family room, throwing my duffel bag on the couch.

Jess informed me via text that she was leaving Penn State around ten a.m., after her media studies class. With a few stops, that would put her in Sandusky well before dinnertime.

It was late, and I should have been exhausted, but the last thing I wanted to do was sleep. I decided to do a room check. It'd been a few years since I'd really investigated the place.

As I entered the kitchen, I was curious if Dad ever spent any time here at all, judging by the six-pack of Miller High Life, some bologna, and a lone bottle of ketchup standing guard in the corner of the refrigerator. The only rooms with any signs of use were the bedroom, attached bathroom, and his office. Although the place could use a good cleaning, it was orderly—nothing out of place. Dad was clearly on the other end of myself regarding organization. He is ... was ... meticulous, while I was always comfortable in clutter. As a kid growing up, I had more conversations with him about the state of my bedroom than literally anything else. He used to tell me to make my bed every morning because at least I would accomplish one thing during the day. Tough love, I guessed.

A stack of bills weighted down by a checkbook sat atop his office desk, along with a picture of my mom a few years before she passed, another family picture of the four of us from around 1990, and an old notepad with *life in-*

surance scribbled on it. I made a mental note to ask Uncle Dan about Dad's life insurance policy.

I went to the kitchen, grabbed a beer, and headed back to the family room, just me and my duffel bag. A good pillow, I thought, as I had no intention of sleeping in any of the bedrooms. As I started to drift off, I was overwhelmed with sadness. Of course, my father first. The regrets I had about not having a better relationship with him the past few years pounded like a bass drum in my forehead. And Sam, who was back in my life for all the wrong reasons. If I decided to keep the funeral home, she'd bolt for a new job somewhere else. I couldn't blame her. Besides paying off my debt that might have been the best reason to pass on taking over the funeral home. It was the right thing to do, at least for her well-being.

I realized it wasn't all bad as I nodded off. There was Jess, and Robby, and Uncle Dan. A lot to be thankful for. But none of that stopped the tears from streaming down my face. I held my duffel bag tight in my arms, longing for unconsciousness.

Chapter 5 – The Death Call

I awoke and looked at my phone what seemed like five minutes later. 4:42. I decided that was about as good as it was going to get and trudged to the guest shower.

In fifteen minutes I was in the car on the way to Starbucks for a double shot. I then headed to the funeral home in hopes of finding Jack. And like always for the past thirty years, Jack's car was parked in the back. I walked in the back door. "Good morning, Jack," I said.

I startled him a bit. "Morning, William. I didn't expect you to be in so early."

"Sleep was hard to come by last night. I was hoping to chat with you if you can make some time."

"Absolutely," Jack said. "I have about fifteen minutes until I have to head out to Blessings Care Center." Blessings was a nursing home for mostly lower- to middle-class clientele.

"Did the call just come in?"

"Yeah. Everything routes to my cell phone now instead of the call center. You know, tightening the belt around here."

"Makes sense. Do you mind if I go with you? I haven't been on a call for some time."

"Actually, I could use a hand, so that's perfect. The office manager at Blessings said to bring two people, but who knows what that could mean. Maybe a large man. You know the funeral business: fun, fun, fun. Let me grab a cup of coffee, and we'll take Pollitt1." Pollitt1 was the newest hearse—from 1997.

It was barely light-jacket weather as we headed out. Jack drove and I rode shotgun.

"Hey, Jack, this hearse looks to be in real nice condition, but why not get a new one?" I said.

"Times are tough. We've cut some corners here and there. I'm sure you've noticed the wear and tear at home base. It sorely needs a makeover. But business has been trailing off for the past few years." He reached inside of his pocket, pulled out a pack of gum, and popped a piece out of the container and into his mouth. He pointed the gum at me. "This here's nicotine gum of some sort. Wife says I need to kick smoking altogether. It was my favorite thing in the world to do. It hasn't been easy. So she makes me chew this god-awful gum. I'd be smoking right now, but that woman is a bloodhound. She can smell smoke on me from a mile away."

"Anyway," snorted Jack. "Sorry again about your Pop. He was a son of a bitch but a great man. This here city'd be a shithole if it wasn't for all the good works he'd done around town. I'm real broken up about it."

"Thanks," I said. "You know, about the funeral home, Dan mentioned yesterday that you want to buy the place. No offense, but with business being the way it is, I thought you'd be more interested in retirement than becoming an entrepreneur."

"Good point. Two things. First, I think I can fix her up. A little. Maybe cater to a certain kind of folk. Traynor can't be the only game in town, can it? And between us boys, I've put away some money. Hell, I can't use it when I'm dead, and my kids sure don't need it. That's a blessing." He snorted again.

"What's the second thing?"

"Retirement. Funny word that: retirement. I've been doing some research on it, and I do believe if I retire, I'm going to have to spend more time with my godforsaken wife. And between us little chickadees, I'd rather put a bullet between my eyes."

"I see your point," I said, pausing. "I found out yesterday that Dad left me the place in the will. Did you know that?"

"Of course I knew. Your Pop and me used to talk about it all the time. That's as it should be. If you want it, go for it. But I figure if you'd like to stick with the advertising bit, I'd be here to pick up the pieces."

Marketing, I thought, not advertising. But Jack didn't need to know the difference.

Jack took a right, and we pulled in a turnaround drive in front of the overhang at Blessings. He exited the hearse, and I followed.

Just before we entered the building, Jack turned to me. "Will, you know this, but normally when we retrieve a body, we wear suits. It's just part of our professionalism. I know you packed light to get here so quickly, so I'll let it slide this time. But tuck in your shirt, will you?" He smirked.

"Roger, boss," I said, quickly stuffing my shirt down into my pants.

I followed Jack through the automatic sliding doors as he headed straight for the reception desk. "Hello, ma'am. My name is Jack Miller from Pollitt Funeral Home. We received a message that you called about a Mr. Davies passing. We're here to retrieve the body as instructed by the family."

The woman looked at Jack, then glanced over his shoulder at me. She took her glasses from the rope hanging around her neck and placed them on the tip of her nose. "Yes, indeed. Thanks for coming," she said as she reviewed her notes. "Mr. Davies is in room one-two-six. That's just down the hall. Make a right and a left, and you'll see it. As per our regulations, we can't move a resident once they've passed on, so do the best that you can."

Jack and I glanced at each other. "Okay," Jack said. "We'll retrieve the stretcher and take care of it. Much obliged, ma'am." Jack tipped his head at the receptionist, and we headed back to the hearse.

As we wheeled the stretcher down the hall, Jack asked, "When was the last time you picked up a body, son?"

"Must have been the last year I worked at the funeral home. The summer before I graduated college. That was in '96," I said. The same year I met Sam, I thought to myself.

We left the stretcher in the hall and as we entered the room, Jack said, "Single room. Good. I hate wheeling out a body in front of a roommate."

The room smelled of antiseptic. Tan and white everywhere except for the sixty-inch television in front of the bed, which wasn't made. There was also no body. Jack walked to the back of the room, toward a small closet. He looked at me and said, "Bathroom. Never a good thing."

He opened the door and stepped aside, giving me a view inside. Mr. Davies, apparently, had passed away while going to the bathroom. He was a large man, easily 250 or 275 pounds. His dark-skinned arms were dangling to either side of him with his right hand touching the floor. His chest was pressed tight against his knees. His head, reddish and purple, was nearly kissing the underside of the toilet.

"Smell that?" Jack asked. "I'm assuming no one did a courtesy flush." He turned toward me. "Okay, Will, go fetch the stretcher, bring it over here to the door, and put it on the lowest setting to the ground. There's no way we can fit that stretcher in the bathroom, so we'll have to carry him out first."

"Can I ask you something first, Jack?" I asked.

He nodded.

"How were you going to do this by yourself?"

"Kid, you don't want to know. Now let's do this."

I brought over the stretcher as instructed. Then Jack went in beside the toilet and grabbed Mr. Davies under the armpits. "Okay, I'm going to lift up his torso and then balance him on his feet. When I do that, you take his underwear around his ankles and pull it up. I'm 99 percent sure Mr. Davies wasn't finished, but just get the underwear on him, and we'll clean him up back at the home."

I was doing everything I could not to lose my coffee from this morning. "Aren't we going to put on some gloves before we do this?"

"Jesus Christ, Will, the man is dead. We aren't going to infect him with anything," snapped Jack. I was thinking the other way around, but I didn't dare say another word.

"Okay, I'll lift him up on three, you get the underwear on, then grab his ankles. I'll take top and you take bottom, and we'll carry him out." He looked at me intently. "Hey, if you're going to puke, make sure you don't get it on my shoes. The wife just bought these for me. All right ... one ... two ... three."

Jack yanked him up and moved to get his weight underneath the body. Mr. Davies, his head dangling like a piñata, dropped about a liter of saliva out of his mouth and onto his chest. I bent to pick up the underwear, trying to look with only my left eye.

"Oh, God," I said in an octave too low.

"Don't lose your shit on me, boy," Jack said. "We're professionals here."

I quickly pulled the underwear over Mr. Davies's privates and gave extra room in the back to encapsulate whatever remained from his nether regions.

"That's good enough," Jack said. "I've got him balanced, now grab his ankles, not the feet, and let's carry him out."

I seized Mr. Davies by the ankles, and Jack had him under his armpits.

We moved the body enough to get away from the toilet. "Stop right there," Jack said and he set Mr. Davies's backside on the white bathroom tile. "This guy has to be topping three hundred pounds." Jack was breathing heavily. "Give me one second." I just stood there, looking at a three-hundred-pound human boomerang.

"Okay," Jack said. "I'm ready … and now." I lifted the feet and Jack moaned, pushing the body at me with excessive force until we had Mr. Davies next to the stretcher. Luckily, we already had it set to its lowest setting to the floor, so we only had to lift him up about three feet. Without saying another word, Jack swung Mr. Davies's head and shoulders onto the stretcher. It caught me by surprise, and only half his backside made it. After securing the chest with the stretcher belt, Jack scooted over to my side and pulled up the rest of Mr. Davies, securing the second belt.

At that, we both sat on Mr. Davies's bed, dotted with sweat and breathing hard.

"Goddamn," Jack said. "How the hell does a decent person let themselves go like that?"

"Judging by the walker and the wheelchair in the corner, I'm assuming Mr. Davies wasn't much for exercise anymore."

Jack put his hand on my shoulder, which sort of grossed me out, and said, "You done good, Will. See all the fun you been missing in your fancy Cleveland office."

"Yeah, this will go down as a career highlight for sure."

At that, we wheeled Mr. Davies out of the room and down the hall. Jack gave the receptionist a half-hearted salute as we passed, and we rolled the body out the sliding doors.

Chapter 6 – Running the Numbers

By the time we delivered Mr. Davies to the embalming room at Pollitt Funeral Home, it was already pushing eight thirty. After scrubbing my hands raw for twenty minutes under scalding water, I grabbed the van and headed to Uncle Dan's office.

While the funeral home was located on the east side of town, the office of McGinty & Associates was in the heart of the now vibrant downtown Sandusky area. In the early 1900s, Sandusky housed two of the largest paper mills in North America. When those companies went bankrupt after World War II, the downtown area fell into ruin. About twenty years ago, a number of concerned citizens, including my father and Uncle Dan, worked together to build what was now a center for shopping, office complexes, and parks, on the waterfront.

As I approached Uncle Dan's office, I was amazed at both the building and the view, almost like he had the pick of the litter as to where to set up shop. I parked in the back and walked up the stairs to the front doors. As I turned around, I had a breathtaking view of bluish-green water and, to the east, the roller coasters at Cedar Point.

I walked in and recognized the receptionist right away.

"Mrs. Kromer? Do you remember me?"

"Why, William, how could I forget? You went the entire sixth-grade year without doing one spelling assignment I gave you for homework, then argued at the end of the year why you deserved a passing grade."

"Well, I remember ditching the spelling, but I don't remember what my argument was. I take it you do?"

Mrs. Kromer scratched her head. "If my thinking is correct, dear—and God knows if it is since I'm almost eighty years old now—that was the year your grandmother died. God bless her soul. It happened at the beginning of the school year. I believe you said that you spent that school year in mourning for your grandmother and dedicated your spelling homework time to praying for her in Heaven."

"And you were nice enough to give me a B in that class even though you knew I was full of it?"

"William, you had such a wonderful imagination. I had a grand old time telling all my friends about your shenanigans. Heck, honey, you were so cute about it I almost gave you an A."

"You were way too nice to me, Mrs. Kromer."

"Honey, please call me Alice. You must be in your forties; we can talk like adults now."

"Well then, thank you, Alice. I'm here to see Dan. I have a nine a.m. appointment with him."

"I'll let him know you're here. Oh, and I'm so sorry to hear about your father. What he did for this community. A true hero."

"Thanks," I said and went over to a small waiting area with magazines and newspapers scattered about the tables. I grabbed a seat and picked up the magazine on top, *Erie County Business*. Uncle Dan was on the cover.

After a few minutes, Alice said he was ready and directed me down the hall.

Uncle Dan's office was an odd mix of small-town hospitality and state-of-the-art technology. You could clearly see the tech—the flat screens, a small data center, new computers on every desk, Bluetooth headsets for the employees—but it all came across as folksy. Maybe it was the wood separating the offices and cubicles instead of the normal fare like what you'd find in *The Office*.

Dan's office was the largest, a view of both the waterfront and half the downtown area. Probably the best view in downtown Sandusky.

As I walked in, Dan opened his top drawer and pulled out two documents, which looked like formal reports. "How you holding up?"

"As well as can be expected. I'm more worried about Denise. She's taking it pretty hard," I said, taking a seat.

"And Sam?"

"I'm sure you can figure it out. The same day she lost her mentor and father figure, she had to interact with me. Yesterday was probably her worst day ever. But Jess is coming in today, and that will help."

"I'm looking forward to seeing her, considering the circumstances," Dan said clearing his throat. "All right, son, well let's get down to it then. Lots for you to review and think about." He handed me one of the reports from across his desk. "I know you've always been a whiz with numbers, I'm sure much better than I, so let's just go through the summary report on page three. Then you can take a deep dive later and let me know if you have any questions. Sound good?"

Alice brought in coffees and set them on Dan's desk. "Will, as you can see this is a five-year performance report. Over that time, revenue has been cut in half, and where there was a nice profit, Abe was showing break-even for the past couple years. But between you, me, and the fence post, he was losing money. I believe he was subsidizing the funeral home with his own funds. Actually, I know he was. A few more months and he would have had to sell the antique hearses, or maybe even the house.

"On page four, you can see the breakdowns by product area. While all the lines are down, it's embalming that's the issue. People getting embalmed were the lifeblood of your father's business. Cremations are up a bit, which is great, but the yield on a cremation is less than a thousand. No embalming, no casket, and generally smaller services and rental fees.

"Okay, let's stop there for a second," Dan said. "Questions?"

I looked down at the report, the numbers flying around in my head, trying to make sense of Dad's business. "Well, from what I can see, the business model might be beyond repair. Even if you doubled or tripled the amount of cremations, the numbers still may not work out. I'll have to do more research, but I'm ninety-nine percent sure that embalmings are not going to make a comeback any time soon."

"I think that's a valid assertion," Dan said.

Dan and I talked for another twenty minutes, half about the business and half about my current business.

"Son," said Uncle Dan, "you could own this from afar and let Jack run it, of course, but I think your father wanted you to either own *and* run the business or just get the hell out altogether, so I think those are your two choices.

The valuation model is included in the back of this report, which includes how the sale would work with Jack, if you decided to do that. Anyway, I've talked enough. Anything else I can answer for you?"

"No, Uncle Dan, this is more than I could ask for," I said. "I just need to review and sit with this for a while. How long do I have to make a decision?"

"There's no real time limit. The funeral home sits in a trust, and you're set as the beneficiary. This all means that you'll get no red tape from probate upon examination of the will. That said, considering Jack and the other employees, I'd make a decision in the next few days if possible."

As I turned to leave, I remembered the one thing I was supposed to ask him. "I almost forgot. I found a piece of paper at Dad's house with 'life insurance' written on it. Do you know anything about that?"

He paused for a second, looking like he misplaced something. "I'm sorry, son. You'll see in the documents I gave you. Your father cashed his life insurance out about a year ago to help pay down some debt. There's nothing left. Maybe the note was about something else."

Pay down debt, huh? Like father, like son.

Back in the car, I spent twenty minutes going through the financial report from Uncle Dan, making a few notes and calling out some odd numbers. Then I called Denise. We decided to have the visitation on Friday from three p.m. to nine p.m., and the funeral on Saturday morning. This would probably be the biggest funeral procession Pollitt had handled in years, so the team needed some time to prepare.

I rang Robby and asked him if he had time for a quick lunch. We decided to meet in an hour at an Applebee's in Elyria, halfway between the two of us. If the timing was right, I'd be back at the funeral home by the time Jess arrived. I also asked Robby to grab a few more clothes from my place, including at least two more of my suits.

Then I called Sam. Surprisingly, she picked up.

"I take it you're done with Dad?" I asked.

"Yes. You said you wanted to see him before hair and makeup?

"No, go ahead and finish him off. I need to head to Elyria to meet with Robby for an hour before Jess gets in."

"Okay, anything else?"

"Is everything okay? I mean, besides the obvious." She sounded mad. I thought I knew why.

"Were you planning on telling me you're taking over the funeral home?"

"I just found out yesterday, Sam. And I haven't decided anything. Uncle Dan gave me all the numbers to review to see if I want to keep it or sell it to Jack."

The line went silent.

"Still there?" I asked.

"I've got to go," she said.

"Wait. Any ruling on COD for Dad?"

"Nothing yet. I need to call Uncle Dan's nephew and check. Bye, Will." The line went dead. I didn't think our relationship could actually get worse, but I was wrong. She seemed to hate me now more than ever.

I pulled off Route 2, passed the mall on Route 57, and found the Applebee's on the other side. Robby's Ford was already there waiting for me.

He was sitting at a booth near the window. As I approached, he stood and we did our normal bro hug, but he held it a little longer than usual.

"How you holding up, man?" he asked.

"I'm okay," I said. "Everything seems strange. Seeing my father dead. Seeing Sam twice in one day, knowing that she hates me. What's not to like?"

"How'd she look?"

"Sam? You know what she looks like."

"C'mon, man. Is she letting herself go, or does she look as cute as ever?"

"She's still the most beautiful woman I've ever seen. She's lost about ten pounds, from what I can tell."

"Did she put up a front?"

"Actually, she was pretty cool. Now don't get me wrong; she drew the line right away, but she could have gone passive-aggressive on me. I think she's really trying to be supportive when she probably wants to slap me." I paused. "And she's in a tough position right now—one of the reasons I wanted to chat with you."

We ordered two Diet Cokes and some onion rings and sent the waitress away.

"Any word from PopC?" I asked.

"Nope, but I just followed up this morning with an email. I'll call them tomorrow," Robby said. With everything going on at the funeral home, we still desperately needed that business to come in, long shot or not.

"Sounds like a plan," I said. "Here's the deal: My dad left me the funeral home in his will. He asked me to run it for a year and see if I like it. I honestly don't know what I should do. Jack—you remember Jack, right?" Robby nodded. "He wants to buy the place if I don't want to run it. I talked to him today and he seemed cool either way; he just doesn't want to retire. Selling it would solve a lot of my financial problems and keeping it might be a lost cause considering the current state of the business. Do you mind running through some of these numbers with me? I could use a second opinion, and you're the only one I trust."

Robby thought for a second and said, "First of all, good on your pop for giving it to you. I know you figured he would, but you never know. Either way, you'll make a good decision. Second, of course I'll run through the numbers with you, but I need something stronger than a soda to review spreadsheets."

I waved the waitress over and ordered a Tito's and Red Bull for me and a Jack on the rocks for Robby.

I gave Robby the overview from Uncle Dan and went into a few specific points regarding embalmings versus cremations.

"I know you aren't a funeral expert, but you've lived and breathed charts, trends, and analytics since we started the agency. Tell me what you see."

"Okay, I get the whole embalming versus cremation thing. Embalming is going away, which means your dad's business model, which was built on embalming and the services around it, is in extreme trouble. That said, whenever you see something like this in a trend line, it means one of two things happened. First, you check the numbers. They may be wrong. But let's say for shits and giggles they aren't wrong. Then the only other explanation is an event."

"Event? What do you mean by that?"

"Something powerful that changes the entire direction of the business. In this case, it could be economic. Let's say the economy became so bad that people stopped using funeral services at all. Unlikely to start, but since last year was pretty good for the economy around here, less than a one percent chance. So if we rule that out, we're talking about an event that changes the entire landscape of the business. A good example of this was when Chipotle had to deal with that case of salmonella poisoning and the press got ahold of it. That event completely reset their business. It took them years to make it back to their original revenue numbers."

"So in this case, something like a horrific PR incident, like something about my father that started making the rounds in the public, and people started boycotting?" I asked.

"Yes, something like that," Robby said.

"Except we would know if that happened, wouldn't we? Heck, I just ran into my old sixth-grade teacher who couldn't stop raving about my dad saving the downtown area."

My phone vibrated. Sam texted that Jess had arrived early to the funeral home. She must have left early. I motioned to the waitress to bring the check.

"I have to go," I said. "Jess arrived in Sandusky early."

"You do this every time and leave me with the check," Robby said, half joking. He knew I barely had enough money for morning coffee.

"It's one of my better qualities," I said.

"So do two things," Robby said. "First, double-check the numbers to make sure they're right, and second, start sniffing around to see what happened between a year and a half ago and two years that might have changed the direction of the business."

At that, he got up, we hugged, and he followed me out to the parking lot so I could grab my extra clothes out of his car.

Chapter 7 – The Life Settlement

I found Jess and Sam in one of the visitation rooms waiting for me. Sam looked mad, maybe for me not being here when Jess arrived, but I simply couldn't tell anymore. The reasons were piling up.

"I have to go work on Mr. Davies," Sam said as I approached. "Bye, honey," she said to Jess. "I'll see you later."

Then Sam handed her off to me, and I gave Jessica a long embrace. "I'm sorry about Grandpa," she said.

"I'm sorry too," I said. "He was way too young to leave this earth." I paused. "Thanks for coming so quickly." I stood back and took a good look at her. "You look great, Jess. So, other than this depressing news, how have you been?"

"I like the change," she said, referring to the move from community college to main campus life at Penn State. "A few of the classes are horrible—statistics, for example—but I love my journalism and media classes. Hey, I found out today that I have to put up a blog site for my Future of Media class. Do you know anyone that knows how to create a blog?" she said with a smirk.

"Thanks a lot," I said with a half-smile. "I'm sure your Uncle Robby can help you with that." The more I heard her talk about college, the more selling the funeral home seemed to be the only option.

Janet entered the room. "I'm sorry to break up the reunion, but Mr. Davies's daughter is here to discuss the plans for her father. She was going to come in tomorrow morning but she's here now to meet with someone." She paused. "This was your father's role. Do you want to meet with her, or do you want Jack or myself to do it?"

"No time like the present, I guess. I'll take it." Then I turned back to Jess. "Why don't you come, too, Jess?"

"I'm not sure how comfortable I am with that."

"If you don't want to do it that's fine, but if you feel up to it, I'd love it if you could join me. Jack and I picked up this woman's father this morning."

She paused. "Okay."

"Where is she, Janet?" I asked.

"She's sitting in your father's office. I put the file on the desk. You'll see the checklist. Do you need me in there for support, to make sure you remember everything?"

"I think I can handle it, but don't go too far away, okay?"

Janet smiled. "Of course."

I led Jess over to my father's office. We walked inside and a woman looking to be in her late forties, early fifties rose to meet us. "Hi. My name is Will Pollitt. I'm so sorry for your loss," I said shaking her hand.

"Thank you. I'm Sarah Evans, Timothy Davies's daughter. I appreciate you meeting with me on such short notice."

"No problem at all," I said. I brought Jess into the conversation and said, "This is my daughter, Jessica. She just arrived from Penn State. We had a death in the family as well. I'm not sure you've heard, but my father, Abe Pollitt, died a few days ago."

Mrs. Evans gasped. "I'm so sorry. I didn't know that. I met with Abe about six months ago to do some preplanning. I was settled on Traynor Funeral Home, but I liked Abe's approach and switched. How did he die, if I may ask?"

"We don't know for sure, but we believe it was a heart attack, Mrs. Evans" I said.

"Mrs. Evans is fine, but you can call me Sarah."

"Thanks, Sarah. Do you mind if Jessica sits in with us?"

"Of course not."

Sarah took a seat across from the desk. I grabbed Mr. Davies's file from the desk and sat next to her. Jessica took a seat next to the window.

I leaned in, "Sarah, since you've done the preplanning with us, we only have to run through a few items. You've already picked out the casket, the church, and we have a preliminary flow. Janet has written up the obituary. I'll need you to review this and get back to us before noon tomorrow with any changes. Then we'll make sure we get it in the paper, which will also go on-line so you can share it with your family."

"Thanks, that all sounds fine, but I'll just review the obituary now, so we'll be all set," Mrs. Evans said.

Jess and I waited in silence for a few minutes for Mrs. Evans to review the obit. As I sat, I realized this was the room Dad died in. To my left in the trash can sat two halves of a broken coffee mug, his favorite mug. Someone forgot to empty the trash, I guess. Denise's belief that Dad didn't die of natural caus-es started to prick at the back of my neck, and I almost had to excuse myself. I looked at Jess, who was gazing out the window, which seemed to calm my nerves a bit. I busied myself by running through Janet's checklist to make sure I didn't forget anything.

Mrs. Evans made a few minor changes to the obituary and handed the paper back to me. Then I pulled the last form from the file I was holding and handed it back to Mrs. Evans. "Sarah, the financial part of this is never easy to talk about, especially so soon after your loss, but I've learned it's better to just get this out of the way now. Are you okay with that?" She nodded. "You've already noted in your preplanning that you want to make monthly payments to cover that final amount, which is completely fine. We just always like to remind the family that you can pay in full within a week after the funeral and save ten percent."

Mrs. Evans reviewed the itemized list of charges and said, "Yes, I think I'd like to take care of it. I can do that now," she said as she pulled out her check-book. This completely took me off guard, since the total amount of services came to approximately eight thousand dollars. From my limited experience, people like Mr. Davies and Mrs. Evans didn't have that kind of money to pay in full.

"Okay," I said. I went behind the desk and sat down in Dad's chair. I opened the second drawer and found a stack of invoices. "The total will come to eight thousand one hundred and twelve dollars."

Mrs. Evans started to write the check out saying, "My father took out a life insurance policy many years ago, but we cashed it in a few months back. There were just too many medical bills, and I honestly didn't know how long he was going to live. At the time, it seemed like a great idea, but since he passed so soon, not so much now."

"Really? I didn't know you could cash in a life insurance policy until earlier today. My father did the same thing," I said.

"I didn't either. It was called a life settlement. Dad was approached by an insurance guy right before he moved into Blessings. He wanted to buy his life insurance policy. It was a five-hundred-thousand-dollar policy, and after a bit of paperwork, we took home about one fifty. He was living with me at the time, and I just couldn't take care of him by myself anymore. He really needed 'round-the-clock care. And even though Blessings isn't the best place in Sandusky, it still costs about two hundred fifty dollars a day. Can you believe that? Anyway, the life settlement made all that possible."

I was fascinated by this and asked, "Your dad sold his life insurance policy and received, in cash, about one-third of the lifetime value? So you're saying that it's not a good deal now because your father passed so suddenly after you cashed in the policy."

"That's correct. I suppose if we didn't sell the policy, I would be receiving half a million dollars," she said as she handed me the check.

"Thank you, Sarah. I'll give all the information to Janet, and she'll call you tomorrow to confirm the rest of the details. Again, I'm very sorry for your loss."

"And I'm sorry for your loss as well. I guess all of us are having a pretty shitty week," she said and immediately turned to Jessica and said, "Sorry, dear, I didn't mean to curse in front of you."

Jessica stood, walked over from her chair, and gave Mrs. Evans a warm embrace saying, "No, Mrs. Evans, you said it right; it's all pretty shitty indeed."

They both smiled, and Mrs. Evans left as an instrumental version of John Lennon's "Imagine" played softly from the speaker system.

JESS ASKED TO HAVE dinner with Sam and me. My two favorite women in the world, but one of them hated me. Afterwards, Jess went to meet a couple of friends she hadn't seen for a while, which gave me a few hours to continue reviewing Uncle Dan's report on the funeral home.

As I headed for Dad's office, I stuck my head in to see Janet. "Do you have a few seconds?"

"Of course," she said. Janet stood up and followed me over to Dad's office.

"I'm trying to figure a few things out, and I think you are the best person to ask."

I sat in my dad's chair, and Janet took the seat across from me.

"No problem at all," she said.

"I started reviewing the state of Dad's business. Dan's company put a nice little report together for me, but a couple things don't add up. Now if I'm reading all these numbers correctly, over the past five years, the business has been cut in half. Does that sound about right to you?"

Janet sat and pondered the question. "Last year was brutal. Your father had to let go of four people. Through all the bad times before last year, your father was the picture of optimism, always giving motivational speeches to the team, talking about how we were going to turn things around. You know he was quite a speechmaker, your father. Anyway, all that stopped at the beginning of last year. You started to see the concern in his face every morning. He aged more in the last eighteen months than the previous ten years. You know how he was such a young-looking man for his age. Your mother's death took a toll on him." Then she looked over her shoulder and whispered, "I'm not sure who on the staff knows about this, but he sold the cemetery last year. Did you know that?"

"No, I didn't," I said.

"He had to sell the cemetery to cover what payroll he had left. I even told him I'd take a pay cut, but he wouldn't hear of it."

"Do you know who he sold it to?" I asked.

"Traynor Funeral Home," she said. "It seems most of the business we used to get goes to Traynor now. We get a lot fewer church folk as customers, and those that aren't religious don't see much value in our embalming services. But I'm sure you already knew that."

"I had a pretty good idea," I said. "This helps a lot, Janet. The cemetery sale answers a couple questions I had." I scratched my head. "Dad's reputation, the funeral home's reputation, still good in the community?"

"Your father is ... was ... the most liked man in this community. Even though you and I knew that he could really be a son of a bitch at times, when he was out in public, he could do no wrong. He could charm the knickers off a nun. This city considers him one of the key architects behind all the success to downtown and the waterfront. But maybe he was losing his touch a bit over the past few years, and it could have affected the business." Janet started to get emotional.

"Thanks, Janet," I said. "That was all very helpful."

She stared at me for half a second, got up, and left the office.

Chapter 8 – The Family Meeting

I had a few hours to kill before dinner, which gave me some much-needed time to look around Dad's office. It was a nice-sized office. Basically a big square with a door for visitors and a back door that led into the hall, then down to the embalming room, and a small closet left of the window facing the street.

While the room was clean at first glance, it was the kind of clean where you don't move the pictures or lamps when you dust, and maybe only sweep around the heavily trafficked areas. It needed a good wall-to-wall cleaning, especially in the corners where most of the dust bunnies were collecting.

I sat back and studied the ancient mahogany desk in front of me. Three drawers on each side, each one bigger than the last, from top to bottom. There also looked to be a middle drawer, maybe where a new desk would house a keyboard tray, but it didn't open.

The drawers were fairly organized. Office supplies in the top drawers and files in both bottom drawers. The left drawer contained files for Pollitt employees over the years, while the right drawer contained information on the bigger funeral home expenses. There was a file for makeup, one for embalming fluid, and a rather large one for the roof replacement, which happened about a decade ago. There must have been over a hundred files in all, each one precisely labeled with Dad's handwriting.

I made a mental note to run through the employee files at some point, then made my way to the closet. Locked. Janet had given me Dad's keys the night before so I could get into the house. At first glance, you'd think they were a school janitor's keys. There had to be at least fifty keys, all shapes and sizes. It took me ten minutes to find the right key and unlock the closet door.

I opened the door and found a chain hanging above my head, seemingly connected to a light. I pulled the chain. There were four shelves that wrapped around the three sides of the closet, and each one contained stacks and stacks of small black notebooks, maybe the size of a Moleskine. I'd seen Dad write in notebooks like these over the years but never knew where he kept them.

Knowing my father, I started with the bottom left side and guessed correctly, that was the oldest, and they went progressively newer until they wrapped around to the other side, then started all over again on the left side of the next shelf up. The top shelf was only half-filled with notebooks. Unfinished business, I thought, feeling a bit of sadness in my chest.

I picked out the first one and opened the front flap. My father had beautiful cursive handwriting, and I was excited that I could easily read every word.

November 15, 1974

Today is my first day as a funeral assistant at Frisch Funeral Home. In every success book I've ever read, it said that the most successful people in the world write down their daily activities. I figure this is as good a day as any to start. Mr. Frisch was nice enough to give me this job as an apprentice. I think he took a shine to me, or felt sorry for me, I'm not sure which. Probably the latter, with two small kids at home and a young family just fighting to survive.

While he's never said it, I think his master plan is for someone like me to take over the business someday. Mr. Frisch has no kids, and he has to be at least sixty-five or seventy years old. He already has me signed up to take some night classes at Cleveland Mortuary School, almost like he's in a hurry for me to get my embalmer's license.

I can't say it was ever my dream to be in the funeral business, but it's not a heck of a lot different than the other sales jobs I've had. You're always selling in this business, even when you're not selling. This morning, I watched Mr. Frisch talk to a grieving widow, telling her that her husband is in a better place now and she will be okay. To take it one day at a time. Great sales job he worked, especially when she purchased the custom wood casket over the basic steel.

Well, that's all I have for today. Hopefully I'll write some more tomorrow.

I closed the book and pressed it against my chest. I'm not sure what I was currently feeling, but it was something akin to winning the lottery or pulling a Mickey Mantle from an old pack of baseball cards. Before I became too excited, I selected one of the notebooks in the middle to see if they were continuations of my dad's diary.

Bingo. The first entry was March 2003. I returned that one to its spot and grabbed the last one on the top shelf, then flipped to the last page with words on it: December 2017. *Okay, good*. Taking what information I had at my disposal, I'd say there were two or three journals after December missing. Maybe he had them at his house.

Now that he was gone, I was desperate to know everything about my father. How did he start? How did he let the business go like this? What was his relationship like with Mom? Did he talk about me at all? Did he write about my gambling and debt problems? And the obvious question: why wasn't I this curious about my father before he died?

AS I WAS DRIVING TO meet Jess and Sam at the Cameo, a small pizza joint on the west side that Denise and I used to frequent as kids, it hit me that it was Wednesday. Since just after the divorce, I'd never missed my Wednesday Gamblers Anonymous meeting. I parked near the intersection of Monroe and Fulton streets where the Cameo was located and pulled out my phone. After a bit of Google magic, I found one GA meeting at eight p.m. at the St. Mary's Church Hall down the street.

My chest tightened as I closed the car door and headed to meet Jess and Sam. It'd been over two years since the three of us ate together. I wasn't sure if this was going to be good or bad, but I made a promise to myself not to act like a jerk.

I opened the door to a bar area, then zigzagged my way to the restaurant seating. As I approached a lectern with a *Please Wait to Be Seated* sign on the front, there were two women standing near it. Their backs were turned.

I put my arm around the taller one. "Hey, there," I said. "How was your afternoon? I forgot which friends you met with."

"It was great," Jess said. "It was Tracy and Zoe. They actually took the afternoon off to meet with me. They are super sweet. We're going to meet up tonight."

The hostess came over and led us to a four-top table in the corner. Jessica snuck into the back corner, while I sat underneath the Blatz sign and Sam sat under the vintage Pepsi-Cola clock.

"The waitress will be right back to take your order," the hostess said. "But I'll get you set up with waters." The hostess left, and we all sat in awkward silence.

"Well," Sam said. "Jessica tells me you put her to work this afternoon."

"Word travels fast," I said. "Actually, it was more for me than for her. I needed reinforcement. That was my first family meeting in what, like twenty years." I looked at Jess. "So, how did your dad do?"

"I was impressed," Jess said. "You put her at ease right away, and by the end of the meeting she was talking your ear off about the insurance thing. I think you have a future in the funeral business," she said, smirking.

"The most impressive part was you hugging her at the end," I said. "You and I make quite a team you know."

"Don't go recruiting her just yet," Sam said. "I'm not sure we'd want the entire family in the funeral business, especially since she's found her passion in media. By the way, Will, I've done plenty of family planning meetings. I could have done it, or you could have called me to help."

There was a lot I wanted to say to this offer, but I simply said, "Thanks, Sam. I should have known that."

"Will there be a next time, Dad?" Jess asked.

"Your mother already knows this, but your grandfather left the funeral home to me in the will." I paused. "This is a decision I'm not taking lightly, and it affects many people, including your mother, and of course, Robby, with our marketing business."

"Is there a timetable for a decision?" Jess asked.

"I think sooner than later would be better for everyone involved. I spent a good chunk of the day going through the financials. I also talked to Janet for a bit today. But your mother and I still need to talk about it."

"Oh," Jess said. "Would you like me to leave so you can?"

"No!" both Sam and I said simultaneously. She looked away and I smiled at Jess. "No, we can talk later about it. I think right now we'd like to spend some time with you."

We spent the next forty-five minutes peppering Jess with questions. No boyfriend, but she had been seeing a few people. Grades were okay but could probably be better. She liked all her teachers, except for statistics, because she hated the entire concept of math. She liked the campus, but it was too big and a few of her classes were twenty-five minutes away by foot. She had picked up a part-time job working the night desk at the campus Catholic church two nights a week. Sam and I were both concerned with the "night" aspect of the job, but Jess convinced us that it was all pretty safe.

After finishing off a large thin-crust, Jess received multiple texts from her friends. Apparently, there was going to be a large gathering at Daley's, the historic Irish pub downtown, and she asked to leave. "Are you two going to be okay without me?" Jess asked.

"I think we can handle it," I said. "Have a great time."

"If you are going to be later than twelve, please text me," Sam said.

"Mom, I'm twenty-one now."

"I don't care if you're a hundred and one, I'm your mother, and I need to know that you're safe," Sam said.

At that, Jess hugged us both and left. I looked at my watch. 6:15.

"I think I've had enough of the soda. Would you like a beer?" I asked Sam.

"I'm not sure this is a good idea," Sam said.

I felt more nervous being here with Sam than on our first date. I really wanted to spend some time with her and wasn't entirely sure how to proceed.

I took a deep breath. "Look, Sam, you have been put in a very difficult situation. Not only do you have to deal with the death of your mentor, but you have to deal with me who's let you down so many times. And then you find out today that I could take over your place of work." I paused. She was listening. "I'm not sure how to handle all this, and the only thing I'm asking from you is that, at least for this week, you give me the benefit of the doubt. After all Dad's funeral stuff is over and we figure out the workplace thing, I promise I'll leave you alone, well, except for issues with Jess."

She looked at me, trying to see if I was telling the truth. Pretty much her normal look since the second time she found out I was gambling. She let out a long, deep breath. "Okay," she said. "I'll do my best, but I make no promises. I still don't trust you as far as I can throw you. But yes, I'll have a beer."

I waved the waitress over and ordered a pitcher of the local brew.

"I was hoping to ask you a few questions about the business, if you're okay talking about it," I said.

"I think I can," Sam said. "I'm not a fan of you running the business, but it's my fault I'm in this position."

"Why do you say that?"

"I'm the one that went to work with your father. I could have hunted around for someone else to work for, but he gave me a shot to embalm right away. Do you know how many licensed female embalmers there are in the US?"

"No, but I bet you do."

"Fewer than ten thousand, about a third of the number of men. Although it's getting better—the majority of my class at mortuary school were women—it's still an uphill battle."

"You know, I haven't had a chance to really talk to you about this, but I'm proud of you. After all the shit I put you through, you finished your schooling and became the best embalmer in the state."

"Well," she said, "You don't know how good I am, but thanks for the compliment. You're just trying to get on my good side."

"Is it working?"

"Jury's still out."

"I do know, by the way. I didn't talk to Dad all that often, but I always asked about you when I did and he was very honest in his assessment. Would you like to hear it?"

"Only if it's good."

"He said your understanding of the human body, from an embalming standpoint, was the best he'd ever seen. And you know he taught night classes at Cleveland Mortuary for some time, so he should know. He also said you could probably do all the makeup for the funeral home as well."

She smiled. "Did he say anything constructive?"

"He said you were great in planning meetings but hated to upsell, specifically caskets. He said you always sold the cheapest one."

"I never saw the point of an extravagant casket. I did sell a custom wood casket one time, but I felt awful afterward and had to go take a shower."

"Regardless, he thought a lot of you. More than he thought of me, that's for sure."

"Now you know that's not true. He just didn't know how to talk with you once you started to go through your addiction issues."

I wasn't sure how much he knew, but he obviously knew enough to share it with Sam.

I quickly changed the subject. "I've been going through the annual numbers, and something's not right." I filled Sam in on the same information I'd relayed to Robby and Janet.

"Did anything strange happen around the beginning of last year, or any time last year?" I asked.

Sam started playing with a crumpled straw wrapper on the table. "Well, there's the death of your mother. But there were other things after that. I can't remember exactly when it started. Maybe right around Easter of last year. Or even before that."

"You noticed less business?" I asked.

"Not at the time. That came later, and it was very noticeable. I was doing fewer embalmings every month." She paused. "No, I noticed a change in your father. He was often irritable. Sometimes I'd see him sitting and staring sadly into space. And you know your father, he rarely sat, and he definitely never acted sad, even when he was. Remember when your mom passed away and how sad your father was, but he never showed it? It's almost like he'd been keeping all these emotions inside for years and they were starting to break free."

"What happened around Easter?"

"A few months after, maybe around this time last year, I asked him about it. He shrugged it off entirely. Said he was just getting old. Of course, that was a lie. I just couldn't figure it out."

"I found his collection of diaries today. With your timetable, I'll go back in and see if there are any clues as to what was going on. Did you know he wrote a diary?"

"He was writing all the time, and he loved his little black notebooks, but I didn't know it was a diary."

"You won't believe it. He has black notebooks going back to when he was a funeral apprentice for Frisch, all the way back to '74."

"Let me know if you'd like any help. I loved your father and I want to know if something was going on." Sam looked at her watch. "I'm sorry, Will, I need to be somewhere else."

Does she have a date? It's been two years; she probably has a date ... I need to let it go.

I pulled myself together. "That's okay. This was great. Honestly, I wasn't sure this was going to be a good idea, but it's been nice talking again. Thank you."

"There were a hundred possible outcomes for this night, and that this one ended with me not killing you is probably for the best," Sam said smiling.

I waved the waitress over for the check.

Sam and I walked outside together. Her car was right in front, while mine was three cars down. We stood in front of each other for a while. *Do I shake her hand? Do I kiss her on the cheek? No, don't kiss her.*

I went with the awkward wave. "Okay, I'll see you tomorrow. Be careful driving."

Sam closed her car door and drove away.

Chapter 9 – Twelve Steps

The GA meeting was next to the old church I attended as a child. Apparently, some woman passed away a decade ago and left millions to the church, and in her honor, they built an attached hall. Now it's used for donuts and coffee after mass, feeding the homeless on Monday nights, and AA and GA meetings.

I walked into a circle of chairs. In each one sat the standard yellow book with *Gamblers Anonymous* printed on the cover. I threw my jacket over one and went to the coffee station. A little after eight p.m., a man, looking to be in his late fifties, tall and thin with a salt-and-pepper goatee, asked everyone to find a chair in the circle. I walked over to him and introduced myself before the meeting began. His name was Pete S. He thanked me for coming and said there was plenty of room.

The last of the smokers came in from outside and the meeting began. There were eleven of us in total, just two women. Men drastically outnumbered women at most meetings I attended.

Then Pete asked, "Do we have anyone here that's never been to a Gamblers Anonymous meeting before?" No one said anything. "That makes it easy then." Pete opened his booklet, turned the page and said, "My name is Pete S., and I'm the facilitator of this group. As you all know, gambling for the compulsive gambler is defined as follows: Any betting or wagering, for self or others, whether for money or not, no matter how slight or insignificant, where the outcome is uncertain or depends upon chance or 'skill' constitutes gambling."

Pete went on to read portions of the next three or four pages of the book. Unnecessary, but mandatory for all GA meetings. I've heard this so much I can almost recite it by heart. Stuff about the founders of GA, commentary on the twelve-step program, description of the nature of gambling addiction.

I don't buy into everything, and I'm not a big fan of twelve-step programs, but for the last two years these meetings have helped. Then Pete said, "We'll go around and do short, and I mean short, introductions and then Roger P. will speak. He's been nice enough to volunteer as this week's speaker."

I was third up. I stood and said, "Hi. My name is Will P., and I'm a compulsive gambler."

"Hi, Will," the group said in unison.

"Two years ago, I ruined my marriage trading online, realized too late that I had a problem, and have been coming to GA meetings since then. I'm from Cleveland and go to my usual GA meetings on Wednesday, but today I'm here in Sandusky. So here I am. Thanks for being so welcoming."

It took about twenty minutes to go around the room. There's always someone who takes too long, and Brenda B. took about ten minutes with her introduction, which would have been longer, but Pete finally insisted she stop.

Then Roger P. gave his personal testimony. Roger was about my age, married, now divorced, with three kids. Within his driving territory for his job, he liked to hit all the casinos. He loved table games, but craps was the big problem. He liked playing the come line and needed to have all the points going at the same time. When someone was on a roll, life was good. But Roger was playing these multiple points with maximum odds behind each point and did this at every casino he visited. He started out losing one or two thousand a trip. With each visit, he bet more and more. A few times he went home a winner, but the losses added up to over a hundred thousand dollars in just one year. Then the story ended like most usually do. He lied to the wife, borrowed money he didn't have, got himself into a bigger hole, and finally sought help when he lost his credit rating, wife, and kids, and had a loan shark or two trying to kill him. Ah, the life of a compulsive gambler. The good news? Roger hadn't gambled for over a year. He just started seeing a woman and luckily still has his insurance job.

Roger ended with a speech about living in the present, something he was adamant on improving. With gambling, he was always looking forward to the next bet or the next roll of the dice. It was almost impossible for him to live in the present. To be happy with his wife and his kids without thinking about what would be next.

After Roger was finished, a few others gave a short testimony. Brenda wanted to talk more but Pete told her she'd be able to go next time. At the end, we all stood and held hands and read the Serenity Prayer out loud. Before we were excused, Pete told us the collection plate was over by the coffee, and since the group supported itself, donations were gladly accepted.

I walked over and refilled my coffee cup, throwing a five-dollar bill on the collection plate. I thanked Pete and walked out the glass doors. Roger was outside smoking. I approached him.

"Roger," I said, putting out my hand. "I'm Will. I wanted to thank you for your testimony. When you were talking about living in the present, it was like you were peering into my soul. Everything for me is ... was ... always about the next trade."

"Yep. Thanks. Welcome to Sandusky, Will," Roger said, taking out another cigarette.

I pulled a cigarette pack out of my jacket. There were three cigarettes inside the dented box. I took one out and started digging for a lighter. Without saying a word, Roger flicked his lighter and held it out for me.

"Thanks," I said.

"Judging from the shape of that cigarette, you don't smoke very often," Roger said.

"Guilty as charged," I said. "It's my emergency pack. It's been a tough week, so I'm allowing myself to smoke and drink at will."

"I take it that's why you're in town?"

"Yep, death in the family."

"My condolences," Roger said.

"Thanks. Hey, you said you work in insurance. I have an odd insurance question if you don't mind."

"Shoot."

"Have you heard of a life settlement? The first I heard of it was earlier today, and I didn't think something like that existed."

"Oh, I can tell you anything you want to know about life settlements. It's hotter than Bitcoin, and my first piece of advice is to stay away from them. The devil's handiwork those are."

"Are they new?"

"Not exactly. They've been around since the early 1900s, same as reverse mortgages, but now the big insurance companies, always looking for a buck, have created all these subcompanies that sell life settlements, and the industry has made it look like legitimate business. If you stay up late enough, all the commercials you'll see are for either Viagra or life settlements."

"How exactly do they work?" I asked.

"An insurance agent or broker, working for one of those large subcompanies, will scour the coverage area looking for anyone with, let's say, a five-hundred-thousand-dollar policy or greater. Then they'll get that data and cross-reference it with financial issues. Like maybe you haven't been paying your bills on time, or maybe you had to downsize from a house to an apartment. Then they'll take that list—did you see that movie *Glengarry Glen Ross*? Well this would be like the Glengarry leads, the good leads. Anyway, then they do their ambulance-chasing. They'll call or visit or send emails and go fishing."

Roger pulled out another cigarette and continued. "They'll tell you that you can get your insurance money now before you die and it's all legal. This is especially promising for those who have lost their beneficiaries or maybe hate them and don't want to leave anything to them upon death," he said smiling. "Once the broker gets them interested, he runs the numbers with the subcompany on high, or maybe a couple of them, and they'll quote him a figure. Generally, you'll see something between fifty K and a hundred fifty K for a five-hundred-thousand-dollar policy, or maybe two hundred to two fifty for a million-dollar policy, depending on a number of factors. They use a very complicated formula to ascertain the current value and then give a 'fair offer' to the life insurance holder, which is generally quite a bit more than the cash surrender value of the policy. But in the end, the person who sells their life insurance policy receives some percentage of cash from the insurance company."

"So what's the catch?" I asked.

"The insurance company or third party that buys the policy is betting that you'll die sooner than the math tells you. So let's say you sell your five hundred K policy for a hundred K, and you're healthy as a horse. But then the next week you die. The insurance company just made four hundred K, getting the entire death benefit of the policy, and all they had to give you was a hundred K. But if the individual would have waited that week and not sold, the person's beneficiary would have received the full five hundred K in cash.

"The long and short of it? I guess if you really need the money and this is your only way, then fine. Kind of like those check-cashing places. But I've stayed entirely away from that business. There are a lot of better ways for an insurance agent to make money than betting on when someone will kick the bucket. It does feel a little like gambling. Make sense?"

"Totally, great explanation. Thanks!"

"If I may ask, how did you come across a life settlement?"

"My dad was in the funeral business. One of his customers paid for their father's funeral with life settlement money."

"I'm surprised this is the first time you've seen it," Roger said.

We exchanged phone numbers for support, which was pretty much standard practice at GA meetings, said our good-byes, and I headed for the parking lot.

On my drive back to Dad's house, Roger's last comment hung in the air. *I'm surprised this is the first time you've seen it.* I made a mental note to review Dad's diaries and customer notes again to see if this had come up before.

Chapter 10 – The Ultimatum

It was six thirty the next morning when I arrived at the funeral home, and both Jack and Janet were already there. I found them in the coffee room. "Why are you two in so early?"

They looked at each other and smiled. "How do you think shit gets done around here, boy?" Jack said. "We can't mosey in at eight like normal people and expect the world to cooperate."

Then Janet turned to me and said, "The phone's been ringing nonstop since I walked in at six. Looks like people are just finding out about your father, so we should expect a full day of calls and visits, even though visitation isn't until tomorrow."

"Got it," I said, and headed for Dad's office.

This time it took me only five minutes to find the right key to the closet. I opened the door and pulled the chain on the light. I went to the top shelf where I thought the most recent notebooks were. The diary writing tailed off starting in 2015. There were twelve notebooks for 2014, eight for 2015, and six for 2016. I could only find two for 2017.

I pulled out the 2017 notebooks and prepared for a full review. They were unlike the diaries I'd found from previous years. In these, Dad skipped days at a time and generally only posted about picking up bodies or visitations or funerals that interested him in some way. The death calls he detailed were the most interesting, and I appreciated his writing style.

Janet buzzed me from her office. It was a call from Uncle Dan.

"Hey, son," Dan said. "There's a luncheon of the downtown city leaders today. The group is called the Sandusky Alliance—SA for short. Your father helped create it. Anyway, I'd like you to join us today."

"Sure, I guess," I said. "You don't think I'd be out of place?"

"No, no. Not at all," Dan said. "If you decide to take over the funeral home, they'll probably want you in the group anyway. It's good timing."

"Okay," I said. Dan gave me the location and I told him I'd see him there.

Sitting at my dad's desk, I tried to think what he would do during this portion of the day if he were still alive. When I was younger and used to follow him around the funeral home, one of his main activities was walking around the place and talking to all the employees. He would see how they were doing and ask them questions, both business and personal. I remember him telling me, *Will, a true leader never hides in his office. A leader needs to be visible. A leader needs to care about his employees. And you have to be consistent about it. You have to get out there every day and talk to them.*

My first stop? To see how Sam was doing. I found her in the embalming room.

"So, how was your meeting last night?"

"I'm not sure we're at a point where I can talk about my after-dinner meetings with you," Sam said.

"You're right. Sorry I brought it up," I said. "Actually, I was hoping to talk to you about the funeral home for a few minutes."

"That's fine," she said, looking at Mr. Davies, who was completely naked lying on a working table. In looking at him from this perspective, I had no idea how Jack and I pulled him off the toilet. "I don't think Mr. Davies is going anywhere at the moment."

"I could use a refill," I said, looking into my cup. "How about we go upstairs to the kitchen?"

In the kitchen, Sam began looking at the different coffee flavors, and I closed the kitchen door. I didn't want anyone to listen in at the moment. While Sam's coffee brewed, I leaned back against the sink.

"I'll get right to the point, Sam. I haven't made a decision yet, but I'm still considering whether to take over Dad's business. And I know exactly what that means for you." I took a deep breath and exhaled. My brain kept telling me to take the money and run, especially for Jess's sake, but something in my gut told me that was the wrong decision. "Now, I don't want this to seem like an ultimatum, because it definitely isn't, but I'll only do this if you decide to stay. If you tell me that you can't work with me, I'm not going to do it."

Sam poured some half-and-half into her cup and had a seat at the kitchen table while I popped a breakfast blend into the Keurig. "It certainly sounds like an ultimatum, a weird one, but an ultimatum, nonetheless. You're making your decision completely dependent on what *I* decide to do?"

"You should be flattered," I said.

"Oh, grow a pair, Will," she said. "You need to make this decision independent of what I do. That's what your father would want you to do."

I took a seat across the table from Sam. "I'm not so sure of that, Sam. You're the best there is at what you do, and outside of being good with people and understanding the mechanics of the funeral business, I don't know shit. I've looked at the reports. I've looked at the numbers. There might be some things I can do to turn this around, but you run the core business. There are some things that are going to need to happen quickly around here, but none of that can happen if I have to find a new embalmer who can't do half the things you do."

Sam looked down at her coffee. "This is not ten years ago when I helped get your marketing business off the ground. Now I love what I do and don't want to stop by any means I know I'm good at it and it's truly meaningful work, but how do I know you won't take the business and screw everyone over."

Sam always knew how to get to the point quickly.

"Honestly, you don't. I might come in here and screw it up. Since we split up, I've been getting help. It's a daily grind, but as long as I focus on the right things, go to the meetings, ask for help when I need it, I'm beating this thing. Could I lose it? Yes. Do I think I will? No." We both sat in silence. "How about this, Sam? Just give me a month. Thirty days is all I ask. After that, you and I talk. If you aren't happy, I walk."

Sam stared into my eyes. Then she stood to walk out, stopped, and looked back at me. "Okay," she said and left the room.

Chapter 11 – The Alliance

The Sandusky Alliance meeting was a block away from Uncle Dan's office. *Larraby Tours,* the sign said. Again, a beautiful view of the bay. Seemed like a waste to put an office here and not a restaurant with a patio, or maybe one of those outdoor shopping areas that are popping up everywhere, but what do I know? I parked the van and knocked on the door.

A man, a little over six feet tall, pulled the door open and stood to the side, welcoming me in. I started to introduce myself but was quickly interrupted.

"Will, you don't have to knock, just come on in," he said.

It was a ten-foot hallway that led to a larger office area. Four cubicles, all connected, with phones and laptops and personal items cluttered around the monitors. I turned back to face him as he closed the door and walked toward me.

"You don't remember me, do you? That's okay. Mark Larraby," he said putting out his hand. "I was assistant coach on your baseball team too many years ago. I think it was a team sponsored by your father."

I still didn't remember but I went with it. "Mr. Larraby, I'm sorry I didn't recognize you. What was that, thirty years ago?"

"More than that," he said. "I was just out of college helping my dad with the team, and you were a little shit. Anyway, we're waiting for a few more to drop by, but most of the group is already here. Follow the hall to the back, and I'll be there in a minute."

I made my way down the hall to a conference room. In the front was a large table that seated ten or twelve. In the back was a table covered in food—sandwich spreads, meats, cheeses, olives, and three guys loading up plates. As I walked into the room, they stopped what they were doing and called out my name, each putting down their plates on a side table.

"Welcome, Will," the first man said. "We're so very sorry about your father. I'm Mitch Dreason," he said, holding out his hand. The other two gentleman were Bob Kasper and Barry White. I chuckled when I met Barry, a tall thin man who looked nothing like the R&B singer, but I said nothing.

Uncle Dan and Mike Walker, owner of Walker Cleaners, entered the room, followed closely by Mr. Larraby. Everyone filled up their plates, grabbed some coffee, and sat at the conference table. I was at the head of the table, feeling a bit uncomfortable that I was probably sitting in my father's chair. It felt like I was meeting with the cast of *Cocoon*, minus the women.

Mr. Larraby began the meeting. "Before we start the official meeting, I have two announcements. First, we want to recognize the loss of our good friend Abe Pollitt, who served with us in this group for many a year. Second, welcome to Will, Abe's son. I think everyone here knows, but Will runs a successful marketing firm in Cleveland and is currently considering whether to run his father's funeral business here in Sandusky."

The comment took me off guard. I didn't know that they knew about my father's will. Dan quickly chimed in, "Your father shared his most intimate details with this group, so everyone here has known for years what his succession plan was. I just want you to know that it didn't come from me," he said, smiling.

"No worries at all," I said, but I didn't like it. It seemed everyone knew my father's plans but me.

"Did your dad tell you much about what we do here at Sandusky Alliance?" Mark asked.

"I'm sorry," I said. "To be honest, I just found out about the Alliance from Uncle Dan."

Mark smiled. "No problem at all, Will. So you know, this is not a formal meeting of SA, but Dan thought it would be a good idea that you got to know us a bit, and we all agreed."

"SA is the group behind the resurgence of Sandusky's downtown area," Dan said, looking up at the ceiling, then back to me. "At least we like to think so. Pollitt Funeral Home is an important part of Sandusky, and we want to see that continue. Everyone knows that the funeral business is a tough one these days, with all the cremations, but we at SA would like to see both Pollitt and Traynor Funeral Home stay a part of this vibrant community." Dan paused, probably giving me time for that to sink in. John Traynor and Dad had a rivalry for years, and it was never a friendly one. Dad believed that Traynor cut corners in both its funeral execution and its sales practices to create a profitable enterprise. I was actually good friends with John Traynor's son Alex in high school, but that never went over well on either side.

Bob Kasper cleared his throat and began to speak. "I believe Dan has told you that Jack Miller is interested in buying your father's funeral business. That's true and not true at the same time. While Jack has some money, he doesn't have close to providing you with fair value if you choose to sell the business. Our idea—and Jack is well aware of this—is to provide a loan to Jack to get him to a point so he can pay you the value of the business, which we believe stands at one-time revenue, or about eight hundred thousand. Minus your father's outstanding loans, that would leave you with approximately half that."

Geez, they even knew the revenue numbers. Talk about coming to a meeting with your pants down. But holy shit. Four hundred thousand would solve all of my debt problems and keep Jess in school. Valuing the company at one-time revenue, for this business, was almost too good to be true.

Bob paused long enough for me to get a word in. "Anything this group isn't aware of?" I said, looking at Dan.

"Will, this group knows everything about Sandusky, which means this group knows about your father's business in its entirety," Dan said without concern. "And we all know about each other's business, intimately. Let's just say, if one of us goes down, we're all affected. It may sound strange coming from Cleveland, but groups like SA thrive in just about every small city in the Midwest. Regardless, let Bob finish, and then we can all chat." Dan nodded back to Bob.

"We're willing to provide a no-interest loan to Jack so he can continue your father's business. Again, only if you decide not to run it yourself. Jack, with our assistance, can then continue your father's tradition of quality funeral service at Pollitt Funeral Home."

"Sounds like a great deal for Jack *and* me if I decide not to take over the business," I said. "What's the catch?"

Dan smiled. "I told you he's smart, didn't I, gentlemen? Yes, William, there's a catch, which is the real reason why you are here. Even though we want both Pollitt and Traynor in Sandusky, we don't believe Pollitt can survive on its own in the current business climate. The only way your father kept it going was by selling a number of assets. He sold most of his real estate portfolio over the past few years as a cash infusion for the business. Basically, Abe Pollitt, the individual, was the only reason Pollitt Funeral's business stayed open."

The choreography was amazing. Everything seemed so relaxed between the group, but I've been in thousands of meetings and knew better. This had a clear agenda. Now it was Barry White's turn to speak.

"We'll stop beatin' around the bush," Barry said. "Jack would do a great job running the funeral home, but he can't grow the business. I've been told you know Jack pretty well, so you know this to be true. We have an alternative proposal for you to consider."

Ah, here it comes.

At that, Barry deferred to Mitch. "We're good friends with the Traynor family. Now they'd be willing to purchase Pollitt Funeral Home. Being that you've been competitive with Traynor for years, probably knowing this since you were just a small boy, this might be an uneasy proposition for you. That's understandable. Alex Traynor, he's John's son who took over the business, is about your age if I'm not mistaken. You used to be friends, right? I told Alex that you'd only consider if you received a premium over-stated current value and the name Pollitt stayed on the sign for perpetuity. Alex knows we're talking today and wanted to approach you personally, but we all here agreed it would be better coming from us."

Alex Traynor. Yes, we were friends our first two years of high school. Maybe best friends. But he went off to summer camp in between our sophomore and junior years and turned into a different person. We stopped hanging out after that. He was truly gifted with computers. And I mean Bill Gates or Mark Zuckerberg gifted.

But Mitch was wrong about one thing. If Traynor ever took over Pollitt Funeral Home, I'd never want to keep the name on the sign. Never.

Dan took a long drink from his coffee cup and said, "I wanted you to hear about this before you made any decisions. This was something I couldn't tell you in our meeting yesterday since there are a few moving parts that I had no control over. But no more surprises from here on out."

I can't say I was in love with all this discussion behind my back, but I kept that to myself. "Well, gentleman, I truly appreciate your concern for my father and for the business," I said. Then I looked at Dan. "So all this isn't just discussion, can you get something in writing about both offers so I can make a proper decision?"

"Absolutely, my boy," Dan said.

I sat through another thirty minutes of business dealings around the city, but they kept everything high level. I thanked each of them and left the way I came in.

As I approached the van, there he was, leaning against a car nearby.

"How's it going, William?"

"Hi, Alex. It's been a long time," I said. We shook hands. It was Alex, but it wasn't. The timid boy I knew in high school was all grown up now. Same height as before, but the man definitely worked out with his biceps and veins protruding out from the sleeves of his Ralph Lauren polo shirt.

"Sorry I couldn't be in the meeting. I really wanted to. I'm sure they explained," he said.

"Yes." I paused. "I appreciate the offer. Gives me something to think about for sure." This sounded like a much better response than *Fuck off*. I could feel the anger building inside of me. We had been best friends. We had an incredible amount in common. Both funeral home kids. Both obsessed with numbers. We probably spent the entire summer after our freshman year smoking and talking in our old hideout just outside the Traynor facility. Although he turned into a jerk a year later, I had no real reason to be this upset at him. Something just didn't feel right.

"We can talk now about it if you want," Alex said. "I did the numbers myself and it's a fair offer. I'm sure you could use the money." He gave me a look like he did, in fact, know something. I must have made a facial reaction because he quickly added, "Uh, we did our homework on you and the business before we put the offer together. How about we go get a drink and chat it over? There's a great little place just around the corner. We could trade stories about the trouble we made in high school."

"That was a long time ago." I paused. "Thanks, Alex, but I need to get going. I'm sure you understand."

"Okay. Of course," Alex said, looking me over. "Let me know if you want to talk sometime, about the deal or whatever." He went to walk away and then added, "Oh, and sorry about your father."

Chapter 12 – The Reunion

As soon as I arrived back at the funeral home, Janet caught me. "Oh, good, you're here," she said. "Mr. Davies's daughter, Mrs. Evans, called and said she has a problem with the funeral date. I just told her you'd call her back ASAP."

Janet handed me a small sheet of paper with a number and smiled, resting her hands just above her belt. "Do a good job."

I walked back to Dad's office and sat down to make the call.

"Mrs. Evans? Hi, this is Will Pollitt from Pollitt Funeral Home returning your call."

"Thanks for calling back so quickly," she said. "Here's the situation. A good chunk of our family is overseas, and they all seem to be having trouble getting travel visas." This was totally understandable to me as the current administration had been limiting travel visas for certain countries. "We don't think they can make it to Sandusky until next week. Would it be possible to postpone the funeral?"

"I'm sorry to hear that, Mrs. Evans. Yes, we can help with that. Do you think next Friday would be enough time? If possible, I'd like to reschedule only once."

"I think so. Thanks. What else do you need from me?" she asked.

"Nothing. We'll take care of the rest."

She thanked me again, and I gave Janet the news so she could make all the calls: the church, the cemetery, the florist, the newspaper, updating the online obituary and notice, and about ten other little things that most people would never think of.

Then I called Robby, who picked up the phone after two rings.

"Any word yet?" I asked.

"I talked to Sarah Arnold this morning. She told me she was very impressed with our presentation and that they haven't made a decision yet."

"Vibe?"

"Not good. I think they've already made the decision, but it's not official yet. You know all the hoops they have to go through at a company like that to select an agency of record. We got them thinking, and they're intrigued, but I bet they'll play it safe."

"You're probably right, but thanks for keeping on them."

"Yeah, I'll ping her again tomorrow without trying to be too annoying," Robby said.

He paused.

"Hey, I can wrap up early here. How about I come to Sandusky for dinner? I was going to come early for visitation tomorrow to keep you company, but I got all my homework finished and have nothing else to do."

"Robby, you don't have to do that."

"Whatever. I'll text you when I'm on the way."

"Great ... thanks. Hey, I forgot to ask you. Have you ever heard of a life settlement?"

"Sure. Why?"

"Really? I met with a customer yesterday whose father cashed one out. I thought it was really strange and I'm curious to know how prevalent they are in this area."

"I'll call my uncle in Elyria. He deals with all kinds of insurance, and I think he dabbles in that as well. I'll let you know."

We ended the call. Sitting in Dad's office, I wasn't really sure what to do. I texted Jess.

Plans for dinner? Robby's coming in. Would you like to come?

The three dots showed up right away.

Thx, Dad. I already have dinner plans tonight. Sorry.

That's okay. Remember to be at the funeral home by noon tomorrow to prepare for visitation. It goes pretty much all night.

Of course, she texted. *Love you.*

You too.

I headed down to the embalming room. Sam had just finished with Mr. Davies. She heard me coming and looked up.

"Hey," she said.

"Hey," I returned. "Did Janet tell you about Mr. Davies?"

"No, what?"

"We need to postpone the funeral services until next Friday. Apparently, they're having trouble getting family into town from overseas," I said.

"Visa trouble?"

"How did you know?"

"It happens more than you'd think. The past few years we've run into a bunch of issues with anyone coming in from the Middle East, Africa, China ... the list seems to be growing. Especially with the poor. Where is the family coming from?"

"I didn't ask," I said.

"You should ask next time you talk to her. It's good to know for future reference."

"I will."

I paused.

"Robby is coming in tonight, and we're heading to dinner. Would you like to come?"

She stopped what she was doing for a split second and then continued. "No. I don't think so."

"It's fine, Sam. We are all grown-ups here. You and Robby love each other. I'm sure he'd love to catch up with you."

She just looked at me. "Maybe," she said, then paused. "All right."

"Cool. I'll text you when I know the time. Probably around six or so."

As I reached the exit, Sam called, "One more thing."

I turned around.

"I got a call from the coroner, Jim McGinty, an hour ago. He's calling the death a heart attack, like we all figured."

Well, seems like Denise was wrong after all. I nodded. "Did he say anything else?" I asked.

"Not a thing."

At that, I left her to finish her work and headed back upstairs.

ROBBY WALKED THROUGH the front door just as Janet, Jack, and I finished our final preparation for Dad's visitation. Both Janet and Jack knew Robby, but they took a few moments to get reacquainted. Janet walked quickly away, and Jack lingered a bit. Then Robby followed me into Dad's office.

"You need to take a look at this," I said, unlocking the closet door. I opened the door and led him in to see the shelves of Dad's notebooks. "Would you believe that Dad kept a diary all these years, going back to his days as an apprentice?"

I handed one to Robby. He flipped through the pages. "Unbelievable. This is a gold mine," Robby said.

"Read this one," I said. "Sit down. I'll wait."

As Robby read, his smile became wider, then he giggled, then laughed out loud. "Holy shit, Will. I can't believe this is true. How many stories are here?"

"I have no idea. I've only read through a few. But I'm guessing hundreds, maybe a thousand or more."

"You know ..." Robby was cut off as Sam walked into the room and put her hands over Robby's eyes, standing behind him.

"Who's your favorite girl?" she said.

"Scarlett Johansson?"

"Close enough," Sam said. Robby stood up, picked Sam up off the ground, and spun her around 180 degrees.

"Hey, girl. It's so good to see you." Robby looked at Sam from head to toe and back up again. "You look gooood. Have you lost weight?"

"Always the charmer, you. Will said I could crash your little dinner party."

Robby tilted his head back like he was dodging a bullet. "What year is this?" he said. "Did I miss something?"

"Stop being so dramatic, you ass," I said. "I can be a grown-up."

"What? Did you steal someone's maturity level over the past few days?"

"It's cool," Sam said. "We went to dinner with Jess the other night, so we got the uncomfortable moments out of the way."

"You did?" Robby said. "Well, I need a drink. Let's get the heck out of here. I'll drive."

I wanted to show Robby the development downtown, so we zigzagged through the streets until we came to a bar called Tony's, good for drinks and burgers, a stone's throw from Uncle Dan's office. As we approached the door to Tony's, I noticed a bright SA sticker illuminated in the window.

We waited in front of a sign that said, *Please Wait to Be Seated (unless you're drinking at the bar)*. Then a very attractive woman, looking maybe late thirties, came over and said, "Hi, there, how many?" She grabbed three menus and seated us in the corner near the window overlooking the street. We took our seats, Robby in the middle with the chair to the left of me open.

As she placed the menu in front of me, she looked at me, squinting her right eye to get a better look. "Billy?" she asked.

"That's me," I said, looking back at her, pointing my finger, trying to remember.

"Shit, Billy. It's Xena, from high school. Remember?"

"Oh, my God," I said, standing up and giving her a hug. I remained standing. "I go by Will now."

Xena was always a looker in high school, but she was stunning now. I couldn't tell if she had work done or not, but everything seemed to be working. The long black hair, voluptuous breasts, and everything else were raised a bit higher than usual for someone in their forties.

"You look great. How have you been?" I asked.

"Not bad. I'm so happy you came in. We've been making some changes to the menu, and I'd love to get your opinion. Marketing, right?"

"Yeah. How long have you been here?" I asked. I wasn't sure if she just worked here or if the bar/restaurant was hers, so I treaded lightly.

"I rounded up some funds to buy this place a few years ago. Got in at a good time before it started to get real nice around here and real estate shot up."

"Congratulations, Xena. That's fantastic," I said. "I'm sorry, this is Sam and Robby. Sam works at my dad's funeral home, and Robby is my partner at our marketing agency in Cleveland."

"Nice to meet you both," she said, shaking hands. "I forgot, I'm so sorry to hear about your father. I only met him a few times here and there, but he took real good care of my Aunt Rita a few years back. God bless his soul." She paused. "Anyway, your server will be over in a second. Thanks so much for coming in and great seeing you."

"You too." I sat back down.

"Xena? As in *Xena: Warrior Princess*?" Robby asked. "You graduated with her? She looks ten years younger than you."

"I couldn't tell," I said, smiling. I wanted to change the subject quickly. "So apparently they have great burgers here."

Once the server came around, it was beer and a burger for each of us. I was hoping the dinner would feel like getting the band back together, but it was the opposite. I watched and listened to Robby and Sam catch up, smiling and laughing and talking old times. They were always so close, and the divorce pretty much made Robby choose time with me over Sam. I should have let them go to dinner without me.

"I almost forgot what I wanted to tell you," Robby said. "I ended up stopping to see my uncle in Elyria about the life settlements."

Sam looked confused. "About Mr. Davies and the life settlement thing. I told Robby," I said. She nodded.

"Yeah. So, we had a real nice chat about it. He said the business is gangbusters in this area. All kinds of shit is going on. Some folks can't afford their meds. Some need cash to get out of the cold and go to Florida. Some need a down payment for assisted living. So they cash out their policies and get what they get. My uncle said for some one-million-dollar policies, he's seen a payout of half a million from one of the insurance companies. Kind of like hitting the lottery."

"When you say gangbusters, how prevalent is it?" Sam asked.

"Not sure, but my uncle said it's the biggest thing in insurance right now. He has a couple of insurance buddies that dropped property and casualty altogether and went into settlements. I guess it all depends on how long you have to wait."

"Wait for what?" Sam asked.

"Wait for your customers to drop dead," I said. "It's probably a lot of cash up front for the payouts and then you have to wait for them to die."

"That's what my uncle said. These cash-rich insurance companies deliver the big payouts and then have some formula for when the customers will kick the bucket. It's the craziest business I've ever heard of ... even crazier than my cousin who wanted to open a strip club that sold all-you-can-eat chicken wings as a way to get repeat business."

As we left, I said goodbye to Xena, who asked for my number to follow up on any recommendations with the service, food, or branding. Why the heck not, I thought, so I gave it to her. Robby dropped Sam back off at the funeral home, and we headed to a liquor store to get a bottle of Jack and a bottle of Tito's.

Chapter 13 – The Suit

After tossing and turning most of the night, I got in the shower about four a.m. I dressed in the best suit I had, a black custom one with subtle crimson pinstripes. Dad would approve.

Denise texted. *Are you up?*

Yep.

She immediately called.

"Sorry to bother you, but I got to thinking about Dad's suit."

"What about it?"

"Remember that one that Mom absolutely loved him in? The charcoal one with the light orange pinstripes?"

"How could I forget? He wore it in every picture with her. She loved that suit." I chuckled. "I always knew Dad was looking to get some when he put it on."

"That's too much information, but anyway, he should be presented to the public in that suit."

"Sam already got him set in the navy suit," I said.

"Will."

"This is important?" I asked.

Denise said nothing but I could hear her breathing.

"Okay, I'll take care of it. By the way, the cause of death came back for Dad. Heart attack."

"I don't care if they said heart attack or stroke or anything else. Something doesn't feel right." She paused. "Don't forget about the suit." She ended the call.

I immediately went to Dad's closet, found the suit, and headed out the door.

I jumped in the car and texted Sam the news about the suit.

I pulled into the back lot at the funeral home just before six. Janet, Jack, and Sam's cars were already there. *Going to be a busy day.*

I grabbed Dad's suit and walked in the back door. Sam was waiting for me.

"Are you kidding me with the suit? Everything's set, and he's in the casket. I set the features last night."

"Yes, I know. But this is important to Denise. I should have remembered the suit thing, but I didn't. What do you want me to do?"

"I've got one body down there and one on the way, and as far as I can tell I'm your only embalmer. So I'll need your help redressing him," Sam said, taking a right toward the stairs to the embalming room.

As I followed her down, she was barking instructions. "Be sure to watch the hair, and don't touch his face at all. The shirt's okay, right?"

"Yes, the shirt is fine," I said, handing her the suit.

"No, you hold the suit," she said as she inserted her thumb and index finger into the scissors. She cut the back of the suit jacket, creating two parts. "Okay, let's do this."

We walked over to the casket and there he was. Looking as dignified as ever. Not a day over sixty. Sam and the makeup team did a fantastic job. When Dad wasn't smiling or frowning, he had a resting smirk, almost like he knew something you didn't. He was smirking at me now. *What do you know that I don't, Dad?*

Sam used the casket crank to lift Dad to his highest setting. She took off his shoes. "You okay?" she said.

"Fine," I said, even though I wasn't.

She undid Dad's belt, unbuttoned, and unzipped his pants.

"Rigor has passed by now, so he shouldn't be too rigid," Sam said. "If you can lift up his legs, I'll pull the pants off and grab the other pair of slacks."

I did as she told me. I grabbed my father's legs between his calf and ankle and lifted them up to my chest. Then Sam tugged his pants toward me with a back and forth motion until they were past his bottom. I moved my hands as she pulled the pants past me so she could get them off his feet. I could smell a hint of Sam's perfume as she passed.

Sam set down one pair of pants and grabbed the other. "We'll just do the same thing in reverse."

She balled the pants up like I used to do with my running tights in high school cross-country and began to insert Dad's feet. As she did, I looked down at my father's thin, hairy legs. On the back side was some staining. A bit of blotching.

"What's that?" I asked Sam.

"What's what?"

"Below his legs. The blotching."

Sam tilted her head. "You can put his legs down for a second." She grabbed a pair of plastic gloves and put them on. Then she lifted up Dad's right leg while I stepped aside.

She bent her head down, coming within three inches of the back of his leg. "I honestly don't know," she said. "I would have seen it before. It's covering a large area."

Sam lowered the leg and moved to the left. Then she pulled up Dad's jacket, shirt, and undershirt. "Yep, there's some spotting here as well."

"Some kind of rash?" I asked.

"If the blotches occurred after death, which I'm assuming they did, it's not going to be like poison ivy or bacteria. It would have had to come from the inside out."

She took the gloves off inside out and threw them in the biowaste disposal. Then she grabbed her iPhone. "Lift his legs up by his feet so I can get some pictures of this." She took pictures of the backs of his legs and the side of his back.

"What are you going to do with those?"

"I know a guy that works in pathology at the Cleveland Clinic. I'd like to send some blood and tissue samples to him, as well as these images. He owes me a favor anyway."

"Why? McGinty already did the autopsy."

"True. But your Dad told me he didn't trust him. Not sure why. Maybe he missed something at one point. Sandusky is a small town, after all. I'm sure McGinty isn't an all-star coroner or anything. Regardless, the blotching is concerning."

We took the next fifteen minutes getting Dad dressed in Mom's favorite suit.

"Thanks. I really appreciate it," I said.

"Let's keep the blotching we found our little secret for now. At least until I find out some more information."

Chapter 14 – The Breakfast Place

I stopped in the kitchen to grab another coffee, then peeked my head in Janet's office. She was watering a small tree that sat on the floor behind her desk. Gorgeous red flowers. The tree was missing a couple of branches, but not so much you noticed.

"Good morning. Need anything from me?" I asked.

"Not a thing, dear," she said. "Just get your game face on. Half the city of Sandusky will be here in a few hours."

"Yes, ma'am," I said heading back to Dad's office.

I unlocked the closet and randomly chose one of Dad's notebooks. I pulled it out and carefully marked the spot, then sat down in Dad's desk chair. I flipped to October 23rd, 1983.

The call came in around 2 this morning. House pickup. Dispatch from EMS told me to bring two guys to the scene. Two bodies. I was given no additional information.

I called Jack and met him at the funeral home at 2:30. We each took a wagon.

Jack beat me there. He was already out of his car waiting by the gurney. I pulled up behind his wagon.

The house was a duplex, and apparently the two bodies were in the upper section of the house. Perfect news for any funeral director. As per procedure, Jack and I went to take a look before bringing up the gurneys.

The EMT was waiting at the door. I recognized him immediately. Bryan Newton from the downtown office.

I asked, "Why didn't you take them to the morgue?"

Bryan responded, "I wanted to leave this one for you." Never good news.

Bryan led us up the stairs and through a short hallway, which opened into a living area. No bodies yet. We continued to follow him to the bedroom.

Jack said, "Ten bucks they're in the bathroom."

I said nothing.

Bryan stopped short of the bedroom but moved aside so we could enter.

All the lights were on. There were two sheets covering the bed, but the form underneath looked like a trapped elephant. More realistically maybe a baby hippo. Whatever it was, the sheet was raised about three and a half feet toward the ceiling.

I looked back to Bryan. "Is this some kind of a joke?"

Bryan was holding back laughter but said nothing.

I walked over to the left side of the bed. Jack took the right.

"Well, shall we?" I asked Jack.

We both took an end and peeled back the sheet. There was a large naked man. Probably 225. Maybe sixty-five or seventy. Bald, but with hair everywhere else. His face was blue, and his eyes were open. Straddling him was a woman, approximately the same age. Also naked. Also large, probably two hundred.

From the looks of it, they were mid-intercourse.

Bryan was now laughing uncontrollably in the corner. Apparently, our faces gave him all the ammunition he needed.

"Did they die at the same time?" I asked Bryan.

He answered. "I can't be sure without a few more tests, but I think she died first and then he continued on, and then had a heart attack or stroke."

"How long?" I asked Bryan.

"I think this happened about three or four hours ago. Their son apparently still lives with them. He came home from the bar around one thirty and found them. He called us and then went back to the bar."

"Game plan?" I asked Jack.

Jack responded, "I think we move them both over to the left first. Together. Then we pull her off him and onto her back."

Worked like a charm and she slid right off, and we dropped her on her side to the right of the man.

After that, it was a relatively normal night, where Jack and I carried two two-hundred-plus-pound naked individuals down twelve steps and then another six steps from the porch to the wagon.

I PICKED UP MY HEAD and saw Jack's towering figure take the majority of the space where the door should be.

"You look quite mesmerized with whatever you're reading."

"Yeah, just some of Dad's old writings. Did you know he kept a diary? He was talking about you in this one from about thirty years ago."

"I saw him writing a lot but never knew he actually kept a diary. I'm surprised he never said anything."

"You know Dad. He always talked business. Never anything personal."

"Indeed."

"Did you need something?"

"Just letting you know that I picked up two bodies this morning and they're with Sam. Everything went according to plan. Anyway, I'm starving so I'm heading around the corner for breakfast."

"Breakfast sounds great. Do you mind some company?" I asked.

"Not at all. Let's ditch this pop stand."

We walked out the front door and headed west. Down the sidewalk, we passed what little rush hour traffic existed in Sandusky and took a right into Carol's Café. Carol's has been open since before I was born. My dad and the funeral home have pretty much kept Carol's in business since that time.

We walked through the door and Carol was sitting behind the counter at the front. She saw me immediately.

"William, it's so good to see you. I already desperately miss your father."

"Thanks, Carol. Last time I asked about you, Dad said you were retired."

"Don't I look retired?" she said, smiling. "Your father was right. I did retire. For a whole day. The most boring day of my life. So I decided to spend the rest of my retirement here. Then when I die, my son can just push me out the front door, and Jack here can collect me." She gasped. "Oh, William, I'm sorry. That's not an appropriate thing to say with your father just passing."

"It's all good, Carol. You know there is nothing inappropriate you can say to a funeral director. And as long as you let us handle your arrangements when you pass, you can say whatever you want."

She chuckled. "Of course you'll get my business. What? Do you think I'm going to the Traynor home? Something's not right about that family."

"No comment," I said. "Anyway, you know a good place we could go to eat? Jack and I came in looking for directions."

Carol came from behind the counter and slapped the side of my arm. "Why, you stinker. I practically raised you when you were the size of a turnip. You know we got the best breakfast special in the city." She grabbed one menu and led us to the side booth.

Jack and I sat down, and she placed the menu in front of me.

"What, no menu for me, darlin'?" Jack said.

"Oh, you're going to start on me too?" Carol said. She looked at me. "He's ordered the same damn thing for thirty years. Not once has he tried one of our specials. What a boring man he is." Carol gave a half smile to Jack and headed to grab the coffeepot from behind the counter.

She came back and poured us two cups of coffee. "Okay, sweetie, do you know what you'd like or need more time?

"I'd love the special of the day," I said, smiling at Jack.

"You little shit," Jack said.

"I always knew you were smarter than most," Carol replied. "And Mr. Jack?"

Jack smirked at Carol.

"The usual it is," she said and walked back toward the kitchen.

"God, I spent so much time here as a kid," I said. "Remember Carmela who worked the main counter? I used to steal her Life Savers whenever they'd let me back there."

"She put them out on purpose for you," Jack said. "She just adored you, kid."

"I always wondered why she left them out like that." I paused and took a long drink of coffee. "I've been wanting to ask you a few questions, if you don't mind, Jack."

"Shoot, kid."

"Well, first, kind of a shitty position for you to be in right now with the funeral home. That you have to wait on me to make a decision seems unfair."

"Son, I don't love the business necessarily, but I love what I do. I love being around people that aren't my wife. So I'd like to keep that way of life going. If you want to take a shot at it, no skin off my back. I just hope you keep me around."

"Jack, I promise if I decide to take the business, I'll force you to stay."

"That's fine, son." Jack chuckled. "But enough talk about that." Carol came by to top off our coffees.

"Got it. My main question was about Dad. Janet said his behavior changed last year, about the time when the business turned worse than worse. Do you know if he was sick? Was there something going on that you noticed or knew about?"

Jack's disposition changed. I caught something in his eye for the briefest of moments. But then it was gone. "The financial situation was no secret. How could it be? He let go of Shelly and Rich and a few others. He sold one of the vans, the cemetery. Told us he couldn't give us raises. But I don't know how much I noticed last year. The fall was like walking down a hill over the last five years. It wasn't a cliff." Jack took a drink. "We were all hoping and praying that things would flatline, no pun intended."

Carol came by and put the special in front of me and two eggs over easy with link sausage for Jack. She turned to me and said, "If you need anything else, honey, just let me know," ignoring Jack. Then she walked back behind the counter.

"Geez, Jack," I said. "She either hates you or she's in love with you. I think it's the latter."

"Oh, my boy, you have no idea. If I wasn't married all these years, I would have given her a good one a time or two. But I've never cheated once on my wife and never will. I've tried to kill her, but never cheated," Jack said, concentrating on cutting his sausage links into dimes.

The special was a scramble. Green and red peppers, onions, corned beef, bacon, and eggs. I was halfway through and already felt like ordering seconds.

"Now that you mention it," Jack said, "the one thing that was noticeable was Abe and Dan stopped getting together as much last year."

"My Uncle Dan?" I asked.

"The same. You know what made me think of it? When he came to meet you at the funeral home the day Abe passed. I mean, I've seen him around and we've always been friendly, but it was odd to see him back at the funeral home again."

"They had some kind of a falling-out?"

"That I can't speculate on. All I do know is that Dan was around all the time, and Abe and he got together for breakfast and such, then they didn't."

"When was this?" I asked.

"Sometime early last year, I suppose. About a year ago then, maybe a bit more."

Jack and I finished breakfast, and I said goodbye to Carol while Jack just looked at her and smiled. Then we started back to the funeral home.

Chapter 15 – Visitation Prep

As we walked back in, Jack headed for the visitation area while I headed to Dad's office. Sam was waiting for me with her purse in hand.

"Going somewhere?" I asked.

She grabbed my arm and pulled me into Dad's office, shutting the door. She whispered, "I'm going to take these blood and tissue samples of your father to Cleveland myself. I'll be back in a few hours. I don't trust a courier with it, and my contact at the Clinic said he can get to it today."

"You're going to miss the visitation. Why do you need to leave now?"

"I looked at your dad's posthumous blotching again. Something's not right, and it's grating on me. I want to get this checked out as soon as possible. Plus, my contact has some time to start on it today."

"You sound nervous."

"No, not nervous. But I want someone to double-check this. Your father would do the same thing."

"Do you have a copy of the autopsy to give to your guy?"

"Yes. It's on my phone. I'll be back by early afternoon, probably right at the start of visitation."

"Got it. Text me if you need anything."

Sam made her way down the hall.

We were just a few hours from the start of visitation, and I figured Denise was already here. I found her at the coffee machine. She heard me coming and turned around. We said nothing, just approached each other and hugged.

"You okay?" I asked.

"Fine, I guess," Denise said. "Oddly enough, I'm thinking about Mom today. Remember her visitation? Dad was running all over, making sure everything was just right, acting like it was someone else who died. I don't think he ever got over her leaving us so soon."

"I know he didn't," I said. "I mean, he was the same man. The same hard worker. The same guy that could walk into a restaurant and go table to table talking to everyone, but he lost the spring in his step. I thought he would get it back at some point, but from what I'm finding out, I don't think he ever did."

"He talked to her every day. Did you know that?"

"What do you mean?"

"Sometimes I would stay with Dad, and every night I would hear him talking in his bedroom. I didn't know if he was on the phone or praying or what. But I found he would sit at his desk and face Mom's closet, and talk to her like she was there. It was both extremely cute and deeply sad at the same time." She paused. "He would talk to her like she was standing right there. One time, it sounded like she was trying on clothes, and he was telling her what looked good and not."

"Did you ever talk to him about it?"

"Not once. People deal with life in their own ways. We all do. I think Dad had to do that to survive. And who knows? Maybe she was there in spirit. Regardless, he probably needed the therapy."

I walked over to the Keurig, popped in a light roast, pushed down the top, and selected a large cup of coffee. "When this is finished, why don't we head over to the visitation room and do a quick run-through?"

"Okay," Denise said.

We walked over together and stopped at the open doorway leading into the visitation room. This was visitation room one, which today opened into visitation room two as well. For normal funerals, just one room was needed. For this one, we probably didn't have enough space even with removing the soft barrier between the rooms.

Dad was laid out in the back of the room two surrounded by at least fifty flower arrangements. *Dad would hate it*. He always preferred charitable donations instead of flowers. We included this in the obituary, but no matter what you do, people still like to send flowers. The same people that walk by each arrangement at the visitation to see who spent the most on a display perhaps.

As Denise and I walked in, we split at the back of the room. I went left and she went right, with about seventy-five to a hundred chairs in the middle. Tables against two walls were covered with individual pictures, photo albums, and keepsakes. I caught one picture of Dad holding Jess as a baby that made me tear up a little. Jack and Denise did a nice job setting up the room.

We met back up at the casket and held hands. "We switched the suit, as requested. Does this work for you?"

"I'm sure it wasn't easy for Sam. I'll tell her thanks later."

"I'm sure she'll appreciate that, but she was fine doing it," I said, lying a bit.

"Okay, boss," Denise said. "What's the rundown?"

We moved to the right of the casket, about ten feet from the kneeler. I placed Denise closest to Dad, and I stood to her left. "I think I want you last. That way if I can't remember someone's name you can whisper it to me like in *The Devil Wears Prada*. I don't have your memory." I turned to face her. "If Jess wants to stand in line, she'll be on my left. Do you have any thoughts about Sam?"

"I think you should tell Sam that Dad would probably want her in the lineup," Denise said.

"Okay, I will. Janet said there'd be some early lunch in the kitchen. I just had a big breakfast, but you should probably eat now. God knows if we'll get a chance when people start coming."

Denise and I hugged again, this time a bit longer, and she headed to the kitchen.

I turned and saw Jack walking toward me.

"Son, someone is here to see you. I told them the situation here but he was very persistent."

"Did he give a name?"

"He just said Roger from the other night. That you would know."

"All right. Thanks. Jack, would you please do one final check of the visitation room before we open the doors, and I'll go meet with Roger?"

"Yessir," Jack said, saluting me.

I walked to the front outside the visitation room entrance, but no one was there. Then I went to check outside. Roger was standing to the side by the outdoor ashtray that looked like a giant landscaping light.

"Hi, Roger," I said as he exhaled smoke.

"Hey, Will ... I'm sorry to come here, but I didn't want to call and didn't want to bother you during your visitation. I caught the obit in the paper and put two and two together pretty easily. Sorry about your father. How's everything going by the way?"

"As well as could be expected. Judging by all the flower arrangements in there, we should get quite a gathering of folks to see my dad." I paused. Meeting with fellow GA'ers outside of meetings was always weird. Almost like getting caught cheating on your wife. Generally, it happens by accident. At the grocery store or at a bar. Going to see a fellow gambler without a call is generally inappropriate. "What can I do for you, Roger?"

"You know how we were chatting about the life settlements. I was curious after our conversation, so I wanted to make sure I didn't tell you anything to mislead you. Anyway, I have a buddy that tracks life insurance packages in the county. If they get sold, like in life settlements, there's a public record of it. You can basically see everyone who has a policy out, who's buying the policies, and all that."

Roger put out his cigarette, pulled out another one, and lit it. He offered me one. I declined.

"So I asked my buddy for the stats from Erie County. No big deal, I ask him for stuff all the time for my insurance business. He gave me the numbers from the last ten years. If you look at year ten, and then nine and then eight, you see ten and fifteen percent growth year-to-year in companies buying life insurance policies, a.k.a. life settlements. Then starting about seven years ago, it goes batshit crazy. Like fifty to seventy-five percent up. Tell me, that gentleman you were asking about most recently, was he a minority?"

"Uh, yes, actually. He was a large black man," I said.

"Figures. Now I don't know what it's like in other counties in other states, but in Erie County, about five in ten life insurance policies are bought by the big boys from minorities—blacks, Indians—dots, not feathers—Asians, Hispanics—all kinds. There's not all that many minorities to begin with in this area, so it's extremely unlikely that this is just chance."

"Odd," I said, "But why did you want me to know about this?"

"You seem like a nice guy. You probably got willed the funeral home from your father, right? Uh, no need to answer. You're a part of the circle of life here, from insurance to death to burial, and if I was in your position, I would want to know."

With that, Roger put out his smoke, walked to his car, and drove away.

Chapter 16 – The Conspiracy

As I walked back inside, my head was swirling, and with the visitation about to start, I couldn't get five minutes to think about any of it. Dad's business goes to hell last year, which was also the same time he started acting like a jerk to people. Now those two things could be tied together. But why would he want me to take over his business? I could understand if I didn't have anything better to do. Why didn't he sell it years ago before he sold all his personal assets to save a failing business? Sure, he was doing a great service for families, but was it all worth it? It must have been to him.

I did the calculations again in my head. The most the funeral home was worth, on paper, was about four hundred thousand dollars. Mostly real estate value. Yet Alex Traynor was willing to offer me double that to go back to Cleveland. It was almost too good of an offer. Almost like he knew the exact amount I needed to say yes. Only an idiot would say no to that. Alex knew I was a lot of things, but he wouldn't take me for an idiot. Desperate, yes, but not an idiot.

Now today with the blotches on my dad's legs and back. The coroner's results would have shown something for blotching like that to appear. It had to be more than just a heart attack. If that was true, then maybe the circumstances behind my father's death were different than they appeared to be. Maybe Denise was right.

And Jack's comments about Dad and Uncle Dan being on the outs. But if Dad and Dan weren't getting along, why did Dan have all Dad's information? Why did Dad share his final will and testament with Uncle Dan when he could have easily chosen someone else?

And then Roger came out of nowhere to tell me about some conspiracy where they—whoever *they* are—were buying life insurance policies from minorities in increasingly higher numbers every year. This was something I'd need to confirm, because if it was actually true, it was hard to imagine the evil lurking behind that strategy.

It was forty-five minutes to start time, which meant people would begin showing up any second. I walked into Dad's office and sat back in his swivel chair. I took one of his notebooks, tore out a sheet, then proceeded to scratch out some of my thinking on the last few days in Sandusky. I folded the sheet and placed it in my back pocket. Then I leaned back and closed my eyes.

There was a knock on the door.

"Come in," I said.

Denise walked in with a small plate of food—a turkey sandwich and some pasta salad.

"Before you tell me you're not hungry, just save your words, and I'll watch you eat this," she said. "It's probably the last bit of food before you drink vodka tonight."

She pulled up a chair and watched me eat the sandwich in silence. Jack peeked his head in the doorway. "Better get moving. Cars are parking as we speak."

I pulled out my phone and texted Jess. *Hey, Jess. People are coming for visitation now, so be here as soon as you can.*

I took a large bite of the turkey sandwich and left the plate on Dad's desk. Denise and I walked out of the office and into the visitation area, heading to our spots. And there was Jess, kneeling in front of my father. I stood there watching her. She made the sign of the cross, stood, and placed her hand on my dad's. Then she turned around and saw me, her eyes already wet with tears. She took two quick steps and gave me a hug I haven't felt from her in years.

"I'm so sorry, Dad," she said.

"Me too, honey. Me too," I whispered in her ear. I pulled away. "And I'm sorry I texted you. I should have known you would already be here."

She pulled the phone out of her purse, saw my message, then turned her phone on airplane mode. "I haven't really done this before, Dad. I didn't do this when Grandma passed."

"No problem. It's super easy. You'll be standing to my left the entire night. When someone comes up to you that you don't know or can't remember their name, just say, 'Hi. Thanks for coming. I'm Abe's granddaughter.' And that's it. Did you get something to eat?"

"I had something an hour ago," she said.

"When you can a bit later, sneak out of line and grab some food in the private kitchen area. Then you can come back."

I turned to Denise. "Denise, before we start this thing, let's take a moment." I gathered the three of us and we walked up to Dad's casket. I turned my head over my shoulder, "Hey, Jack, can you just give us a minute?" Jack nodded and held guard outside the door.

I grabbed Denise's hand with my left and Jess's hand with my right. From the back, I heard someone else coming and turned. It was Sam. "Oh, good, Sam. Can you come up here, please?" Sam came up to the casket and took Jess's other hand.

Without having to say anything, we all bowed our heads in unison. "Dad, what is there to say? We love you, and we are going to miss you very much. You were a good and decent man. One of the best this city has ever seen. They were lucky to have you. I wish we could have a few more moments to see you in action, especially holding court at a party or a restaurant. Everyone loved you, Dad. Please give Mom a big hug for us. I'm glad to know that you two are together again. Thanks for everything, Pop."

We stood there for a second, and then Jess looked over at me and kissed my cheek. "Good speech, Dad."

"Thanks, honey. Okay, let's get this started." Jack peeked in the doorway and nodded. Two seconds later, the line was coming toward Jess. Sam was walking away. "Sam," I said. "Dad would have wanted you in the line with us."

"Maybe in a little bit. Right now, I'll just make sure Jack has everything under control."

I pulled her to the side. "Trip went okay?"

"Yes," she said. "Should have something back tomorrow."

For the next six hours, half the city showed up to pay their respects to my father. Of course, Uncle Dan was there. He stayed a few hours. The entire Sandusky Alliance team showed up, trading stories in the back. John and Alex Traynor stopped by, which was a bit awkward, but I respected them for it. About twenty of my high school graduating class showed up. Even my old college roommate, Alan, who worked at the FBI in Cleveland was there. Xena came too. She asked me out again, you know, to talk about her restaurant.

Robby showed up about an hour before visitation was over. He drove to Toledo during the day to see one of our clients, which I was eternally grateful for. We needed to keep that account. Since I'd been off the grid, Robby was dutifully holding down the business.

As the final group left out the front door, Jess said goodbye, leaving with Tracy and Zoe. We agreed to meet back here tomorrow at eight a.m., plenty of time before we left for the church at nine-thirty.

Robby was waiting for me to wrap things up. He knew I needed a drink. I gave Denise a hug and we said our goodbyes, then I spotted Sam running out the door.

"Sam," I said. "Robby and I are grabbing a drink. Can you join us?"

"I don't think so," she said.

I put my hands on my hips and gave her a look. She almost smiled. "I learned some things today and I need to get your take. Just one drink?"

"Okay, where?"

"Jerold's down the street."

"I'll meet you there."

"Great."

I gave Robby quick directions, and we both got in our cars and headed to Jerold's. As I pulled in the parking lot, I noticed the sign out front hadn't changed since I was a kid. The bar was an institution in Sandusky and used to be known for freely letting in minors. I went to Jerold's more times before I turned twenty-one than after.

The bar was half full with several people who came straight from Dad's visitation. I waved and headed in the other direction. Sam was at a corner table.

"Hard to escape," she said.

"This is the closest bar to the funeral home. We probably should have had a few drinks using Dad's casket as a table. He'd have appreciated that."

Robby came in and sat in one of the two open chairs. "It's too bright in here. Did Sandusky put a ban on black people?" he asked.

"What do you mean?" I said.

"Let me ask you this. How many black people did you see at Warrior Princess's restaurant?"

"I don't recall any," I said.

"Of course you don't. Because there weren't any. How many brothers did you get at your visitation?"

"Hmmm ... there was Mr. Williams that owns the flower store. And Ray Jones that used to drive the hearse for Dad. A couple ministers that I didn't know. Did I miss any, Sam?" She shook her head.

"Okay," Robby said. "How many black people do you see right now?"

I looked around. "I don't see any, but it's so hard to tell these days," I said, smiling.

"You ass—it's a big zero. Sandusky has to be the brightest town in America."

"I think it's just coincidence," Sam said.

"I'll tell you what," Robby said. "If you two walked into a bar or a restaurant, or went to a visitation, and saw only four white people, you'd surely notice it and wouldn't be talking about any coincidences. I need a drink."

Robby turned around and waved to the waitress. "See? She's white too," Robby said, smiling.

The waitress took our drink orders. Vodka tonics for Sam and me. Double Jack for Robby.

"Sam, do you mind telling Robby what we found today?" I said. She looked at me like I was crazy. "It's okay; Robby will be the only other one to know."

"Know what?" Robby asked.

"Okay, but this is it. Only the three of us will know, and no one says anything to anyone," Sam said, looking straight at me.

"Okay, okay," I said.

Sam relayed the information about Dad's blotching.

"What are you thinking?" Robby asked Sam.

"Jim McGinty is Erie County coroner. That's Dan's nephew. He did the autopsy and called it a simple heart attack. I know he ran tissue samples, because Abe came to us without many of his internal organs left. It's just odd."

"You think there's some hanky-panky going on?"

"I don't know, but Abe never liked McGinty and always questioned his findings. Well, at least since I've been at Pollitt."

Listening to the conversation, I realized how much I missed watching Sam talk. She got these little creases in her forehead when she was passionate about something, and they were in full force when she was explaining things to Robby.

The waitress brought our drinks over. I raised my glass, and Sam and Robby followed. "To Abe. A good man and a good father. You'll be missed." We clinked glasses.

"You'll never believe this," I said. "Roger, the insurance guy I met at GA. He showed up today and said he did some research on life settlements in Erie County. Apparently, about half of all the insurance policies in this county are bought from minorities."

"What does that mean?" Sam asked.

"It's either a huge coincidence or the insurance agents in this area are targeting minorities at an incredibly high rate, trying to get them to sell their five-hundred-K and million-dollar-plus policies. He thinks there's some conspiracy going on, and as a funeral director and a human being, I should look into it."

"You mean a conspiracy how there are no black people in this county either?" Robby said.

I pulled out the sheet of Dad's notebook paper from my rear pocket. "You want to talk conspiracy. Well if you really want to get crazy, I have one for you," I said, rubbing the creases out of the paper. "All right. My brain is worthless right now, but here's what I've put together. First, Sam you attested to this, and so did Janet and Jack. Sometime last year, my father turned into an irritable prick. Second, this happened at the same time that the business really tanked. Both Sam and the financial numbers from Uncle Dan confirm that. And third, sometime around then, although we don't know exactly when or why, Dan and Abe had a falling-out."

"I didn't know that," Sam said.

"Me either," I said. "Jack mentioned it today at breakfast. Besides this week, have you seen Dan around much?"

"Now that you mention it..." Sam said.

I swallowed the rest of the vodka tonic and waved at the waitress for another round.

"Fourth, my father didn't trust the coroner, who happens to be Uncle Dan's nephew. Dad didn't trust him so much that he started to create backup tissue samples from Pollitt customers. So either Dad was going crazy, which is always a possibility, or he knew something."

"What the heck, man?" Robby said.

"Right?" I said. "And now we have this life settlement insurance thing, which may not be related at all. Dad did have the words *life insurance* on a notepad at home. I checked with Uncle Dan, who said that Dad cashed out his policy a while ago to pay down debt. But then if Uncle Dan and Dad had a falling-out, he probably wouldn't know what it means anyway. Related or not, GA Roger thinks there's some local conspiracy going on. And Robby, now your comment about your uncle has me thinking."

"What's that?" Robby said.

"You said your uncle's buddies were dropping the insurance they sold to get into the life settlement business, right?" I asked.

"Correct."

"And then you said the part about how they sign these people up and wait for them to die. Well, what if they get tired of waiting?"

"I know where you're going with this, Will," Sam said. "That's lunacy."

"Look, I'm just trying to bring out the facts so we can make sense of them."

"Let me get this straight, Will," Robby said. "This conspiracy from your GA buddy about them targeting minorities as the scam. You're saying that might not be the scam. The scam is that they sign them up and then find ways to accelerate their death?"

"It's a possibility, right?"

"That has to be a movie," Robby said.

"Hell, Robby, you've just been complaining about there being no black people in Sandusky. Maybe they're killing them off."

At that, the three of us just stared at each other.

"I don't think this drink is near strong enough for that kind of theory," Robby whispered.

Sam looked down at the paper. "So, any other points to consider off of this scribbled sheet?"

"Not really," I said. "The only other thing I noticed was that Dad was writing in his diary a lot less starting at the same time the business tanked, and he became visibly frustrated with something."

"Okay," Sam said. "What do we do with all this?"

"Well," I said. "For starters, I think you should send some more of those blood and tissue samples Dad collected to your contact in Cleveland. Then you can match those up with the coroner's report, and we can see if it sheds some light on Dad's paranoia."

"I can take the life settlements thing," Robby said. "After the funeral to-morrow, I'll go see my uncle again. Maybe we can take a ride down the rabbit hole to see who's funding all the settlements in Erie County."

"Perfect," I said. "Sam, do we collect ethnicity information when we sign up a new customer?"

"Janet doesn't. And your dad never did it on intake, as far as I knew. But," Sam said, smiling, "the embalming records do."

"Bingo," I said. "The problem is the data on this might be a bear. We'll have to go back, let's say a year before the business tanked, and cross-match minority customers with life settlements. Robby, what do you think your uncle would need to find out if someone sold their policy?"

"I'll check, but probably just name and address would do it," Robby said. "It's all public record, so it shouldn't be that hard." Robby paused, rubbing his hand back and forth over the stubble on his chin.

"What's this SA scribbled on your paper?" Sam asked.

"Sandusky Alliance. That's the group my dad belonged to that helped to revitalize downtown. Do you know much about it?"

"Not really. They have a pretty good reputation, from what I hear," Sam said.

"Xena is a member. I saw the SA logo on her door when we went to eat there. I'm supposed to give her some feedback on the restaurant, and I'll find out some information on SA at the same time."

We all paused. I broke the silence. "Either we're all going crazy or there's something here, so whatever we do, we can't mention anything to anyone about this."

Chapter 17 – The Camera

It was after eleven when we left Jerold's. Robby followed me back to Dad's place. We parked and headed for the door. "Nightcap?" I said.

"Thought you'd never ask."

We loaded up, same as the night before, Tito's and Jack Daniels, and saddled up at the kitchen table.

"You know," Robby said. "I think you should do something with your dad's diary."

"Like what?"

"If you were a small business and I was your consultant, and you showed me a gold mine of content like you have with your dad's diary, I would tell you to create a blog out of it. Or perhaps a podcast."

"I see where you're going, but these are the innermost thoughts of my dead father. They were never meant to see the light of day. It would almost be like a betrayal."

"Don't be so quick to see it that way. Even with all this crazy shit going on, he left you the funeral home in dire condition. Either he was crazy, or he actually thought you could turn it around. And he knew you had marketing chops, so you'd be getting creative." Robby paused and took a drink. "I don't know, Will, I think this is exactly what he would want you to do with it."

"Let's say I agree to do something. How would you proceed?"

"First thing is to get the whole thing transcribed. From looking at your dad's handwriting, I think we could pay a freelancer to scan each page, and the computer will do most of the work. Some of the metadata would be captured, like the date, as well as some broad categories. We can preprogram the software to tag it if a certain word or phrase comes up. Then once that's done, either you or I would go through and rate each one, as well as mark some not for use. As for titling, the software will automatically create a title, which we can edit after the fact."

"Sounds like you've been thinking about this quite a bit."

"A little. But I'm stuck between a podcast and a blog. A blog would seem like the natural fit, but I could also see this being like a *Serial*-type podcast where people would want to know what happens next. If that's the case, you could just go in chronological order and can the ones that don't tell a compelling enough story. *Tales from the Crypt* or some shit like that." Robby laughed. "But—and this is a huge but, my friend—you have to be willing to change the business model, like we discussed the other day."

"Why's that?" I asked.

"Because this is a bold move. If you deliver this consistently over time and build an interested audience, it's going to target a different clientele, which will be asking for different products or services. Hell, just like you pitched PopC. Could be merchandising, sponsorship, and advertising, maybe even an event, but that's down the road. Funerals would come in different shapes and sizes for sure. Anyway, Suzie Q Homemaker from Sandusky probably isn't going to give a crap about the blog, but other people will. It could be amazing. But it could also create a shitstorm, especially in Pleasantville here."

I PULLED INTO THE FUNERAL home at five thirty a.m. and Sam's car was already there. *Is she a workaholic?*

I walked in the back door and headed down the stairwell. "Sam, you there?"

"Yes, I'm here."

I saw the body she was working on. Sam was standing next to a naked elderly white woman, probably over eighty years old. She didn't have an ounce of fat on her. Her breasts sagged down and to the sides, almost brushing the table. Sam was standing next to the centrifugal pump, which was busy draining blood from the woman's system and replacing it with embalming fluid.

"Did you set the features last night?" I asked.

"You've been paying attention," Sam said. "Yes, I actually set the features right before I left for Cleveland yesterday, so Mrs. Reeves here was looking as close to her picture as possible. Then, as you know, the day got away from me. I need to get Mrs. Reeves here finished and then Mr. Talbota over there."

Sam pointed her head to the far mortuary table, where an elderly Latino man was waiting his turn.

"Okay, I'll leave you be in a second. I remembered something last night. As I told you, Jack said that Uncle Dan didn't come around much anymore, but Dad could still have been seeing him. When Uncle Dan read Denise and me the will, he mentioned that Dad changed it many times over the years, most recently a few weeks ago. And the letter accompanying the will sounded like Dan and he were still the lifelong friends they'd always been."

"So maybe there's nothing there. Either Jack was wrong, or Dan just didn't come to the funeral home when Jack was around."

"I think you're right. Strange though. This whole thing. Ride in the limo with Jess, Denise, and me?"

"Uh, okay."

"I know that would mean a lot to Jess. And don't forget that list of bodies by ethnicity when you get a chance."

I headed back upstairs, grabbed a cup of light roast from the Keurig, and beelined to Dad's office. I closed the door and sat back in the swivel chair.

"Talk to me, Dad. What was going on? What aren't you telling me and why?"

I leaned my head back and closed my eyes, then spun around for a few rotations. I opened my eyes, trying to see the world more clearly.

"Couldn't be," I said aloud. Straight above me, next to the recessed ceiling light, was a small black indent covered with clear glass or plastic. I rose from the chair and went to the door, opening it a crack to see if anyone was coming. The coast was clear.

I closed the door, carefully stepped on the swivel chair, and stood on the old mahogany desk. I reached up to feel the clear material. I knocked on it. Plastic for sure. It was the size of a fifty-cent piece. I strained to see what was inside but couldn't make it out.

Standing there, I removed my iPhone from my pocket and zoomed in on the circle, taking multiple pictures. Then I gently stepped back down onto the swivel chair and sat. I had taken five pictures, with one getting the best view of what was inside the hole. "You've got to be kidding me," I said aloud.

I was right. It looked like a tiny camera, something like you'd see in the eye of a teddy bear that watches over a small child. Something new parents would use when hiring their first babysitter.

My first instinct was to go ask Janet or Jack about it, but I just sat there. If anyone knew about it, they would have pulled the video footage from the night my father died. They must not have known, or they would have said something.

I left the office and walked out the front entrance. Just above the door I spotted the original security camera Dad installed a decade ago. I then headed to the back entrance to find another camera hanging off a light fixture that illuminated the parking lot.

I heard a car pulling up. It was Janet. Six fifteen on the nose. She parked and headed toward me.

"What are you doing out in the trees?" she said.

"I actually remembered we have a security system. I was looking at the cameras."

"I had a security system," Janet said.

"Oh yeah?"

"Your father cut the service middle of last year. He said they didn't serve a purpose, but it was really a cost-cutting measure."

"So these don't film anything?" I said, pointing up at the camera.

"Nope. As useless as your father was in the kitchen," she said with a smile.

"So this entire place has *no* security system at all?"

"That's correct."

We walked in the back entrance. "You need anything?" she asked.

"I'm fine," I said. "Well, I will be."

"Do you have your speech written?"

"Shoot. I actually forgot."

"Go in your dad's office, close the door, and get it done. I think the entire city will want to hear your thoughts on your father."

"I'll do that now. Hold my calls, please," I said with a smile.

Janet turned left, and I went back to Dad's office, shutting the door.

I walked back to the desk and looked up at the tiny camera. This added a whole new dimension. First, why would Dad want one there? And second, how did Janet not know about it? Janet knew everything about Dad. If Janet didn't know, then Dad didn't want her to know.

Unfortunately, I didn't have time to think about this now. We were just a few hours away from Dad's mass, and I was to give the eulogy after communion. It took me forty-five minutes to scratch out three blue notecards that included word prompts for the stories I wanted to tell. In my marketing career, I had the opportunity to give speeches all over the country, so I was comfortable with getting in front of people. But this was different. This was my dad. It *had* to be memorable.

Chapter 18 – Closure

There was a knock on the door. It was Jack. "Everything okay in here?"

"Yeah, sorry. I was working on my dad's eulogy. What's up?"

"I need the keys to the van for the flowers," Jack said.

"I was thinking about that, Jack. You know that my dad wasn't a flower fan, which is pretty strange for a funeral director. Anyway, I think we should skip transporting the flowers to the cemetery. Agreed?"

"This is a funeral director's funeral, correct? Probably the most famous funeral director that's ever been in this city, county, and state. And there are going to be hundreds of people there. Boy, this is advertising as much as anything else, so we're doing this one by the book. Flowers and all. I'm taking every goddamn flower I can find to the mausoleum today."

"I didn't think about it that way, Jack. Thanks. I forgot about the marketing aspect." I stood up and tossed him the keys. He caught the keys with his left hand and headed out to the back lot.

A few seconds later, Robby texted. *Check your email.*

I scrolled to the email app on my phone and saw it immediately. It was from Sarah at PopC. They want us in for a meeting on Monday morning. *Who sends an email on Saturday?* But holy crap. A meeting meant we were down to either the final two agencies or we got the project.

I texted Robby back. *OMG.*

Can you make the meeting? Robby texted.

Are you crazy? Absolutely.

I'll respond back and get a time. CU in a bit.

I sat back in my chair and smiled. "Not bad, huh, Pop?" I said out loud. Getting the PopC account would change everything.

Don't count your chickens, I heard him say to me. *You can get excited when the deal is done.* Dad must have told me not to count my chickens before they hatch a thousand times growing up. Whether it was cross-country or math competitions or school, Dad was adamant on me never getting too excited until the task was over.

I read through my notes on Dad's eulogy one more time. I cut out a couple small sections, knowing I'd probably ad lib a bit as well and I wanted to make sure I didn't go too long. Nothing worse than a funeral mass that never ends.

People were starting to mill around outside the visitation area. In the front, Jack was hard at work lining the cars up behind our limo and securing the magnetic purple funeral flags to the tops of the cars. After one of the longest weeks I'd ever had, the funeral was finally here.

As I walked out the office door, I ran into Uncle Dan. He was talking to a couple of my distant cousins whom I only saw at funerals and weddings about the new development going on downtown.

"How you holding up?" he asked.

"I'll be glad when the day is over."

With quite a few facts still shaky in my head, I pulled him aside. "In the past few months did you notice anything strange about Dad's health? I'm trying to figure out if he was hiding some health issues from me and the heart attack was just the last straw."

Dan scratched his head. "You know your father. He kept his well-being to himself. So, no, I didn't know if he was having any doctor-related issues."

"When was the last time you two got together?"

"Not sure exactly, son. A few weeks ago, I presume. Coffee or breakfast or something," Dan said.

"Thanks," I said. At least this confirmed my suspicions. Uncle Dan had a perfect memory when it comes to meetings with anyone. He could tell you to the day the last time he met with any one of his clients. That he was fuzzy about seeing my father the last time spoke volumes.

"Any thoughts on whether you want to keep the business or not?" Uncle Dan asked.

Who asks a question like that the morning of your father's funeral? "I've been thinking plenty about it. If you were me, what would you do?"

"That's not for me to say," he said. "But considering your own business and the state of your father's business, I'd probably sell it and get as far away from here as possible."

Dan loved Sandusky more than his kids, so his comment took me off guard. Either something was going on or he didn't want me here. *I'm becoming paranoid for no reason.* I took a deep breath in and out. "That helps," I said. "I'll catch up with you later." I shook his hand and walked to the side of Dad's casket. I figured it was the best place to stand for the next twenty minutes just in case a few people wanted to pay their final respects. I saw Denise in the back of the room, and she came to join me.

Jess walked in, smiled, and approached us, giving a long hug to both Denise and then me. Then she sat in a seat in front of Dad's casket. Jack approached a few minutes later. "You ready, Will? Denise?"

"Yes. Thanks," I said, taking a seat next to Jess.

Jack turned to face the audience. About three-quarters of the chairs were taken, with another dozen people standing in the back. "Welcome, everyone," Jack said. "We're going to say the final prayers, then you can all head to your cars while we let the immediate family say their good-byes. Then we will all process to St. Mary's Church on Central Avenue."

Jack then led us in a Hail Mary and an Our Father, and a minute later it was just Denise, Jess, and me with Dad.

"Let me know when you're ready?" Jack said to the three of us.

"Where's Sam?" I asked.

"She's right outside," Jack said.

"Could you have her join us please?"

I held Jess's hands while we were waiting. "You know," I said to Jess. "Your grandfather was never one for showing emotion. But you know the first time I ever saw him cry?" I paused as she waited. "At the hospital the day you were born, he and your grandmother came to see you. I passed you to Grandma and she smiled and told you how pretty you were, then she passed you to Grandpa. He just looked at you, and the biggest tears you ever did see started rolling down his cheeks. And for the next five minutes or so, he just held you, smiling and crying. He loved you so much, Jess."

Jess started to cry, and I began to cry. Sam entered the room and stood to the side. When we saw her, Jess and I opened our hug to invite her in, and the three of us held each other ... then we walked over to the casket where Denise was waiting for us.

The four of us locked hands and took one final look at Dad. I nodded at Denise. She nodded back. I turned my head at Jack. "Okay, Jack, we're ready. Sam, will you lead Denise and Jess out to the limo please? I'll be there in a second."

Without saying a word, Sam took Denise and Jess by the hands and led them out the door. I took two steps back and let Jack do his job. Jack removed the casket key from his right jacket pocket, inserted it into the back of the casket, and turned it multiple times to the right. Dad's legs began to lower. Then Jack did the same on the left side, and Dad's head sank down into the casket. He pulled forward the cloth hugging the outside of the casket and pushed it inside. Then he removed the flower arrangement from the top right side that said, *Beloved Father and Grandfather*, and placed it on the chair to the right. Jack pushed down on the casket side above Dad's legs while I locked it with the key. We moved to the head of the casket and paused.

"Abraham. You were a good and decent man and a great friend. You will be missed," Jack said. Then he motioned me over. "Would you like to do the honors?"

I loosened the lever above Dad's head and gently began to close the casket over his head. "Love you, Pop," I said, shutting the cover, and pushed down hard while Jack sealed it with the key.

"Okay. I'll see you at the church," I said and headed to the limo, walking past six of the Sandusky Alliance board members, minus the Traynors, who were waiting to push Dad's casket into the hearse.

Chapter 19 – The Revelation

The next hour was a blur. The ride over. Walking into church. Watching Dad's friends push Dad up the aisle in front of the altar. There were a lot of "greats" and "goods" in the homily, but nothing memorable. In talking to the pastor in preparation, he seemed like a decent person, but he didn't know my father at all outside of funeral masses, which was unfortunate.

After communion, the pastor called me up to make the speech. I was sitting between Denise and Jess, and squeezed both of their hands as I rose, then bowed in front of the altar, stepping up to the lectern.

I stood and looked out at the crowd. The church was easily three-quarters full. About four hundred people. I looked down at Jess, Denise, and Sam, and saw Robby smiling from the third row. Xena was there. Fifth row right. The Sandusky Alliance team decided to sit next to each other near the back. This time, both John and Alex Traynor were present. I pulled the notecards out of my inside pocket and set them on the lectern.

"First of all, on behalf of the Pollitt family, I want to thank each of you for your presence and your kindness over the past few days. For those of you who do not know me, my name is Will Pollitt, and I had the very distinct honor of being Abe's son.

"Since most of you are from Sandusky, I have a feeling that you've all heard about what Abe tried to do for the city. He loved this city and gave almost everything he had to it. This week, I was approached by many of you wondering where this city would be without Abraham Pollitt. But you know that part of the story. You've been here. You've seen him. You know that side of Abe.

"You probably have also seen Abe in action, let's say, at a restaurant or at a city planning meeting or perhaps at a funeral when you lost a loved one. Abe had that special gift where he could look you in the eye, shake your hand, and be totally present with you. He wasn't distracted with what was coming next; he was focused on you and your well-being. Growing up, I remember that going out to dinner was a four-hour affair. We would enter the restaurant. Mom, Denise, and I would grab our seats, and Dad would make it around to every table, greeting everyone with a handshake and a smile. An hour later, Dad would sit down with us. After we ate, we'd repeat the cycle. But you've been here. You've seen him. You know that side of Abe.

"Here's something you may not know. My dad woke at four-thirty a.m. every day. Sometimes, if there was a death call in the middle of the night, he would skip sleep altogether. When Denise and I would be getting ready for school, Dad was there with his coffee to talk to us. Sometimes he made us breakfast. Once in a while it was edible. Many times, he packed our lunches. When we would arrive home after school, Dad would be there and make time for catch with me in the backyard or to go for a run with Denise. After dinner with the family, which was critically important to him, he'd leave to go back to work. Usually a visitation at the funeral home.

"The side of Abe you know? He worked all the time. He was everywhere in the city. He accomplished as much as any other person in the history of the city of Sandusky. And yet he never missed a moment to be a father. A true, loving, and present father.

"Some people live their lives always searching for a better life. My father simply chose that his best life was always there for the taking, in front of him every single second of every day.

"Dad, thank you so much for being the true definition of a man. We love you and will truly miss you, but we promise to continue your mission of being present every single day to those who are most important to us."

I brushed the tear away from my eye, put the notecards back in my inside coat pocket, and headed to the pew. As I sat down, Jess grabbed my hand and Denise whispered into my ear, "Truly wonderful, Will. Heartfelt and organized, just like Dad."

Heartfelt and organized. *Such an odd pair.* Yes, Dad was organized, but in a way that only he would recognize as organized. Neat for sure, but not organized. It used to drive my mom crazy, especially when he filed bills for the family. He always thought it was funny to change the headings on file folders as an extra layer of security. I remembered having a long conversation with him about it a few years back.

"Shit!" I said under my breath. Denise elbowed me.

"Will!" she said, giving me a look like I was disrupting class. "What is wrong with you?"

The pallbearers gathered around my dad and headed back out the front of the church.

"I left something at the funeral home that I wanted for the mausoleum," I whispered to Denise. "I'll meet you at the cemetery, okay?"

"What if you're late?"

"I won't be late. I promise. Tell the driver not to wait for me."

I turned to Jess and Sam. "I have to grab something from the funeral home, and then I'll meet you at the cemetery." I kissed Jess on the cheek and flagged down Robby, who looked as puzzled as I'd ever seen him. I waved him over to the side entrance.

"Where's your car?"

"In the back," he said.

"Can you drive me to the funeral home? Quickly."

Without a word, we hustled out the side entrance, found his car, and he drove off in the direction of the funeral home.

"Take a right here and a left at the next street. That will save us five minutes," I said.

"What are we doing, Will?"

"I don't know, but I think I realized that something important is in Dad's files."

"What about them?"

"When I finished Dad's eulogy, Denise said it was heartfelt and organized, just like Dad, which I thought was a weird thing to say. Dad was super organized, the opposite of my desk at work, but often he used weird organization patterns because he liked to throw people off as a level of security. Make a right at the next light. He would drive my mom crazy with it sometimes; he would label a file vacations that was actually work receipts if he was trying to hide something. Anyway, I think he left something for me to find, but only for me since I think I'm the only one who ever asked him about his filing system. I'm pretty sure even Denise doesn't know."

Robby made a left and headed to the back entrance of the funeral home.

"Just pull up to the back door. We don't have much time. Stay here," I said, opening the passenger door before Robby came to a complete stop.

I ran into the funeral home, headed for Dad's office, and went behind the desk. I opened the drawer where the files were marked from A to Z. Legal. Licenses. Life Insurance. *There it is*. I grabbed the file. I also took a small picture of Dad, Mom, Denise, and me that was on his desk. Then I headed out the door and jumped back into Robby's car.

"The cemetery is just off Perkins Avenue. Take a right and an immediate left, and we can probably beat them there," I said, breathing heavily.

"So which file is it?" Robby asked.

"Remember that Dad scribbled the words life insurance at home, and I couldn't figure it out? Well, I think he left that for me, without being obvious about it. I immediately thought it had to do with his life insurance or all this life settlement shit going on, but I think he wanted me to find this file."

I opened the file, and I knew I was right. I felt both elated and horrified at the same time. I said nothing.

"Well, what's in it?"

"It's the secure server and password information to the camera above his office desk."

WE PULLED IN THE BACK side of the cemetery, twisting through a labyrinth of headstones and large crypts left by the rich and famous of Sandusky. Calvary Cemetery was the oldest one of its kind, dating all the way back to the late 1700s, before Sandusky was incorporated as a city.

Even though he owned his own cemetery, Dad chose this place at the exact middle of Calvary Cemetery because Mom always preferred it. Today, the two of them will be reunited.

As we were approaching from the back, the hearse and limo were parking at the north end of the mausoleum, which was easily the largest one on the property, home to over two hundred bodies. My mother had been present at thousands of death rituals, from burial to cremation, but she always wanted to be entombed above ground. So, of course, that's what Dad did.

Robby parked, and we hurried to the mausoleum entrance. The ten minutes from the funeral home to the cemetery had given me plenty of time to tell Robby how I found Dad's office camera, and how I believed, but couldn't be sure, that no one else knew about it except for my father—and now, the two of us.

I made it to the door in time to hold it open for Denise and Jess, who both gave me strange looks. But the strangest one came from Sam.

"Where did you go?"

"It was something important," I whispered. "I'll fill you in."

Only about a quarter of the funeral mass audience had made it to the cemetery. Most, I imagined, were at the meeting hall, waiting for us and eating and drinking their fill until we arrived.

The ceremony lasted just minutes. The pastor said a final prayer. I assumed it was a prayer since I was lost in my own thoughts. Half were about this wild-goose chase my dad was sending me on, and the other half were about my mom while I stared at her tomb. Laura Rose Pullitt. Beloved Wife and Mother.

After the pastor was finished, Jack said something about everyone heading over to the hall to continue the celebration of Abraham's life. And then it was just the five of us, me with Denise, Jess, and Sam, with Robby standing off to the side, doing his best to look supportive.

Just before the administrator closed the chamber, I took the photo from Dad's office and propped it between the casket and the side of the interment space.

"That's what I went back for. Dad always loved that family picture," I said to Denise in my best poker face. She nodded in appreciation. I was now confident Denise had been right about her suspicions with Dad's death, but I didn't want to fill her in until I was sure.

There were only three cars outside when we left the building: Robby's car, the limo, and a dark SUV just up the hill. The administrator, I presumed. Our driver, who was waiting at the side of the limo, opened the doors for us to head to the meeting hall. I told Robby to follow us there.

We sat in silence for a while, then Jess said, "Mom. Dad. I'd like to go back tonight if that's okay."

I instinctively looked at Sam. When Jess's mom was around, my opinion took second place. Not that it ever bothered me.

"Are you sure, honey? I can get you up early to head back in the morning. There won't be any traffic on Sunday morning," Sam said.

"I know, Mom, but I've been putting off a couple big projects, and I'd like to spend the whole day tomorrow working on them. And," she paused, "I'd really like to get back. If you don't mind."

Sam looked at me. My turn to talk.

"Okay," I said. "Just make a few rounds and say good-bye to your cousins, and you can head back to your mom's place and grab your stuff."

The meeting hall was five minutes from both the cemetery and the funeral home. The driver pulled out in front to drop us off.

"Jess, go in with your Aunt Denise. Your mom and I will be right in," I said. Jess gave me an odd look. I'm sure seeing her parents talking with each other was a weird experience. It was for me anyway.

There was an alcove off the front entrance. I pulled Sam off to the side, and we headed over. There were two ladies extinguishing their cigarettes as we approached. "I'm so sorry for your loss," they both said in unison. Robby was approaching and I waved him over.

The three of us huddled together. "I want to start by saying I am officially freaking out right now." I looked at Sam. "Robby already knows this, but I found a hidden camera in Dad's office this morning. I checked with Janet who informed me that he turned off all the security cameras some time ago. Is that right, Sam?"

"It was about six months after I started working for him. Yes. Apparently, he said it wasn't necessary anymore, but we all knew it was to cut costs."

"Perfect. That's exactly what Janet said. So this camera in his office is new. And separate. And I just found the information on how to get access to it."

"That's what you went to get after the funeral?" Sam asked.

"Yes. I had a theory, and it turned out to be right. I had to know," I said. Sam nodded and Robby smiled.

"So, after you do the rounds here and make sure Denise is okay, we'll go review it," Robby said.

I hesitated.

"What is it, Will?" Sam asked.

"Oh," I said, snapping out of a trance. "It's fine. I just need to prepare myself for seeing my father die on camera. And God knows what else."

Chapter 20 – The Reception

As I made my way into the reception area, the only place I wanted to be was a casino. Before I became hooked on day-trading, my game of choice was blackjack. I became pretty adept at counting cards and knowing when to bet. My problem was, even though I knew when to leave the table, I never did. Ah, the life of a compulsive gambler. But even when I was losing, the blackjack table was where I felt most comfortable.

I certainly didn't feel comfortable at the reception. With everything I found out about my father in the past few days, this seemed like a big waste of time. That said, half the city of Sandusky was present to honor the man, so I told myself to suck it up and deal with it.

The room was buzzing, groups of people seemed to be either laughing or crying. A heated discussion near the back drew my attention and I headed that direction. Uncle Dan with Alex and John Traynor. Uncle Dan was drunk. In all my years of knowing him, I've never seen him even slightly intoxicated in public.

"Thanks for coming, gentlemen," I said.

Uncle Dan set his drink on the table and gave me a big bear hug. "Nice speech today, my boy," he whispered loudly in my ear. He backed away. "I'm sorry, Will, but I have to go attend to a few matters." He walked through the crowd and out the door, stumbling once along the way. *Odd departure.*

John Traynor cut in front of Alex, reaching out his right hand to me with his other hand on his walking stick.

"My deepest sympathies," he said. "Your father and I did a lot of good in this town and he will be missed."

Probably not missed by you. "Thanks," I said.

He looked around while making sure Alex stayed behind him, blocking him with his cane. "I've been told that our offer has been delivered for your father's funeral home. I'm sorry I couldn't be there in person, but you know how committees can be."

"Yes, thank you," I said. "It is a very generous offer. It gives me a lot to think about." I wanted nothing more than to tell him to fuck off, but selling the funeral home would take care of so many things—Jess's tuition most importantly—and give me a fresh start to live a life free of debt, scrubbing the previous sins of excessive gambling and poor decisions away.

"Alex here tells me you're good with numbers. If that's true, you know that the offer is more than fair value for Pollitt Funeral Home. We will take good care of it, while you manage certain financial issues on your end at the same time. Especially that daughter of yours. A win-win wouldn't you say?"

He knows. He knows about everything. How embarrassing.

Mrs. Kromer from Uncle Dan's office was coming from behind the Traynors. I reached out and shook John Traynor's hand. "Thanks again for being here."

I slid past both Traynors toward Mrs. Kromer. "Hello, Mrs. Kromer," I said, hugging her.

"Honey, it's Alice. I know it's hard to get used to."

"Of course. Alice," I said. She was short, soft, and round and, outside of the gray hair and wrinkles, exactly the way I remembered her. The body odor was a bit much, but no one cares about BO with sweet old ladies.

A line was beginning to form behind her. Xena was next.

She was dressed in a thin black sweater that hung below the waist, with black tights and black boots that rose just above the ankle. At first glance, she looked a little too dressed up for a funeral and had more makeup on than when I had seen her at her restaurant.

Alice walked away, and Xena came up to hug me. She pressed her body against mine and then backed away as if something was wrong.

"Sorry. Mrs. Kromer has a bit of body odor going and left some for me," I said.

"I thought it was a new type of cologne," she said, and we both chuckled. "How are you holding up?"

"It's been a long week. I'll be happy when this is over. I could certainly use a few drinks tonight."

"Look," she said, "I know you have a lot going on, and this is absolutely the worst timing, but I'd still love to get together to pick your brain. What about tonight, and you can drink as much as you want?"

"Wow. I'm impressed. You always were tenacious."

"You have no idea," she said.

I hadn't been with a woman in over two years, and the last one was about twenty feet away talking to my daughter. When it came to reading signals, I was as rusty as could be. But the only way Xena was going to be more obvious was taking her clothes off in front of me. Outside of my sad and lonely sex life, I wanted to ask her questions about the Sandusky Alliance. Who would know better than she as a member and a downtown small business owner?

"I can probably make that work. What time?"

"It's Saturday night dinner rush. It'll calm down around nine, and I'll be able to leave. How about you come to the restaurant around then, and we can figure out a plan?"

"I'll be there."

She smiled and said, "Great. Good luck the rest of the day. You've almost made it through."

As she walked away, Sam walked over. "That's ballsy of her to wear that outfit to a funeral," she whispered. The comment surprised me. Either Sam had a drink or two or was becoming more comfortable around me.

"She's in all black. Very respectable for the occasion, I would say."

"You know she's into you."

"Yes, but I didn't think you and I were on talking terms about our outside relationships."

"If you would have asked me a week ago, I didn't think you and I could talk about anything face-to-face."

Sam held her gaze on me for a second too long and then said, "I came over here to tell you your daughter is leaving."

Sam and I walked to the back of the hall where Jess was talking with her friends. "Do you have time to meet with Robby and me after she leaves?"

"Just text me where you'll be, and I'll meet you."

Walking over to Jess all I could think about was the Traynor's offer and Jess being able to stay in school. She was finishing talking to Zoe when Sam and I approached. "Hi, Zoe. How have you been?"

"Fine, Mr. Pollitt. I'm very sorry for your loss," she said.

"Thanks, Zoe. Did you, Jess, and Tracy have some fun this week?"

"Considering the circumstances, it was great to get together again. Felt like summertime."

"How are your parents doing?"

"Mom's doing great. She's still teaching. Dad's been sick for a while and isn't staying with Mom anymore," she said.

"I'm sorry to hear that. Do you mind if I ask where your dad is staying?"

"He's at Blessings Care Center. Been there for a couple weeks now. Doctors said the chemo didn't take. They're trying some different things, and Mom and I are hopeful."

Zoe looked like she was about to break down. "You let me know if you need anything, okay? I'll be in Sandusky more often, and I'd be happy to help if you or your mom need anything," I said.

"I will. Thanks."

"I'll text you when I get back," Jess said to Zoe, giving her a hug. Zoe walked away.

I turned to Jess. "I'm sorry about that. I didn't mean to make her feel uncomfortable. I had no idea."

"It's fine, Dad. We've actually been talking about it a lot. It was like a support group weekend. I guess it was really hard times for them a couple months ago, but they came into some money and things are better. Zoe had an old iPhone 5c and just got a new one. Can you believe that?"

"Wow. Hard to believe anyone could live with only a 5c," I said sarcastically. "They came into money? Like winning the lottery or something?"

"I'm not sure. Zoe said something about her father's insurance policy."

Sam and I looked at each other. We were thinking the same thing.

"Now you be super careful driving back to school. Remember to watch the trucks on 322. And don't stop for gas anywhere near Clearfield. That girl was taken from the Clearfield Mobil station last year. And—"

Jess came over and hugged me. "Dad, I'll be fine. Thanks for caring. I love you."

Jess and Sam left out the back door. As Robby and I walked out the front, I noticed what looked like the SUV that had been at the cemetery. It was backed into the parking lot of the Convenient Food Mart. Something wasn't right.

"Robby, stop here and pretend to talk to me. Look—but don't look—at the Convenient Food Mart across the street. I saw that same SUV at the cemetery."

I turned with my back facing the food mart so Robby could look past me and see the parking lot.

"The one with the tinted front windows?" Robby asked.

"Correct."

"If I'm not mistaken, I saw an SUV like that at our funeral home stop before the cemetery."

"Where did you see it?"

"What's that restaurant next door?"

"Carol's?"

"That's the one. There was an SUV parked there. I noticed it when we made the turn. I mean, who uses tinted glass on an SUV? That's so 2008."

"Okay," I said, and we walked toward Robby's car. We got in. "Just start driving so we don't look suspicious. Make a left out of the parking lot."

Robby made a left, heading west. "What do you want me to do?"

"Either I'm going crazy or that SUV has been following us all day. Here's what I want you to do. About a mile on your left is a cornfield. Just after that is a street called Braynard. Make a left there. Braynard goes for about a mile with a cul-de-sac at the end. Most people don't even know about it, but I used to date a girl in high school who lived there."

Robby set his hands at the ten and two position. "There's no way, man. Why would anyone be following us?"

"Why the hell did my dad have a video camera above his desk? Do you think he was a secret YouTuber or something? Here's the cornfield. Now take the left."

Robby took the left.

"Now all you have to do is make the turn around the cul-de-sac and come right back out the way we came."

The street went over a slight hill and led us to the turnaround. There were four huge houses all sharing a large pond in the back. Two of the houses had huge Cleveland Indians flags in front. They were predicted to win the AL Central Division again this year.

Robby made it around the turn and was now headed back to where we came from.

"If we pass it, just look forward like no big deal," I said.

"We won't pass it," Robby said.

As the words escaped his mouth, the SUV with the tinted windows came over the hill and passed us on our left.

Chapter 21 – The Lookout

"Shit," Robby said. "Shit, shit, shit."

"I knew it."

"What now?"

We came to the stop sign at the end of Braynard. "We need to get lost. Make a left here and an immediate right."

Robby did so.

"What if they have a tracker on us?" Robby asked.

"What?"

"A tracker. Like a little GPS monitoring my car. There's no way that SUV took a left down that cul-de-sac without some kind of tracking device on our phones or the car. Or possibly the cell signal."

"God, you're as paranoid as me."

"Of course I am. I'm a black man. Ever driven in Alabama?"

"How would we find out?" I asked.

"Maybe if we park somewhere in the open. Then we can view the car from a distance and wait to see if the SUV shows up."

I tried to think of all the places in Sandusky where something like that would work. "I got it. The mall. Go straight through the next stop sign and make a right. And push it."

A few miles later, we reached the Sandusky Mall. It was four big boxes connected together like Tinkertoys. The first one we approached used to be a Sears, but all that was left were the stained white of S, E, A, and R that remained after taking the sign down.

"What a dump," Robby said.

"All the action is over there." I pointed at a nice set of stores that included Target, Old Navy, and Duluth Trading. Duluth was having some grand opening party, what with all the balloons. "Park here."

Robby parked next to a handicapped spot. We hustled out of the car and headed toward a BAM, which I guessed was the new name for Books-A-Million.

"This store has two levels, both facing out to the parking lot. We can go upstairs and watch from there."

No one was in the store. It was eighty degrees and sunny on a Saturday afternoon. No sane person would be at the mall. We jogged to the escalator and took two steps at a time, reaching the top and making a right toward the front windows.

I spotted a sitting area between two bookshelves that had a clear view of Robby's car. I sat on a bench, while Robby leaned back into a large tan beanbag.

"How long do you think we have to wait?" Robby asked.

"Shouldn't be too long. Maybe five minutes. With all the turns we made, I'm ninety-nine percent sure he couldn't have followed us. Let's just hope we're being paranoid."

"Sam looked good today."

I smiled. "I didn't notice." She looked better than good.

"I'm sure you didn't. You still in love with her?"

"Of course I am. I'll always be in love with her. That's part of the reason this week with her has been half amazing and half utterly depressing."

"Outside of all this conspiracy shit, why depressing?"

"Just being around her. I want to hold her and tell her I'm sorry a million times until she forgives me," I said.

"Well, she's talking to you. And not in a bitchy way like the previous year and a half. You're making progress."

"She's dating someone, isn't she?"

"Don't go there," Robby said.

"I knew it."

"It's been two years, man. She works at a funeral home. Sandusky is a small city. She must be bored out of her mind. Hell, I'd probably be desperate enough to switch sides if I was in her position."

"Shhhh," I said. "Look."

Robby sank into the beanbag while I hovered behind some Harry Potter merch.

"And there it is," Robby said.

"Tracker," I said, as the SUV parked in the back of the lot, three rows over.

"I need to get out of this city fast," Robby said. "It's always at this point in the story where they off the black guy."

I sat on the floor with my hands around my knees, low enough to make sure we wouldn't be seen.

"We know we're being tracked, but we aren't sure how. Could be your car. Could be our phones. Who knows? So first, we need to get to a safer spot while Columbo is watching our car. We also need to get Sam as well. She's the only other person we can trust at this point."

"You think?"

"I don't want to take any chances. Come with me," I said, and Robby followed me to the information counter in the back corner of the store. There was a young man, probably just out of high school, sitting behind a crate of the latest James Patterson thriller.

"Hello, sir," I said. "My phone just went on the fritz, and I need to make a quick call. Would that be okay?"

"Suit yourself," the boy said. "Dial eight to get out."

"Thank you."

"Who are you calling?" Robby asked.

"Patience," I said. I dialed the number and the phone rang. She picked up after four rings.

"Hello?"

"Sam, it's me."

"Where are you calling from and why are you calling the home line? I don't have this number listed. I was going to let it go to voice mail."

"I'll explain later. Do you remember the place we went on our second date? We had a basket of mozzarella sticks and PBRs. But don't say the name."

"Of course I remember," she said.

"Can you meet us there in thirty minutes?"

"Uh, okay, I guess."

"Park your car on the other side, then walk through the alleyway between the two stores. And don't bring your cell phone." I hung up.

"She is going to think you're crazy," Robby said.

"Too late for that," I said. "Let's go."

We took the back elevator down one floor and headed into the mall walking area. I saw the restroom sign to the left and followed the signs to the back. There were two vending machines, a drinking fountain, and a set of lockers. Bingo.

I opened one of the lockers, and both Robby and I placed our iPhones inside, then locked it, putting the key in my pocket. We headed back out and found a knock-off Radio Shack, but a thousand times worse.

"Can I help you?" asked the boy behind the counter, who looked eerily similar to the boy at BAM information. His name tag said Owen, Store Manager.

"Hi, Owen. Yes. I need to buy the cheapest laptop you have. Something like a Chromebook, perhaps? I just need it for connecting to the internet and watching videos," I said.

At that, Owen smirked a bit. He was thinking porn. Of course he would be. Owen walked Robby and me over to a long table with eight laptops in a line.

"This one works. I own it myself. It's an Acer mini-lap. 802.11AC Wi-Fi plus Bluetooth 4.1, Windows 10 Home 64-Bit, MaxxAudio Pro, stereo speakers, 3-cell lithium-ion battery, includes USB 3.0 with PowerShare, one HDMI, one SD card reader, and one headphone jack. Video camera works pretty good, as well, if you're doing some kind of video chat." He smirked again.

Way too much information. "How much?"

"Two forty-nine."

"I'll take it."

I looked in my wallet. I had a hundred, and four twenties. Pretty much all I had left in free cash. I looked at Robby. "I have $180. Do you have cash for the difference?"

Robby slipped out a hundred from his wallet and gave it to me. We paid and left the store.

"Where to now?" Robby asked.

"When the Target was being built about twenty years ago, this mall put in an underground walkway from here to there. They thought it would help get more people to the mall. It actually did the opposite. The bar where we're meeting Sam is called Dewey and Pete's. I think it's a chain."

"You took her there on a second date?"

"Heck, I still had spots when we were dating. What the hell did I know about class?"

"Don't we have to go back to the car for the life insurance folder?"

"I left the folder in the car, but the contents are inside my jacket pocket," I said, opening up my jacket to him.

I checked my watch, which showed about ten minutes until Sam would arrive. As we walked under the road, we could hear the cars above our heads and then saw a bit of light after about a hundred feet. There were ten steps up to the exit. At the top it looked like a bus stop, with a two-sided movie poster and a set of trash and recycle cans. We took the alley to the right of Target and immediately saw the back patio for Dewey and Pete's. We entered through the patio, walked by the kitchen, and headed toward the front to ask for a table.

Colleen, a young blonde with a nice smile welcomed us. "How many?"

"Us and one more to come," I said. "And if you have something in the corner that would be great. Do you have a Wi-Fi connection we could use?"

She grabbed three menus. "Of course. We need the Wi-Fi for the fantasy sports crowd on Sundays. There's not great cell reception here." She gave us the Wi-Fi password.

She led us to the corner and set down the menus. "Can I get you started with drinks?" she asked. I ordered the usual for all of us, including Sam.

The table was half booth seating, half chairs. Could fit six or seven if necessary. Robby sat in the middle and was busy getting the laptop set up. I was keeping an eye out for Sam and, more importantly, my drink.

Sam entered through the back patio as well, spotting us as she passed the restrooms. I waved, and she pulled a seat next to Robby.

"You've got me running around the city like it's the Hunger Games or something. Explain," she said squeezing her lime into her vodka tonic.

Robby and I looked at each other and shrugged. "Okay," I said. "The first thing you need to know is that Robby and I are not currently on drugs and this is our first alcoholic drink of the day. The second thing is that we are currently being followed."

Sam looked at Robby. "He's telling the truth, Sam. I thought he was shitting me while we were in the car, but I've seen it with my own eyes."

"When we stopped at the funeral home before the cemetery, Robby spotted an SUV with tinted windows. I saw the same one at the cemetery. Then we believe the same one followed us from the meeting hall. By that time, we knew something was going on, and I had Robby take some weird turns. We passed it again down off Braynard, sped off in the other direction to the mall, and five minutes later, guess who shows up?"

"We were way in front of them, so they must be tracking one of our devices, or possibly my car," Robby said.

"And we don't know if you're being tracked as well, or whether our phones are bugged, hence all the secrecy in getting you here."

"Let's say I believe you for this minute," Sam said. "What now?"

"What we have here is an untraceable laptop that we bought at the mall," I said. "The next step is to tap into the server Dad set up and see what was recorded on the office camera. I guess here and now is as good as it's going to get."

I pulled the sheet of paper out from my inside pocket, unfolded in, and pressed it onto the table. The top of the paper included a picture of the equipment, which was identical to the camera in Dad's office. Below the image was an HTTPS secure site URL, and below that was a password full of special characters, numbers, and capital letters.

"Before we do this," I said, "we promise to keep all this between the three of us. And I mean everything. Whatever is on this footage, the insurance conspiracy stuff, the being followed mess. Everything. Agreed?"

"Agreed," Robby said.

"Of course," Sam said.

"Okay, then. Robby, you have the honors."

Chapter 22 – The Video

Robby typed the URL into the browser and hit Enter. The page was blank except for a box in the middle: *Password*. Robby entered the password exactly as it was written down on the piece of paper from my dad's office.

The screen returned blank, same as the first page, this time saying, *Enter a Name*.

"What is it, Will?" Robby asked.

"Try Pollitt," I said. Robby hit Enter, and nothing happened.

"Abraham?" I said. Again, nothing happened.

"Try Will or William," Sam said. Robby tried both. Nothing.

"How about Laura or Linnie, my mother's name," I said.

This time, the screen changed. Under *Enter a Name*, it read, *You have one more try or the system will lock. Please call administrator.*

"Are you seeing this, Will?" Robby asked.

"No, I was looking at the décor. Of course, I'm seeing this. Isn't there a hint button anywhere?"

"Not that I can see. Will, if this was meant for you to find, you should know the name your dad would use. One only you would know. Some secret between the two of you. Something you shared perhaps?" Sam asked.

"My dad wasn't much of a sharer. We didn't have any secrets. At least nothing that I can remember."

"Didn't your father collect baseball cards, just like you?" Robby asked.

That's it! "God, you're brilliant."

"What?" Sam said.

"My dad took me to a sports card show years ago. I must have been about five or so. He was looking through the 1957 commons from a dealer and found an absolutely perfect Rocky Colavito card. That was Colavito's rookie card. The dealer was selling the cards in that box for a dollar each, but the Colavito was worth a hundred dollars. My dad carefully pulled the card out of the stack and took it to the dealer, who immediately saw the mistake. After a bit of back and forth, they agreed to twenty bucks. Then Dad gave him thirty. A few weeks later, Dad took the Colavito rookie to a professional card grader. It came back rated Gem Mint 10, which increased the value tenfold. I've never seen my dad so excited about anything in his life. I don't think I've ever seen another card from 1957 rated Gem Mint."

"Great story, Will," Robby said. "So what am I typing in here? And make sure you're sure because this could be our last shot."

"It's Colavito," I said, spelling it out for him. "Dad even mentioned it in his will that I should remember the name Colavito. I didn't think of that until just now."

Robby typed it into the space. "Is this correct?"

"That's perfect. That has to be it."

Robby hit Enter and the screen changed again, this time with a list of dates starting with today's date and going down, each line a previous day. Robby hit the page down button to the last line.

"This earliest date is from two weeks ago," Robby said. "You think he smelled trouble and installed the camera?"

I ignored the question. "All I want to do right now is see what happened on Sunday, the night he passed away."

"Do you want me to watch it first, Will?" Sam said, reaching across and putting her hand on my shoulder. Then she quickly removed it.

"I can handle it. But thanks."

Robby clicked on the day my father passed away. A page loaded that had twenty-four icons, one for each hour in the day, starting at midnight to one a.m. "What time?" Robby asked.

"I was told it happened late at night, between ten and midnight. Is that right, Sam?"

"That's what the coroner said, and right now, we have no reason not to believe him."

"Start at eight, just to be safe," I said to Robby.

Robby clicked on the icon above eight p.m. to nine p.m. Another browser window popped up with a YouTube-like video screen. Robby hit the play button. The image was of my father's desk. In the camera view, the desk was at the bottom of the screen with a couple feet free on either side. Dad's swivel chair and the ledge behind the chair was visible. Robby turned up the sound.

"Looks like just image," he said. "There's sound available, but I'm not getting anything. I'll fast-forward a bit."

The video was counting down from 59:59. There was a forward thirty seconds and back thirty seconds button on each side of the play button. Robby kept hitting the forward thirty seconds button. We would see shadows off to the left side, most likely someone walking down the hall, impeding the light, but no one entered the office. It seemed that, if there were no shadows for a while, thus no movement, the camera paused recording, then picked back up when there was movement.

"Okay," Robby said. "Let's try nine p.m."

Robby fast-forwarded through until nine thirty, and my dad entered the room. His back was turned to the camera. He was making a pot of coffee with the old percolator. Then he left the room. Robby hit fast-forward again, and Dad reappeared at 9:50. He poured a cup of coffee into his favorite mug and sat at the desk. He pushed the chair forward and took a quick glance at the camera, almost like he knew we were watching him.

Someone entered the room from the bottom of the screen. The office door that led to the main entrance. Dad was looking at the person, apparently listening. His coffee mug was on the desk, but he was holding it by the handle. His right hand was under the desk. Suddenly, there was sound crackling through the speakers.

"Turn it up," I said to Robby.

Robby turned up the volume.

The first part was inaudible. Then you could clearly hear a voice. Jack. The top of his head was in view. He was talking about the call schedule for the rest of the week.

"Thanks," my dad said. "Now get home. It's way too late to be here on a Sunday night."

"Well you're still here," Jack said.

"I'm just finishing up some financials. Maybe another hour, and then I'm gone," Dad said, but his tone was a bit off, and Jack caught it.

"You okay, boss?" Jack asked.

"Oh, I'm fine. Just tired," my dad said. He paused. "You've always been a good friend."

"Now don't get all mushy on me, boss. I already have to go home to my wife, and I'm feeling a bit queasy," Jack said with a deep chuckle.

My dad smiled. "Now get out of here." And Jack was gone.

Then my dad put his right hand underneath the desk and the sound cut out again. He sat back and raised his head looking at the camera. I could clearly see his eyes. They were the same eyes he had the day my mother passed away. Then he picked up his right hand, made a fist, and proceeded with a circular motion around his heart.

"What's he doing?" I asked.

"That's sign language. He learned ASL about a year ago. He's saying he's sorry," Sam said.

My body started to tingle, like watching a horror movie before the climax. I wanted to look away. To leave. But I was frozen to the screen.

Dad pushed the swivel chair back and stood. He removed something from his pants pocket with his right hand. A piece of paper? A packet of some kind? He opened it slowly, placing it directly above his coffee, and some kind of substance fell into the cup. I had the feeling it wasn't salt or sugar. He brushed the inside of the paper with his index finger above the cup. He then crinkled the paper into a ball and walked out of the room through the back office door, leaving the coffee mug on the desk.

He came back through the same door twenty seconds later. He took his index finger and dipped it into the coffee mug, stirring it clockwise three, four, five times, then wiped his finger on his right pant leg. He picked up the coffee mug with his right hand and held it in front of his torso. He took one deep breath, brought the cup up to his lips, and took what looked to be a long drink.

And he stood there. No sound. Everything was still as a picture, almost as if the video paused. After what seemed like minutes, but was most likely seconds, his eyes widened, and he fell forward. His left side hit the desk hard, turning him midair, and he landed on his back. All that was left in the image was his lower legs, his shoes pointing up toward the ceiling, and half a broken mug next to his leg.

Chapter 23 – Spock

I sank back into the booth.

"Nothing brightens your day like seeing your father commit suicide." I thought I was going to be sick.

"Are you sure he did?" Robby asked. "It could have been sweetener or something and he coincidentally had a heart attack or stroke."

"Will's right," Sam said. "Abe always took his coffee black. I'm so sorry, Will."

"Listen," Robby said. "If that's true, there's a reason behind this. He wouldn't kill himself unless there was something terrible going on."

"That doesn't make me feel better," I said.

"Robby's right," Sam said. "He set the camera up two weeks ago, so he's probably giving us fourteen days of clues or information to work with."

"It's more than that," Robby said. "For whatever reason, your dad needed you to know, without a doubt, that he killed himself. By doing that, we already have some important information."

"Robby, you're brilliant," Sam said. "You know how we've been questioning McGinty's work as coroner? He did a full autopsy and came back saying the COD was a heart attack. Now we know that the coroner, and whoever else is working with McGinty, didn't want anyone to know that your father died by poison or whatever that was he put in his coffee."

"Good point," I said. "But why couldn't he just tell me. Or write something down. Why be so cryptic? It doesn't make any sense."

"Spock," Robby said.

"What?" I said.

"Spock from *Star Trek*. I can't remember which movie it was, but he said something like once you eliminate the impossible, whatever is left, no matter how improbable, must be true."

"That's Sir Arthur Conan Doyle," Sam said.

Robby looked at Sam. "Whatever, whoever, doesn't matter. The point is that it's impossible Abe just killed himself on video for dramatic effect. He did it for a reason. If that's true, he couldn't write all this down or tell you in person. He *had* to communicate *this* way. He was being watched."

"And Will you said that you couldn't find the last few months of Abe's diary installments," Sam said. "Either he stopped voluntarily because someone was watching him or someone took them or he hid them somewhere for you to find."

"Okay." I paused, trying to collect myself. "Let's say you're both right. What's next?"

"Well, first," Sam said, "we need to go through the rest of this video footage and see what's there. And then we need to get those additional blood samples to my contact at the Clinic and see what we can find."

Sam had a good point. There's no way my father would have gone through the extra work of keeping those samples unless he was planning on using them for something.

"Robby and I have a meeting in Cleveland first thing Monday. I can take them to your contact at the Clinic. It's right next to the PopC offices. If someone is tracking our movements, we'll be able to get them there without leaving a bread trail."

"But we've got bigger issues," Robby said. "Like the fact we're all being tracked right now. We need to assume that our phones are bugged, our cars have tracking devices on them. It's also likely that our houses are under surveillance. Will, I bet your dad's house is completely wired up."

"Okay," I said. "But we need to act in a way that shows we don't know we're being tracked. We use our phones for normal stuff. We use our cars as usual. Robby, do you still have that crate of phones from the LG marketing pitch we did?"

"Sure do."

"Good. Get three of those. We can communicate with each other while we figure this out. Sam, I'll come back from Cleveland after our Monday meetings and get one of the phones to you. Robby can program each of our numbers in to make it easy."

"What do we do until Monday?" Sam asked.

"Just try to act normal I guess," I said. "Don't trust anyone, but don't act like you don't trust anyone."

"Great advice," Robby said, shaking his head.

"You got a better idea?"

"No," Robby said. "Sounds right. But what about calling in the po-po?"

"I'm guessing the Sandusky Alliance owns the police. They all play Friday poker together or something," Sam said.

"Agreed," I said. "Probably not safe. But I don't think we have enough evidence to contact my old roommate that works for the Cleveland FBI. He would be our first contact when we have something."

"What can I do?" Sam asked.

"You keep working on any trends you saw at the funeral home with the body count. Perhaps Dad was taking samples strategically and that will tell us something. Can you do that without being noticed?"

"I think so," she said. "I already have your dad's spreadsheets from the last few years, so I'll start there. As for the samples, I'll get those ready tomorrow, and I'll do it in a way no one would notice, even if there's a camera in the embalming room that I'm not aware of."

"Can you imagine the sick freak watching those videos if there is a camera in there?" Robby said with a straight face. "What can I do?"

"You're leaving tonight, right?" I asked.

"Yes. Was planning on it."

"You should stop in and visit your insurance uncle in Elyria."

"What are you going to do?" Sam asked.

"I'll find a place to watch the rest of these videos," I said. "And I have a meeting with Xena tonight. I'd like to find out more about the Sandusky Alliance, and I have a feeling she knows something."

Chapter 24 – The First Date

S am left first, going out the way she came. Robby paid the bill and we walked back through the tunnel leading to the mall. We picked up our phones from the locker and zigzagged back to BAM.

"Should we check if the SUV is still there?" Robby asked.

We took the elevator back up to the second floor and walked the south side to the front windows. I approached the Harry Potter merch and peeked around it to get a view of the outside.

"Yep. He's still there," I said.

"Dedicated, isn't he?"

"Yeah," I said. "He's in line to win asshole of the year."

Before heading to the escalator, I grabbed a large BAM shopping bag from the information counter and placed the computer in it. Then down and out the doors we came in.

"Act like I said something funny," I said. At that, Robby started to laugh, almost barreling over as we approached the car.

"A bit much, isn't it?" I said under my breath.

Robby took the most conspicuous route back to the funeral home so I could pick up the van, then he headed off to Elyria. I ran in and picked up the keys Jack left for me on Janet's desk and headed to the van. It took twice as long getting back to Dad's with the Cedar Point traffic. First weekend of the year, and afternoon rates started at four. I stopped looking for the SUV entirely. I figured it was back there somewhere.

I felt like I hadn't eaten all day. I stopped at Chipotle to get a burrito bowl for early dinner. The kid taking my order looked like a clone from the information-desk kid at BAM. *Everyone looks the same.* I grabbed the order to go and pulled into Dad's driveway just before five.

Stepping out of the van, I thought I'd work on just being my normal self, whatever that meant. I called Denise. She was hanging with some friends tonight and seemed relatively okay. Then I called Jess, who was about thirty minutes outside of State College on Route 322. I grabbed the BAM bag with the computer out of the back of the vehicle.

I tried to act normal once I entered the house, but all I wanted to do was search for cameras. It felt like an episode of *Survivor*, without the prize at the end for being the last one standing. I went to the kitchen, pulled a beer from the refrigerator, and sat at the table to eat my bowl.

I thought seeing the video of my father would bring peace, but it brought the opposite. Suicide? I guess everyone is surprised when someone kills themselves. When I was in college, one of my friends committed suicide, and our entire group of friends was shocked. He was the happiest kid in the world. Apparently not. That's probably ninety-nine percent of suicide situations. No one ever expects it.

But my father was a devout Catholic. He believed that taking your own life was a one-way ticket to Hell. No refunds. Even as a last resort, he wouldn't have taken his own life. But he did. I saw it. He signed that he was sorry, put something into his coffee, and dropped dead.

Patience, Will. Dad wouldn't do this without a reason.

I finished the bowl, grabbed a fresh beer from the fridge, and surveyed the house looking for a safe place to watch Dad's video footage. The closet in my dad's bedroom? The guest bathroom? Anything close to the bay lacked a solid Wi-Fi connection, so that was out. My paranoia ruled out every room in the house. I was afraid to even take the computer out of the bag.

I set the half-finished beer on the counter and headed back to the van. Ten minutes later, I was downtown. I passed Uncle Dan's office, the waterfront area that my father helped to build, the new police station and the library. I parked the van and headed toward the library entrance. Hours until eight p.m. on Saturday. Nice.

Two elderly women behind desks were organizing books. They were talking about something they'd seen on the news regarding refugees. I gave them a smile and proceeded to the computers, which were in the same exact spot when Alex and I used to visit the library as high school freshmen. I actually watched him change his Religious Studies grade from a D to an A minus, just like Matthew Broderick did in *Ferris Bueller's Day Off.*

There were four rows of computers with only two computers being used. There was no one in the third row, and I chose a terminal in the back left.

I moved the mouse, and the computer screen lit up. I double-clicked on the Search function. A screen popped up that looked like Google but was customized for the library. I typed Pollitt into the search engine. It resulted in over a thousand hits, mostly obituaries. I retried the search with Abe Pollitt all in quotes to get an exact match.

There was the obit from a few days ago. A nice summation of Dad's life.

A few more searches and I found what I was looking for, an article from seven years ago: "Sandusky Business Leaders Launch Downtown Development Group."

Apparently, there were four founders: my father, Dan McGinty, Mark Larraby, and John Traynor. Dad and Mr. Traynor were quoted the most, talking about how Sandusky's government wasn't proactive enough with the downtown area. In response, they formed the Sandusky Alliance. SA would be a privately funded group with the mission of transforming downtown Sandusky into "the most vibrant downtown area on the north coast."

The group would fund real estate projects, help market the downtown and downtown-area businesses, and help spur tourism. The article also noted that SA would be initially funded through capital from the four founders but would later take on grants from corporations and individual donations. The first one, a generous grant from Cedar Point, was noted in the article but no amount was given.

I continued searching, mostly around variations of the Sandusky Alliance. Each year, there was a press release that added executive members. First, Mitch Dreason, then followed by the others.

Two years ago, John Traynor stepped down and his son, Alex Traynor, not only took his spot on the board, but became president of the group.

If my count was right, that was a circle of nine. Nine white men, no less. Apparently, there were no diversity quotas in the SA mission statement.

Not sure if it was a coincidence or not, but once Alex Traynor took over, the articles and announcements exploded. New office complex, funded by SA. New restaurant, funded by SA. Construction on the walking pier on Water Street, funded by SA. New distillery project, funded by SA. Each project was a million dollars or more.

In the past eighteen months, SA went from a small organization to one of the most successful city development and marketing groups in the country.

The clock on the screen said 7:45. I went to the Tools section of the browser and deleted my history in case someone wanted to know what I was searching for. I gave the ladies behind the desk a smile as I left and walked down the library steps back to the van.

Xena's restaurant was five minutes away. I took the long way there and parked a block down the street. As I approached the restaurant I could hear the conversations inside. *Business must be good.* I had to walk past a dozen people to get to the hostess. She said there was a twenty-minute wait, so I headed to the end of the bar and ordered a Tito's and tonic.

I felt a hand on my right shoulder. "I like it when people show up early for a meeting." I turned my head to see Xena smiling. She had a black polo shirt on with the Tony's restaurant logo embroidered on the left side of her chest.

"Looks like business is going really well," I said. "There were no open tables."

"Let me get you one," she said, about to head off to see the hostess.

I grabbed her elbow to stop her. "Xena, this is perfect. And I'm in no hurry. I'll be here whenever you're ready."

She smiled. "Tommy," she called to the bartender who had served me my drink. "Anything he drinks is on me," she said, and bolted through the back doors leading to the kitchen.

Tommy came over. "She must really like you, because she never comps drinks."

"I'm an old friend of hers. And don't worry, I'll still tip you," I said, smiling. "I'm Will Pollitt." I reached out my hand to him.

"Tommy Rose," he said as we shook hands. "Pollitt? Are you related to Abe Pollitt who just passed away?"

"My father," I said, taking a drink.

"Oh," Tommy said. "I'm sorry for your loss."

"Thanks."

"When I started working here, I used to see him downtown all the time, but lately not so much. Was he sick for a while?"

"No. Heart attack," I said, cringing a bit at the lie. "When did you start working here?"

"About two years ago. Just after Xena opened the place. Came back home after graduating college. Bowling Green."

"Good school."

"Yeah. But this job was supposed to be temporary, and yet here I am. Money's good though, and I get my days free."

"Xena seems like a good boss," I said, taking another drink. "So when did you stop seeing my father around here?"

"Hard to say. Maybe a year. Or a bit more. Before that he'd come in here or I'd see him walking the streets downtown. One time I saw him walk up and down this street going into every shop. Looked like he was checking in with everyone to see how they were doing."

"Sounds like my father."

Someone was calling Tommy for a drink down at the end of the bar. "Gotta go," Tommy said. "Again, sorry for your loss."

More proof of my father's changing behavior. But why? I felt like I was gathering a lot of information that was leading to nowhere in particular. Maybe the videos would provide some substance.

There was a nice buzz inside the restaurant. Everyone was having a good time. Mostly an older crowd, fifty-plus. Maybe some in their forties.

Xena came around the corner. "You ready?" she asked.

I stood, pulled my last five-dollar bill out of my wallet, and set it on the bar. Whatever Xena and I did would have to add to my credit card debt.

"Drinks are on me," she said.

"Yes. Thanks. The five is for Tommy."

I followed her out the front door, making a right toward the water.

I said, "You sure you're okay to leave when it's that busy?"

"We close at ten, so that's as busy as we'll be. There'll be some who come in the next half hour but not many. Anyway, the team can live without me for an hour."

"If you're sure," I said. Uncle Dan's office was on our left. We hit Water Street and made a right.

"There's this nice wine bar down the street that my friend opened up. You okay with that?"

"Perfect," I said. I could see the sign up on the right. Rosi's Wine Bar. "I remember this area when I was growing up. It's like living on a different planet. So many retail shops and people actually on the street at this time of night. As kids, we were never allowed in this area after dark. No matter what."

I pulled open the door for Rosi's and let Xena lead in. As we entered, she shuffled toward another woman and they embraced, rocking back and forth a bit.

Xena stepped to the right and introduced me. "Dana, this is Billy. I mean Will. He's visiting from Cleveland." We shook hands.

"Nice to meet you, Dana." She was just a bit taller than Xena but just as attractive. They could have been sisters.

"Same here, Will. Glad you two came in."

"Thanks."

"Can we sit outside, Dana? It's amazing weather tonight," Xena said.

"Got the perfect spot for you," she said, leading us into the back. The back doors opened into what looked like a butterfly garden. There were orchids and ferns and plants of all shapes and sizes surrounding six small tables with chairs. The light came from tiny strings of LED lights dangling over our heads. Dana sat us in the corner.

Dana asked, "Can I get you started with something?"

"Surprise us," Xena said. "Are you okay with something in red?" she asked me.

"A surprise sounds just fine to me," I said, and without a word Dana was gone.

I didn't notice before we left Tony's, but Xena had changed her outfit. A maroon blouse, short-sleeved, cut low and showing just enough cleavage. It hung to mid-hip. She had black tights on with the black boots. I figured they were the same ones from the funeral.

"Looks like you are in a better mood than before," she said. "You holding up okay?"

"Yes. Better. Thanks. It's good to be out. I appreciate the invite." It did feel good to be out.

Dana came back with a bottle and two glasses and went through a few minutes on the history of the winery behind the wine.

"Enjoy," she said. "I'm headed back to the front. Mary Ann is covering the back if you need anything. Nice meeting you, Will." Dana left us.

"She seems very nice," I said.

"She's amazing. Divorced mother of two. Her dream was to open a wine bar, and she made it a reality. She opened about the same time I did."

"How long have you known her?"

Xena took a long sip of wine, leaving a hint of lipstick on the glass. "She went to Perkins High School the same time we were at St. Mary's, but I met her the first time at an SA meeting. Being divorced mothers trying to succeed as entrepreneurs, you know, we just clicked and became instant friends."

I wanted to ask about SA but decided to continue with the small talk for now. "How many kids do you have?"

"Two. They both live in Columbus now. My boy is an accountant, and my daughter is still trying to find her way. She graduated from Ohio State a few years back and works as a bartender on High Street." I vaguely remembered Xena becoming pregnant right after graduation, so I figured her kids were a bit older than Jess. I couldn't remember the guy and decided not to bring it up.

"Nothing wrong with tending bar. You could say bartending is one of the more noble professions. Takes good listening and customer service skills."

"She likes Columbus and decided to hang down there with her brother. They live a few blocks away from each other, and as a mom that makes me feel a whole lot more secure. So, you have one kid, right?"

"Correct," I said, taking another sip of wine. "Jess goes to Penn State right now. She just started. Majoring in Journalism and Media Studies. She went back after the luncheon today."

"She's pretty. She looks like her mother. It was strange that you introduced your ex-wife to me as your father's employee when you came into the restaurant."

"You caught that? Of course, how could you miss it? It's been two years since the divorce and that might be the first time I've introduced her to anyone since we parted. Sorry about that."

"No." She chuckled. "You handled it just fine. If my ex was here, I'd introduce him as a piece of shit."

"My condolences."

She smiled. "No need. I'm glad he's gone. That's what happens when you fall in love at eighteen. But I wouldn't take it back for anything. He gave me my kids, and they're my world. Only two good things he ever did. Anyway, forget all that. You promised some feedback on the restaurant, and I'd love to hear what you have to say. I want the one-hundred-percent truth." She said this with a grin, and her right eye squinted a bit. She seemed to be getting more attractive by the minute. *Could be the wine.*

I spent the next few minutes asking her questions and talking about her business goals. Mary Ann came over and asked us if we needed anything. "We're still working on this bottle, but we'll let you know," I said. Mary Ann looked related to the kid at BAM and the worker at Chipotle. Robby was right—Sandusky was like Pleasantville.

"Can I ask you a nonbusiness question?" I said.

"Of course."

"When I grew up in Sandusky, how do I put this? There were a lot more black people. Just seeing Mary Ann there and most of the people working downtown or at the mall. Everybody looks the same. Everyone's white. Am I missing something?" I said the last part loudly, and the couple next to me gave me the eye. I become a loud talker when I drink.

Xena gave a look like she just stepped on a tack. "You need to keep your voice down when you're talking about things like that."

"I'm sorry?" I asked. "Talk about what things?"

"About black people," she whispered.

"What's wrong with talking about black people?"

"You don't know?" she asked.

"Know what?"

She looked at me like I had three heads. "Okay, I'll tell you. But let's get out of here first, okay?"

"Whatever you say. Sure."

We got up, and I walked over to Mary Ann and put the bill on credit. Thankfully, it cleared. Dana gave us half off the wine, so the bill came to less than twenty bucks.

Xena walked out of Rosi's and made a left, then we took a right on Jackson Street and headed for the waterfront. The wind had picked up a bit, but it was a beautiful May evening. Warm for this time of year. The whole situation should have felt fantastic—I was on my first date in forever, enjoying a walk on the harbor—but I could sense something bad was imminent.

Jackson Street dead-ended into the Sandusky Bay, and we walked up to the edge of the dock, which was guarded by ropes that seemed to go for miles in each direction. Several couples walked by, taking in the evening.

Since she didn't say anything, I decided to chime in. "Does this have anything to do with SA?"

Xena looked in both directions as if someone was watching her. "What I'm going to tell you did *not* come from me. I'll deny ever telling you anything. If they find out, my restaurant is done for." The playful Xena was gone. Everything about her demeanor had changed.

"Got it. I won't say anything, Xena. Now what's going on?"

"I don't know the complete history of how SA started. You might know better than I because your father helped start it. That's kind of why I thought you knew. Anyway, a couple years ago some new and some of the old businesspeople got together. They say they commissioned a study, but I've never seen it. It said that, economically, both from organic business and tourism, minorities were to blame for Sandusky's problems."

"African-Americans?" I asked.

"Yes. Black people, Hispanics, Asians, you name it. Even homosexuals. I was at the initial meeting where they talked about it. I had only been in business a few months at that time. It was like being at a KKK rally, but more sophisticated and no hoods. They used percentages and charts that said people who employed minority workers were not only hurting their own businesses but damaging the entire city. They showed stats from other cities the size of Sandusky that said when minorities are less 'out in the open,' tourism in those cities flourished. They said we had to get rid of the unclean masses of Sandusky."

"Unclean masses? What is this, Jonestown?" I said a bit too loudly. I regained my composure. "So what did they tell you to do? Not hire blacks or Hispanics?" I asked.

"Not directly. They basically said if you have to hire them for menial tasks, keep them unseen by the public. I had a wonderful hostess. Her name was Tish. She was black. I had to move her to the kitchen, but she hated it there and quit."

"What if you didn't move Tish? What would happen?"

"There were a few businesses that didn't fall into line. Matt Jacobs ran a fix-it repair shop off Washington. He had a young black girl working the register and a middle-aged Asian man who fixed everything and was always visible to the customers. His shop burned down about a month after the initial meeting. Fire department said it was an electrical problem, but the talk underground was arson."

"They can't get away with that! What about calling in the police? How can SA keep the entire city in line?

She paused. "I don't know how to describe it. They just do. People that make a fuss seem to find a lot of bad luck happens to them and their families."

I thought about my dad and, for some reason, my mother's car accident two years ago. Could it be related?

"So you're scared that if you don't fall into line, something will happen to you or the restaurant?" I asked.

"Yes. Yes," Xena said, her eyes beginning to tear up.

"I'm sorry. I didn't mean to make you upset. I had no idea," I said. "But I have to know. Was my father involved in this?"

"I know your father was at the first meeting. Where the idea was first brought up. But that's all I know."

"Who led the meeting? Who is enforcing all this?"

"I don't know who specifically, but the entire board was up there talking as one."

"Including Dan McGinty?" I asked.

"Yes," she hesitated. "Dan was there."

"Shit," I said.

"You know him well?" she asked.

"Yes. He was my father's best friend. I grew up calling him Uncle Dan. Still do." The thoughts and the emotions were hard to control in front of Xena. I wanted—needed—to leave. I looked at my watch. It was just past twelve. "I'm sorry, Xena. I think I should call it a night, if you don't mind."

"That's fine, Will. I'm sure it's been an incredibly long and stressful day. And you just had a hell of a cake topper, with this conversation."

"Not your fault at all. I appreciate you telling me. It just feels like a punch to the gut."

"Just promise, whatever you do with the information, you leave me out of it. Now that the kids are gone, the restaurant is my new baby."

"I promise," I said.

She started walking east down the dock and waved me toward her. "I live a couple blocks down this way. Can you walk me back?"

"Of course. You don't have to go back to the restaurant?"

"Nope. Tommy closed up for me. He's a good kid."

We crossed the street, away from the water, and hit the sidewalk on the south side of Water Street. Xena owned a two-story condo that couldn't have been more than five years old. I walked her up to the door.

"Thanks again for the wonderful conversation, Xena. Other than learning a few things I wish I hadn't, I had a great time."

She unlocked her door and pushed it open, then turned around to face me. She placed her hands on my chest. Then she leaned her head in, put her lips against my earlobe and whispered, "Would you like to come in?"

The last woman I had any physical contact with was Sam. That was over two years ago. My body was responding in like fashion. All I wanted to do was take her in my arms, push her through the door, and toss her onto the bed.

She pulled away and, with her about three inches shorter, looked slightly up at me. "I'd honestly love to, Xena. I really would. But I can't. For a variety of reasons that I can't get into right now."

Xena put her right hand on my genitals. Then she squeezed. "It feels as though you can," she said. She kept her hand there. "Will, don't worry. I'm divorced. You're divorced. We're both lonely. And I think we're both attracted to each other. No harm, no foul. It could be a wonderful night. For both of us."

I took both her hands and placed them in mine. "A big part of me wants to. You have no idea. But I can't right now. I hope you understand." I leaned over and kissed her on the cheek. Then I turned around, made a left back toward the van, and thought of Sam.

Chapter 25 – Homework

I spent the night on Dad's couch. I tried to sleep in the guest bed but couldn't get comfortable. At one point during the night I almost jumped in the van and headed to the casino in Toledo. I thankfully gave up on the idea and showered instead. Regardless, I didn't have a dollar to my name. Made not gambling a lot easier.

Searching on the phone, I found a coffee shop near Cedar Point that opened at five. The shop was just opening when I arrived.

My mind was on the day before. Could yesterday have been the worst day of my life? There were many to choose from. The first time I gambled away our savings was a top five for sure. Telling Sam the first time was right there as well. The worst was probably when she found out the second time, which ultimately led to us splitting up and then divorcing.

So let's say yesterday was a close second. Realizing that my father committed suicide felt worse than when I found out he passed away. To add to that, he may very well have been a racist who helped lead the entire city of Sandusky down a dark hole.

And then there was Uncle Dan. His involvement was shady as well. And could be much worse depending on what Robby, Sam, and I dig up. Not to mention we were all being watched.

I told myself that yesterday was the second worst day of my life, but I'd keep it open to further consideration, depending on what other information I could uncover.

The coffee shop looked like it had recently received a makeover. New paint for sure. Newish sign. It was called "Coasters." The name was perfect since it was a block off the Cedar Point causeway.

An elderly man opened the front door. He gazed up and nodded like he was welcoming me.

I shut off the van and brought in the BAM bag with the computer inside. The shop smelled of hazelnut. And maybe pumpkin spice? I couldn't tell.

I ordered a large low-fat latte and a blueberry muffin, put it on the credit card, and sat in the corner near the restrooms. The perfect spot, since the barrier between the booths was high enough that it blocked my computer from sight. If the SUV came around, there'd be no way the driver could see what I was doing. At least I hoped that to be the case.

I booted up the computer and signed in to the security camera server. Now, fifteen lines appeared. It included today. The camera was apparently still working.

I decided to go to the first day and watch each video. I didn't want to miss anything. Who knew what kind of clues my dad was leaving me?

A good, solid Wi-Fi connection. I clicked on the first date, and twenty-four blocks appeared, just like before. The first entry of the first day started at two a.m. Dad must have installed the camera that night. Or turned it on that night, since the midnight and 1 a.m. blocks were missing.

At around two fifteen a.m., my dad was sitting at his desk. He was looking at the camera and mouthing something. I turned up the sound, but didn't hear anything.

Then he reached below his desk and seemed to press something. There was some crackling, then I could hear his voice.

"Check, one, two. Check, one, two. Checking for sound." Hearing his voice felt like home. Then he grabbed some files and left out the back door. Two minutes later, the video stopped. Why would Dad install a sound control for the camera?

I clicked on three a.m. There was no video.

It was the same for four, five, and six. Then I clicked on seven a.m., and at about seven thirty, the video picked up my dad walking in and laying the files on his desk. The camera only recorded when there was motion and seemed to shut off after about two minutes of no movement in the room.

That should make it a lot easier.

I checked through each of the first two days. Nothing out of the ordinary in any of the video clips. Dad had one meeting on the first day with a woman whose husband just passed, and had another one the next day with a young mother and father whose child had cancer and was apparently close to death.

There were tears all around in that meeting. I must have gotten caught up in it because the man who opened the coffee shop came over to see if I was okay.

Outside of Dad running in and out of the office, there was nothing else of note except the two meetings.

Before I opened up the third day, I checked my watch. Six thirty a.m. I decided to text Sam. I figured she'd be up, if she'd even slept at all.

Good morning.

Three dots came up almost immediately.

Hi. You're up early.

Couldn't sleep. You know the drill. I'm heading to the funeral home before I head to Cleveland for the PopC meeting. Thought maybe we could review those financials before I do.

Absolutely. What time?

How about noon? I'll pick up lunch.

See you there.

Just an ordinary text conversation, I thought. Nothing wrong at all. Or at least I was hoping whoever was reading our texts was picking up that vibe. Sam knew I wanted her to prepare the samples so I could take them to the Clinic. After a couple years together, we could communicate without using words, mostly through eye contact and gestures. We could read through texts to find the real meaning as well.

I ordered another latte from the old man. A large again. Plus one of those mini-quiches. He asked me if I wanted a loyalty card, but I politely refused. For now.

Two days down. Twelve to go. I clicked to the third day and made my way through. If I was backtracking correctly, it was a Tuesday. Nothing much during the day. My dad was in and out again. During the evening, the camera turned on, picking up some shadows, probably a visitation.

The fourth day saw hardly any activity. Same with the fifth.

It was eleven a.m., and my eyes were already sore from watching the videos. And my wrist was sore. Probably the start of carpal tunnel or some other new technology disorder that affected people who grew up on computers.

I decided to shut things down and grab lunch before heading to the funeral home. As I clicked the corner X to close down day five, I accidentally ran the mouse over the last line. An icon popped up on the screen between the two and three a.m. slot. From today. The picture was blurry. I clicked it.

The video began at 2:30 a.m. Lights turned on from the side. Possibly the hall lights. Then there was some kind of shadow outside the back door. Someone was pacing back and forth.

A person walked around the front of the desk. He or she made a left at the desk and headed in the direction of Dad's closet. It didn't take the person too long to open the closet. They must have had a key. The light inside came on, then darkness. Two minutes later the video went out.

At 2:54, the video returned. The camera picked up movement from the closet door. It opened, then the light shut off. Then the door closed. Two seconds later, a blur went across the screen, as the person crossed between Dad's desk and the ledge behind, brushing his swivel chair. The movement was too fast, and I couldn't pick up any details. Nothing happened until 2:57 when the video ended.

I rewound the video back to the 2:54 mark and hit the pause button as the person came from the closet door. The figure entered the frame at the 2:54:42 mark. Definitely a man. Larger than most. Dark hair. Possibly some gray. The left side of his face was covered by the shadows, so I couldn't get a good look. I played the video in slow motion: 43 seconds, 44 seconds. Still the same view as he reached the chair. Then at 45 seconds, just as he was nearing the end of the desk, the light from the hall hit his face, and I could finally get a good view.

I recognized the man immediately. I was looking at the side profile of Jack Miller.

Chapter 26 – Minority Report

I parked the van behind the funeral home. I'd picked up a few Beef 'n Cheddars from Arby's, one of Sam's favorite guilty pleasures, and the smell had overtaken my senses. I had no idea Arby's accepted credit cards. Sam hadn't arrived yet, so I grabbed the bag and exited the car. I unlocked the funeral home's back door, turned on the main lights, and headed for Dad's office.

The first thing I did was walk back and forth behind Dad's desk, making sure the camera could see me. Then I marked the time: 11:52. I wanted to double-check the camera's time for accuracy.

Then I checked Dad's journal closet. Locked, just like I had left it. Jack either had a key or he could pick locks.

I unlocked the closet door and turned on the light. Nothing looked out of place, but it was hard to tell with over one hundred journals lining the walls. *What were you doing in here, Jack?*

I wanted to give him the benefit of the doubt. He was a great friend of Dad's. Even Abe himself had said so. And Jack had always been so good to me. To our family. He'd been so helpful to me—to us—this week. But everything in my senses told me that something was wrong. *Is everyone in town a part of this conspiracy?*

I heard a knock. I opened up the door and saw Sam.

"Do I smell Arby's?" she asked.

"Maybe," I said.

"Wow, you are really sucking up to me lately. I kinda like it."

"You need to raise your standards if you're impressed with me bringing you a sandwich."

She saw the bag on Dad's desk and started digging through, searching for Horsey Sauce. "Do you mind if I get started? I skipped breakfast."

"Knock yourself out," I said.

Sam took the wrapping off one of the sandwiches and spread it out flat on the desk. She removed the top bun and squirted two packages of Horsey Sauce onto the meat. Then she put the bun back on the top and took a bite.

"Are you looking for something?" she asked with her mouth full.

"Sort of," I said. I sat down at Dad's desk and grabbed a sheet of Dad's notebook paper.

I wrote.

Yes. Lots to discuss. Let's go down and get the samples prepared, and then we can talk outside. Make sure cell phone is off.

I flipped it over and let her read it. She shook her head.

"Will, I don't have a lot of time. Can we review those financials while I straighten up a bit in the basement?"

"Of course," I said. I grabbed the Arby's bag and followed her down to the embalming room. By the time we reached the bottom of the stairs, she was done with the sandwich.

Sam headed over to the meat locker and pulled out a small cooler big enough to hold a six-pack. She placed the cooler in a reusable grocery bag and hoisted it over her shoulder.

She turned to face me. "You know, it's a beautiful day. Why don't we finish lunch and talk financials at the old picnic table behind the back shed?"

"Is that still there? Great idea."

We walked up the steps and out the back door. I turned to relock it, and we walked across the parking lot. I followed her as she passed the shed with Dad's two old hearses and turned right to see the picnic table.

"Looks like this thing needs a little love. Maybe on a free day I'll sand and stain it."

"I think Abe would approve," she said.

We both picked a leg up like getting on a horse and straddled the benches. Sam sat on the far side of the table. I was closer to the shed.

"Do you think we're in the clear?" I asked.

"If they have a recording device out this far from the funeral home, then they deserve to catch us doing God knows what." Sam pulled a few curly fries out of the bag. "So, how was your date?"

"It wasn't a date," I said. I could feel my face turning red. "But I did find out some things. But you first. What did you find?"

"Last night while you were out, I was going through every dead body that's come through here over the last four years. Now keep in mind that I didn't start until two years ago, so I'm going by your dad's records for the previous two. Four years ago, there was nothing special. At least I couldn't see anything. The next year, there was a drastic increase of minorities. It's a small sample size, but African-Americans increased by 250 percent, Asians by 150 percent, Hispanics by 300 percent. I actually went back through the numbers twice because I couldn't believe the percentages."

Sam put a few more curly fries in her mouth and licked her fingers. "Things continued like that until February of last year. Basically, the numbers went right back to where they were before. Maybe even a little less. And that's been the status quo up to today."

She dug into the Arby's bag and pulled out another Horsey Sauce, squirted the contents on a napkin, and dipped in two fries.

"Now, get this. Your dad started taking the blood and tissue samples in January, right before the numbers dropped. So there are quite a few from January, then it gets sporadic all the way to present day. And you'll never guess who the samples were from."

"All minorities, right?"

"Yup. Just a few Caucasians here and there. At least, those are the records I have."

"You are awesome," I said. "Do you have the full list of names that have samples?"

"Who do you think I am?" she said. "Yes, there's a full list in the bag with the samples. Each name is marked with a number that corresponds to one tissue and one blood sample. Oh, and I called my Clinic contact using a pay phone. Can you believe that?" she said, smiling. "Anyway, his number is on there, and you need to text him tonight when you get to Cleveland. You can meet him somewhere. He'll give you your father's results and get to work on the others first thing Monday. He said he might have results same day."

"Perfect," I said. "Sam, thanks for doing this. You didn't have to."

"The hell I didn't," she said. "Now tell me about your date."

"It wasn't a date."

"Whatever," she said.

"So basically I had to swear I wouldn't tell anyone what she told me. She acted legitimately scared that someone was going to hurt her. Or hurt her business. Since she started the restaurant, she's been a member of SA. She went to some meeting. Dad was there, but not in the front. But Uncle Dan was there with the other founders of SA. They presented research about minorities being responsible for all the bad things happening in Sandusky. She was told in no uncertain terms that if she hired minorities, they had to work without being seen by customers."

"What? Sounds like Jim Crow or something."

"It's something like that. And from what Xena said, my dad didn't say anything. She thought I knew all about this because my father helped found SA."

"I think we're picking up on a pattern. You're not thinking your dad was involved in that. He loved everyone."

"Do I think so? Not really. But I can't dismiss it. Obviously, he knew about it. Anyway, here's the second part of what I found. I couldn't sleep, so I went through a good portion of the footage from Dad's overhead camera. I haven't found anything from before Dad passing, but I did find someone snooping around Dad's office early this morning, just after two."

"In the funeral home?"

"Yep. And I recognized the person. Want to take a guess?"

"No guess. Just tell me."

"It was Jack."

She paused. "Jack is at the funeral home in the middle of the night all the time. It's his job. Might be nothing."

"Does he usually unlock my dad's closet door? Stay in there for twenty minutes? Then relock it and leave?"

Sam's features went cold. Or sad. "I love Jack," she said. "I don't want him mixed up in this. I haven't felt like this since ..." I knew what she was going to say.

"Who knows?" I said. "Maybe it won't be a big deal. But right now, I'm treating everything like it's war on the Pollitt family."

I threw all the garbage in the bag. We both stood and headed back to the cars.

As I reached the car, she handed me a slip of paper. "What's this?" I asked.

"I bought a burner phone at Walmart. With cash. That's the number. In case you need me. I didn't want to wait for you to bring one back from Cleveland."

"Good thinking," I said. I felt like giving her a hug but just opened the door to the van and she approached her car. "By the way, you're in charge of the funeral home while I'm out." Before she closed the door, something occurred to me. "Wait, Sam."

"What?"

"This might sound ignorant, but why did Dad hire you?"

"Excuse me?"

"From everything we've learned, the funeral home was under a massive amount of financial stress when you were hired. He was actively laying off the staff, and yet, you were hired." I paused. "With embalmings going down, why did he hire you? Why couldn't he just do the work himself?"

She looked at me like she'd been blindsided. "I honestly don't know. But now that you mention it, I can't remember one embalming your father did by himself after I arrived. He insisted I do all of them. He said I needed the practice."

"I don't know if it's connected, but maybe he couldn't perform for some reason. Or maybe he wanted or needed you at the funeral home. Give it some more thought." I went to close the van door and turned back to Sam. "And be careful."

Chapter 27 – Vito's and Tonic

Leaving Sandusky, I stopped about twenty miles from Cleveland to gas up. If the van was getting more than ten miles per gallon, I'd be surprised.

I texted Robby during the stop and told him I was thirty minutes out. I never thought I'd say this, but I missed my vodka at Vito's. Maybe we'd have time for one or two games of Galaga. At least to feel normal again for a while.

I decided to park in front of my apartment and then walk down to Vito's. I brought the cooler from Sam with me. I texted Sam's Clinic contact, who responded immediately. He agreed to come to Vito's inside the next two hours.

The walk was night and day from a week ago. Just seven days ago, the wind was cold blowing off Lake Erie. Today, it could have been July but not near as humid.

As I approached Vito's, I could already smell the burnt chicken. *Home,* I thought.

I walked through the door and caught Dell with a rare smile.

"I thought you decided to leave us for good," Dell said. "Sorry about your dad. First round is on me."

"I'm sorry, sir?" I said. "There used to be someone named Dell here. Do you know where he went?"

"Suck it, Will. Good to have you back."

Robby was already sipping a Jack Daniels on the rocks in our normal seat. He was midway through, looked up, and nodded at me.

I mouthed without saying anything, *Is your cell phone off?*

"Didn't bring it," he said. "You?"

"Turned it off on the way over. Did you bring the burner phones?"

"Yep," he said, sliding two over to me.

"Before you do that, Sam already got a burner from Walmart. Here's her number. Can you program it in for us?"

While he added Sam's number to our two phones, I replayed the last twelve hours in five minutes. The meeting with Xena. The video and seeing Jack Miller. What Sam found about the funeral logs.

Dell brought me a Tito's and Red Bull.

Robby took another sip of his drink. "You know," he said. "You'd think I'd be most upset about the fact that Sandusky turned into freakin' South Africa circa 1970. But that's not even a close second. Dude, are you telling me that you didn't tap Xena when she pretty much put it on a platter?"

"Just because she grabbed my junk doesn't mean she wanted to sleep with me."

"Oh. Of course. It's not a sure thing. It's sorta like, I'm not sure there was a moon landing. Or I'm not quite sure the earth is round or not."

"It's not that I didn't want to. The general was at attention. He was ready to come out of retirement."

"Then?" Robby waited.

"I couldn't stop thinking about Sam." I felt embarrassed as soon as the words left my mouth.

Robby stood up. "Listen, everyone," he called out, looking around the bar. Of course, it was four p.m. on a Sunday and it wasn't football season. It was just Dell, Robby, and me in the entire bar. "This man right here needs his head examined. Both of them." Then he sat down.

"How'd she look?"

"Who?" I asked.

"Miley Cyrus. Who do you think? The Warrior Princess."

"She looked good. Real good. Wore tights again with the black boots."

"Don't worry. You'll get a second chance."

"We'll see."

"Brother, you and Sam are divorced. As in not together. That ship has sailed." Robby took another sip. "Dell, another round for the good reverend and myself over here, please," he called out. "Enough of that. You're going to shit when you hear what I found out."

"Okay, Nancy Drew. Lay it on me," I said.

"My uncle has access to some secure website that only licensed insurance guys get access to. It took us a while to get the search criteria down, but we got a list of every Erie County resident who sold their life insurance policy in the last five years."

"No way," I said.

"It gets better," he said.

Dell came over, collected our empty glasses and put new drinks in front of us.

Robby waited until Dell was far enough from earshot and leaned in. "For each resident who sold their insurance, we also have who they sold it to, and who that company sold it to."

"What do you mean? Someone buys the policy and then someone else buys it from them?" I asked.

"Just like a mortgage. When I bought my house, I had to get a bank loan. Then two months later, I got a notice in the mail that I was to pay my mortgage to a different bank. Happens all the time in real estate. I guess it's happening more with life insurance as well."

"Got it. So what's so good about that?"

"Well, it's only good because we can follow the money flow," Robby said.

"I think you have a future as a private investigator," I said. I leaned over and grabbed Sam's embalming records from inside the grocery bag and underneath the cooler. "Okay, let's try a couple of these."

There were about thirty names on the list. Each one had a date, a first and last name, an address, ballpark ethnicity, and whether they were embalmed or cremated. There was also a handwritten number next to each one, I'm assuming from Sam, who marked the samples in the cooler for matching purposes.

I scanned the list. "From the look of this list, there are quite a few Caucasians on here. Mostly minorities, but still a good handful of white people. More than I thought at least. My hypothesis may be wrong."

"Let's just see what we can find. Give me a name," Robby said.

"Start with this. Last name Boggs, first name Luther. The date is January 7th of last year."

"Give me a second," Robby said. He flipped through a bunch of pages and selected one. "This is the list from last year. I'll start a year before that."

Robby turned the page so we could both read it as we sat across from each other in the booth.

"I don't see it," I said.

"Nope. No Boggs. Let's go back another year," Robby said, selecting another sheet from his stack of paper. He turned the page again so I could see it. The type was small and hard to see, especially with the dim lights in the back of the bar. "I got it," he said. "Luther Andrew Boggs, Perkins Township, Sandusky, Ohio. He sold his $1.25 million policy for $243,000 in cash to Tranquility Insurance LLC. This was about fourteen months before he died."

"So we have a match."

"Is he black?"

"The form Sam prepared says Caucasian."

Robby scratched his ear. "Do you think he had a Facebook page?"

"Why does that matter?"

"Because I have a sick suspicion about something," Robby said. He pulled out his burner phone and logged into Facebook. Then he searched for Luther Boggs from Sandusky, Ohio, in the Facebook search field. "Yep, here's his profile. Nobody's marked him dead yet. That's so sad that he's dead in real life but still alive on social. Or maybe that's like the Millennial version of the afterlife."

"And your point is?"

"I hate being right. Look at these images," he said, showing me his phone. "Look at this one and this one and, oh man, look at this one."

"Very perceptive, Mr. Thompson. Now why should we care?"

"Because he was gay. He *was* a minority. It fits with the theory."

We spent the next forty-five minutes and three drinks combing through Robby's uncle's information and matching it up with Sam's information.

"What's the tally?" Robby asked.

I was taking down notes on the other side of one of Sam's pages. "We went through sixteen total names from Sam's list. Of those we found fourteen who had received a life settlement. Of those fourteen, seven were black, three were Hispanic and four were Caucasian."

"And ..." Robby said, waiting for my response.

"It looks as though the four Caucasians were either homosexual, bisexual, or transgender," I said.

"That is the correct answer. What does he win, Monty?" Robby said a bit too loudly. Dell looked over, and we looked back. Then he went back to washing glasses.

"This is straight out of *Law & Order*," I said. "Hold on for a second."

Robby finished off his drink while I scratched numbers out on the page.

"Okay. The total payout on the fourteen was about $2.7 million. The various insurance companies retained the full value of those fourteen upon death, which comes to $19 million and change. That's over a seven hundred percent return in less than two years."

"It's a burden to be right all the time," Robby said.

"I think I'm going to be sick."

"Do you think your father was in on this?"

"I don't want to answer that right now. Anyway, we're not done yet. You take these names," I said, pointing at three insurance companies, "and I'll take these. We need to find out who's behind it."

We pulled out our phones and started searching. Dell came over to the table. "Here," he said, putting two huge plates of fries and burgers in front of us. "You didn't ask, but you have to eat something, or you won't be able to make it home."

"Don't let anyone tell you you're not a stand-up guy, Dell," I said.

"Whatever," Dell said, walking back to the bar.

The next fifteen minutes consisted of eating and searching Google with greasy fingers.

"Find anything?" I asked.

"Nothing," Robby said. "Tranquility, Pristine Insurance, and Life Services LLC come up zippo. I can't find a parent company. Nothing on the website or the Better Business Bureau. You?"

"Same thing with Barant Insurance, Retire Well, and 2020. Sites were all built in the last three years, most likely out of the same template. None of them even have an executive team or staffing listed."

"Shady."

A tall, dark-skinned man, most likely in his late forties, walked into the bar, looking lost. He looked at Dell and then saw me. I figured it was the Clinic guy and waved him over. I stood up as he came over.

"Are you Will?" he said.

"Yes. Are you Sam's friend?"

"Jared Kumar. Nice to meet you." We shook hands.

"Have a seat," I said, giving him my side of the booth and I scooted in next to Robby.

Robby reached out to shake his hand. "Robby Thompson."

"Like the old Giants second baseman," Jared said.

"Yes, that's correct," Robby said, smirking at me.

"Thanks for doing this," I said. "It really means a lot."

Jared smiled. "No problem. I owed Sam a couple favors."

I bet you do. I didn't want to think about the fact Sam was dating.

"I have a cooler here of samples that Sam packed for you. There's also a list so you can match up the person with the sample. How long will it take?"

"I can't do this on work time, so I'm going over to the Clinic right now. If it all works out, I can have preliminary results for you first thing in the morning."

"You're a godsend. And please keep this on the down low."

"Absolutely," he said. "I have your father's results and, uh..." He was looking at Robby.

"Robby's family. He can hear anything you have to say."

"Okay, then," Jared said. He sat upright in the booth and folded his hands in front of me. "I found a variety of toxins in your father's blood and tissues. These include saponins, digitoxigenin, oleandrin, oleandroside, and nerioside. The mixture of these toxins most likely stopped your father's heart from beating." Jared scratched his head. "I actually had to do some research on this combination, and I'd put a strong probability that it was oleander poisoning."

"Like the flower?" Robby asked.

"Well, yes, but it's actually a tree. The amounts were small in the blood and nothing showed in the tissues themselves, so I'm assuming your father ingested the poison instead of injecting it."

I looked at Robby. "We saw the video of my father collapsing. He put something into his coffee, drank it, and fell over."

"That would correspond with the findings," Jared said.

"Is that a common poison?" I asked.

"I read that in some places overseas, it's the soup du jour," Jared said, smiling, then immediately went stone-faced. "I'm very sorry for that last comment, Will."

"No worries at all," I said. Then I realized something. "Wait. What does oleander look like?"

Jared pulled out his phone and typed. He showed me a small green bush with red and pinkish flowers. I looked at Robby. "I've seen that plant before. In Janet's office at the funeral home."

Robby just shook his head.

"Does oleander poisoning cause posthumous blotching or staining?"

Jared shrugged like he didn't know.

Then he asked, "Did your father kill himself because of his cancer?"

"Excuse me?" I said.

"Oh my God, you didn't know?"

"That my father had cancer?"

"You'll have to forgive me. I exclusively work in the lab, and I never talk to real patients. I obviously have some work to do in that area."

"Just tell us what you found," Robby said.

"I found a number of cancerous cells in the sample Sam provided. So I looked up your father's record in our database. His doctor in Sandusky is in our network. I did have to hack into it a bit to get at the good stuff." Jared paused. "I probably shouldn't have told you that. Anyway, your dad had an inoperable malignant tumor the size of a baseball inside his skull. He declined surgical treatment and chemotherapy. According to the records from his last appointment, the doctor gave him two to four weeks to live."

"When was that appointment?" I asked.

"I didn't get the exact date, but I remember it being about two weeks ago."

"Anything else?"

"Those are all the findings I have," Jared said.

I just sat for a few seconds, then Robby nudged me with his elbow. "Thank you, Jared," I said. "I can't thank you enough."

"Are these the rest of the samples?" he asked, pointing at the bag next to the booth.

"Correct. They're all yours," I said. "Did you want to stay for a drink before you leave?"

"Oh, no. But thanks. I have to drive downtown and get right to work on these."

I ripped a small corner off one of Sam's sheets and wrote down the burner phone number. "When you're done, you can text me at this number."

Jared stood up, grabbed the bag, and started to leave. Then he turned back. "I'm sorry about your father," he said and walked out the door.

I sat there with my head in my hands. Robby put his arm around me. "I'm sorry, man. I'm sure your dad had a reason he didn't tell you," he said as he got up and moved across from me.

"Dad kept most everything to himself, so even this doesn't surprise me. He never asked for help. Never wanted help. I'm actually shocked that he went to the doctor at all. I can't even imagine the pain he was going through."

"So he's dealing with cancer, knowing it's pretty serious, but maybe feels he has some time. He's taking tissue and blood samples, gathering evidence, and BAM!, goes to the doctor and gets told he has two weeks to live. Then everything moves into high gear. He can't afford to waste any time. He installs the camera. And then ..."

"He poisons himself, on-camera," I said. "And uses poison from a tree that's probably the same one in Janet's office. He also updated his will. And we know that's important because he put the camera password in the will reading as a reminder. But if Uncle Dan is involved in some way, why would Dad give him a new will?"

"Maybe he was being watched like we're being watched. Maybe he couldn't think of another way to get you information," Robby said.

"Seems farfetched," I said.

"This whole thing is farfetched," Robby said.

I looked down at my watch. It was just before seven p.m. "I feel like we're running out of time as well. When's our PopC meeting tomorrow?"

"Nine a.m.," Robby said.

"We have a little more than twelve hours to go through the rest of my dad's videos and try to connect these dots. Maybe they can lead us to the missing journals as well, if there are any. I'd say we go to my place, but I don't trust it. How about yours?"

"Let's go," Robby said.

"We need to make a stop on the way."

Chapter 28 – Inside the Man Cave

"How do you know he's home?" Robby asked.

"It's eight o'clock on a Sunday night. If he's not traveling, he's home," I said.

"If we're being tracked, we can't just pull up in front of his house."

"Hold on," I said. I pulled up Google maps on the burner phone. "Make a right here, then pull into the shopping plaza. There should be a 7-Eleven and a laundromat there." Robby made the right with his Ford SUV and parked in front of the 7-Eleven. "According to this, there should be an alley just to the right of the laundromat. We can take that to his house."

Robby opened his secret compartment underneath the rear seats of the Edge, and we secured the laptop inside. Then we exited the car and quickly found the darkness of the alley. It was about fifty feet to the street on the other side. Along the way, there were garbage and recycling cans, and the smell of sewage.

"What's the house number?" Robby asked.

"Twelve forty-nine," I said. "Should be this side of the street." The alley came out at house number 1235. I looked to see what direction the numbers were going, and we made a left. His house was a brick bungalow, a popular model for this area of Cleveland. Although, for an FBI agent, I thought he'd have something bigger, and in a better neighborhood.

Robby and I stood in front of the house. "Well, what are we waiting for?" Robby inquired.

I asked him, "Am I being paranoid?"

"Hell yes, you are. And for good reason. Remember yesterday when we had to hide out in a bookstore for an hour and then sneak around town?"

"You're right," I said. "Just checking."

We walked up the cement stairs that led to a small brick patio. I decided to ring the doorbell instead of knocking.

"Ten bucks I bet you they think we're Mormons," Robby said.

"Who is it?" asked a woman's voice from behind the door.

"Hi. My name is Will Pollitt. I'm Alan's old college roommate. I'm trying to track him down," I called through the door.

"Hold, please," the woman said.

After a couple minutes, there was a man's voice. "Who is this?"

"Alan. It's Will Pollitt. I didn't have your phone number, and I was hoping to talk to you about something."

The door opened. Alan was in a Notre Dame T-shirt and sweat pants. *Still in pretty good shape.* Still had all his hair, and whatever FBI training regimen he was on was working. "Normally I'd be happy to see you, but this is a bit irregular. We've been having some break-ins around here, and Jules, my wife, has been a little more tentative lately."

"I'm sorry, Alan," I said. "Oh, by the way, I think you know Robby, right?"

"Yes," Robby said. "We met at the funeral." They shook hands.

"I wouldn't bother you unless I thought this was extremely important. Is there a place we could talk? I need at least twenty minutes of your time."

Alan turned around. "Honey, I'm going to talk to these guys in the man cave. I won't be long." He shut the front door and made sure the screen door was closed. Even though there was no one in front of him, Alan looked like he was clearing a path when he walked. He made a left just beyond his front hedges and another left down his driveway, toward the backyard. Robby and I walked a few steps behind him.

"I've been working on this little man cave project for a few years now. Just put in the dart board. It's got a big-screen TV and a mini fridge, but everything in there is pretty cheap just in case someone wants to rip it off." He led us to the back of his garage. The structure looked like an old converted shed. Alan tried the door and it wouldn't open, so he leaned into it a bit with his right shoulder and popped it free. Then he flipped the light switch on the right wall and led us in.

"All I got is beer. Cool?" Alan asked.

"Perfect," I said. Alan pulled three Coors Lights out of the mini fridge.

"Have a seat," Alan said.

The room was small and had a bar on the right side with a mounted fifty-inch television behind it and a dart board on the wall to the left. Alan was sitting in a small sofa chair, most likely something he picked up off of someone's lawn, while Robby and I were on stools. Alan tossed us two Koozies for the beers. When he leaned back, I could easily see the gun bulge in the side of his sweat pants.

"Talk," he said.

"You know the first part when we talked at the funeral. My dad left the funeral home to me in the will. I'm considering it. And then we started doing some digging. Financials and embalming records. We found some things. And now we're really concerned. We actually believe our cars or our phones are being tracked. Before I tell you everything, the reason we're here instead of the Sandusky police is because we think they're involved in some way."

"Okay," Alan said. "Can I ask you some questions first?"

"Sure," I said.

"Are either of you on drugs or heavy medication right now? Have you been drinking?"

"Shit, Alan. No, we are not on drugs, and yes, we just came from a bar but we aren't drunk," I said.

"Just checking," he said. "Now before we go any further, I have to ask if you are recording this conversation."

"No," I said. "Are you?"

"I am not."

"Anything else?"

"You may proceed."

I took the next fifteen minutes going over the situation. My dad's apparent suicide, found on the hidden camera. Xena's description of the SA meeting about minorities. The rampant case of life settlements in Erie County, and that those settlements targeted minorities. That we had tissue samples from about thirty residents that we were having checked. The SUV following us.

He listened intently and asked no questions while I was describing the situation. A few times he scribbled notes on a small notepad he grabbed off the bar. I ended by asking him, "What should we do?"

"First off, if someone has your cell phone number and the phone is on, they can find your location, so make sure your phones are off. Second, I'll have to make a couple calls, but if the life settlements are happening over state lines, say it's a Delaware corporation or any of the companies involved are headquartered out of state, the FBI can get involved."

"You believe us?" Robby asked.

"Well, I believe that you believe you are telling the truth. And that's a big deal for me. Once one of our tech folks can dig into the six insurance companies you mentioned and find out what they are doing, it should tell us a lot." Alan rose from his sofa chair. "If you don't mind, I'm going to step outside for a second and make a call. I'm pretty senior at the Cleveland bureau, but I don't make the final decision and I don't normally deal with financial schemes."

"What do you normally deal with?" I asked.

"WMD. Weapons of Mass Destruction," he said and closed the door behind him.

"We should probably text Sam with the new phones so she can find us," I said. I pulled out the burner phone and texted Sam. *Hi, Sam. It's Will. This is my new number. Robby will text you from his in a bit.*

Three seconds later the burner phone rang.

"Hello?" I said.

"Shit," Sam said. "What took you so long? I didn't know how to get in touch with you with your phone off."

"I'm sorry, Sam, but you'll never guess what Robby and I found by using your data."

"You don't know, do you?"

"Know what?"

"I'd rather not say, but I'll text you the link and then you can call me back." She hung up.

A few seconds later, Sam sent me a link from the *Sandusky Register*. I clicked on it and a video frame appeared, but the image was blurred, and a circle kept going around and around on the phone. No Wi-Fi.

"What is it?" Robby asked.

"I don't know. Sam sent this to me. It can't be good."

We both waited for the video to finish buffering, and finally it played. It was a woman in her late twenties. Thin. Looked like a weather girl. On-screen she was standing behind a *Sandusky Register News* logo. I didn't even know the Sandusky newspaper had roving television reporters. Times have changed.

In the background, people walked on the Sandusky Pier, almost in exactly the same location as Xena and I were yesterday.

This is Rebecca O'Hara with Sandusky Register. We just received word of a warrant out for the arrest of this man [cuts to a picture of me from the PT Marketing website] *William Pollitt, son of funeral director Abe Pollitt, who passed away last week. According to the warrant, Mr. Pollitt assaulted this woman* [cuts to a picture of Xena with her eye swelled shut and a deep gash on the side of her jaw] *Xena Anthony, proprietor of Tony's restaurant just a block from where I'm standing. According to Ms. Anthony, the assault happened last night. The location of the assault was withheld. If you see this man or know his whereabouts, you are to call Sandusky Police at 911 immediately. Subject is considered extremely dangerous. This is Rebecca O'Hara reporting for Sandusky Register.*

"Holy shit," Robby said.

"They know we know," I said.

"I take it you didn't do this to her."

"You're joking, right? That's the lowest form of man."

"Good," Robby said. "Just checking."

I started pressing numbers on the phone and hit dial. "I'm here," Sam said.

"We have to call Jess and get her to safety. Have her call you back from a pay phone or a friend's phone. Shit, I don't know. We're trying to tiptoe around all this, and they obviously found out we know something."

"So you didn't do it?" she asked.

"Sam, under the circumstances I understand you asking me this, and dickhead Robby asked me the same thing. No, I did not do it. Someone is trying to set me up."

"Good. I had to ask," she said. "Yes, I'll talk to Jess."

"Can you contact my sister as well? I have no idea how far this reaches, but Robby and I figure these guys are protecting hundreds of millions of dollars and trying to save their way of life."

"I'll contact Denise," she said.

"Robby and I are at FBI Alan's house now figuring this out. In the meantime, you need to get lost. Where can you go?"

"I don't know. Let me take care of Jess and Denise, then I'll let you know ASAP."

"Be careful. Talk soon," I said, ending the call.

Robby and I just sat there looking at each other.

"Now would be a great time for a joke," I said.

"I got nothing, man. Nothing," Robby said.

The door opened and Alan came back in. He stood in front of me. "Is there something you want to tell me?"

"What?"

"Do you know a Xena Anthony?"

"That escalated quickly," I said to Robby. "I literally just found out there's a warrant for my arrest. I know you're going to ask, so the answer is no, I did not do it."

"What happened?" he asked.

"I had a meeting with her—"

"It was a date," Robby said.

"It was not. Anyway, I walked her from downtown Sandusky to her condo a few blocks away and left her there. It was about midnight last night."

"Can anyone corroborate your story?"

I bit my upper lip and shook my head. "No. I don't think so. There were no other people. I left her and went to my car. It's pretty much her word against mine."

Alan stood thinking. "By law, I'm supposed to turn you in, but you're in luck. The initial parts of your story show promise. We called in one of our tech guys on the phone and had a quick con call. We got hits on two of the insurance entities you gave me."

"What does that mean?" Robby asked.

"It means someone in the bureau found something shady and marked it in the database. We have a meeting first thing in the a.m. to discuss. It will be me, my superior, the white-collar lead, and a couple tech guys."

"That's great. But what do we do until then? I don't know what you call it, but I've got an X on my back the size of New Jersey, and I'm concerned for the safety of my family. They probably want to kill him, too," I said, pointing at Robby.

"My momma always said never to trust your white ass, and here we are. I got a bunch of rich white racists that know technology coming to get me. It can't get much worse."

"I can get you some police protection, but that's going to take a few hours. Is your family in a safe location?" Alan asked.

"We are working on it," I said.

"You guys can hang out here and wait it out a bit if you want."

"You have Wi-Fi out here?" Robby asked.

"No," Alan said.

"In the house?"

"No."

"Shit. It's like 1985 around here," Robby said.

"Any ideas where we can safely watch the videos?" I asked Robby.

"Possibly."

Chapter 29 – Uncle Rod

We gave Alan our burner phone information and walked out the door, snuck around the hedge, and took a right into the alley. I peeked around the corner of the laundromat. There were no cars that we could see. Pretty standard for a Sunday night on the west side. We hustled to the car and took off.

"Where to?" I asked.

"I have to stop at my house and grab a few things first," Robby said. The drive to Robby's condo took less than five minutes. He pulled into the lot on the back side, parking next to a dumpster.

"Stay here," Robby said. "I'll be back in two minutes."

Robby inserted his left foot into a hole in the chain link fence and pushed himself over. *He's in better shape than I am.* Then I lost him in the darkness.

It was almost impossible to sit and wait. I wanted to text or call Sam. And then Denise. How was Jess doing? But I decided to let Sam take care of that. And then there's Xena. It didn't take them long to go after her. They wouldn't think twice about hurting the people I truly cared about. Every additional step of this fiasco was making me think my mother's death was not so accidental anymore. And now I was in way over my head. How could I be so reckless as to try to unravel my father's puzzle without help?

Robby returned with a black Nike duffel bag and set it between our seats. Some of the smell from the dumpster followed him inside.

"Are we going to the gym?" I asked.

Robby unzipped the bag and pulled out a gun.

"Holy shit, man. I didn't know you had a gun."

"There's one in here for you as well."

"Why would you own a gun?"

175

"That's an ignorant question. I'm a black man in white America. And before you ask, yes, I have a license for them."

"I've never held a gun in my hands, let alone fired one."

"It's just in case. Seems like they're beginning to get their hands dirty. We found something big. Now they're in protection mode." He held the gun in his hand, displaying it for me. "This is a Colt M1911 pistol. It's fairly popular and has been for years. It's semiautomatic, so you don't have to load bullets or anything."

He turned the gun to the other side. "This button here is the safety. In this position, with this piece sticking out, the gun won't fire. Once you push it," Robby pushed the button and it disappeared into the pistol, "then you can fire the weapon. Just point and shoot." He held the gun out for me. "Take it, Will."

I reluctantly took the pistol in my hand. It was heavier than I imagined.

"There's a new magazine all loaded up," he said. "It has nineteen rounds, just in case we get into some kind of shootout." He looked at me and smiled. "I'm just kidding. Anyway, I have an extra magazine for each pistol. All you have to do is pull this release when you're out and then insert a new magazine for a fresh nineteen."

"Have you used this before?" I asked.

"Just at the range over on East 55th. Takes some getting used to. When you fire, you get a little pushback as it spits out the empty cartridge. But after that it's pretty easy to use. Hopefully, we won't have to use it, but if you do, aim at center mass."

"This is perfect. Before, I was just a fugitive. Now, I'm an armed fugitive. I don't look guilty at all."

I gave the gun back to Robby, who put it back in the duffel. Then he took out what looked to be a large computer router with a USB charger attached to it. "This little baby I bought last month and have been dying to give it a try. This is portable Wi-Fi. Basically, it takes cell service, makes it wicked fast, and you can take it anywhere."

Robby plugged it into the car's USB jack, put on his seatbelt, and started the car.

"Since we don't have anywhere safe to go that we know of, I figured our best bet is to stay mobile. While I drive, you can watch the rest of the videos."

"I like your thinking," I said.

Robby pulled out his burner phone.

"What?" I asked.

"I need to text Sarah at PopC. We're going to have to cancel our meeting for tomorrow."

"Good call," I said. "Probably not a good look to walk in to our marketing pitch carrying pistols."

Robby looked at me. "You know, with that news piece, there's no way we're going to get the business now. They're going to see it."

I considered his comment. "I know, but right now I'd like us to get out of this alive. And I'm especially concerned about Jess and Denise."

Robby texted.

"She's already replying," he said. "People are so attached to their phones today."

He read the response. "Sarah said she was just going to call me. They just received word from PopC corporate that their offices are closed tomorrow. Someone got shot outside their building about thirty minutes ago. So no meeting, and she'll email me a reschedule time."

We looked at each other.

"I've got a bad feeling about this," I said and pulled out the burner phone. I went to Google and typed in *Cleveland shooting PopC*. There were three articles, one each from Cleveland's three major news outlets.

"Oh God. Read this," I said to Robby, showing him the news brief on my phone.

A man was shot and killed Sunday night in an apparent mugging outside PopC corporate headquarters. Cleveland Police are currently on the scene. The man, whose name is known but cannot be released until family is notified, worked at the Cleveland Clinic, located next door to PopC. There were no witnesses.

"Jared?" Robby said.

"Of course Jared," I said. "It has to be."

"But how did they know?"

"Oh my God, I killed him," I said. "I texted him from my other phone before I switched to the burner."

Robby put the car in drive and peeled out of the parking lot.

"Where are we going?"

"To my uncle's to ditch this car and get a different one," he said. "And you need to call Sam and then Alan."

I dialed the burner phone.

"Will!"

"Sam. What's going on?

"Jess is safe. She's with a friend. She left her cell in her room and borrowed her friend's phone."

"Is she rattled?"

"A little, yes. I didn't tell her much. I just told her to trust me."

"Great. How about Denise?"

"She's going to her friend's house in Port Clinton. She left her phone in Sandusky as well. I have a number I can contact her if needed."

"Perfect. And you?"

"I'm in my car heading east on Route 2. I didn't know what else to do." She sighed.

"This might work. What's your exact location?" I asked.

"I just passed Berlin Road."

"Good. We can meet you in fifteen minutes. I'm texting you directions to Robby's uncle's house now. It's Elyria, north of Route 2."

"Got it. Okay."

"And Sam."

"What?"

"Watch your back. Don't trust anyone." I ended the call.

"Well, we're going to have company at your uncle's," I said.

"I got the gist," Robby said.

I dialed again. This time Alan.

"Where are you?" Alan asked.

"We're headed west toward Elyria. Did you see the killing in downtown Cleveland?"

"Yes. I received the alert about five minutes after they found the body."

"Did they ID the body yet?"

"No name. Just description. Why are you asking?"

"Let me guess. Tall, thin, dark-skinned man. Possibly Indian?"

Silence for a few seconds. "What's going on?" Alan asked.

"Shit! We knew it. That's the guy I told you about. The lab technician from the Clinic. He was going to check COD on the samples we gave him. They must have followed him right after he got the package from us. No samples left at the scene I suppose? Or inside at his station?"

"None that we've found. No."

"For the love of ..."

"Do you have more samples? We're going to need them to put all this together."

"We should have some different samples. Sam might have some others. I'll check with her. But right now we've got more important things to do. Like stay alive."

"Whatever this is, you two knuckleheads landed right in the middle of it. You know those two insurance companies that hit in our system? The white-collar division thinks they can link nine figures to those companies. Nine as in over a hundred million. They want to talk with you ASAP. You need to turn the car around and get your ass back here."

I paused for a second. "No can do, Alan. Right now you need to get your cowboys and a shitload of guns together and bring your ass to us. These guys are serious, and I have a feeling we've only seen the appetizers to this point."

"We're fast but not that fast. We've got agents out on other assignments, and it will take at least twenty-four hours. Maybe more. Plus, we'd never get approval at this point."

"Look, Alan. Outside of taking the law into our own hands, you're all we have. In twenty-four hours, this thing will probably be over, and either I or someone I love, probably both, are going to end up permanently missing. You have this number. Call me back. Robby and I will try not to get killed in the meantime."

I ended the call.

"How far are we from your uncle's house?" I asked.

"About fifteen minutes, maybe less. What's the video status?"

The videos were cued up, and the computer was tethered to the portable Wi-Fi. "I'm going fast and trying not to miss anything, but I'm just finishing Wednesday. After that we have four days left. Thursday, Friday, Saturday, and Sunday, right up to the point you already saw. I need a breakthrough. Between the phone calls, watching these videos, and your driving, I'm close to vertigo."

Twelve minutes later, we arrived at Robby's uncle's place. Robby parked a couple blocks away as a safety measure, and we walked to the house. His uncle was waiting for us on the porch. Older man, maybe in his late sixties. He looked like he used to be taller, but now the top of his back was slightly hunched. He walked up to Robby like he was in a constant ducking position.

"What kind of shitstorm are you two kids involved in?" he said, shaking hands with Robby while they embraced. I shook his hand. "Roderick Beckett. Nice to meet you."

"Will Pollitt. Can't thank you enough for all your help."

"Please call me Rod. How can I help?"

"Uncle Rod, here are the keys to my Edge. It's parked two blocks east of here. We think they've bugged it, but we're not sure."

"No worries, son," Rod said. "I know a guy, his name's Keener. If that thing is bugged, he'll find it inside twenty minutes."

"Great. In the meantime, we need your car."

We saw headlights and a slow-moving car was about to pass the house. Robby and I ducked a bit behind Rod's front door. As the car neared, we saw the make. A black Jeep Cherokee.

"That's Sam," I said, jogging out to meet her.

She rolled down the passenger window. "You okay?" I asked.

"Yes. What's the plan?" she asked.

"We'll be right back," I called out to Robby and Rod and hopped in Sam's car.

"Go straight for two blocks and park behind Robby's car. We don't know if his or yours or both cars are being tracked." Sam parked, then we exited and started to head back toward Rod's house. Sam made her way around the front of the car toward me and embraced me, completely taking me by surprise.

"This is crazy, Will," she said. "I can't stop thinking about Jess."

"Me either," I said. "And I have more news that you aren't going to like. Your friend Jared. After we met with him and delivered the package," I paused, looking at the ground, "someone killed him."

Sam's hand immediately lifted and covered her mouth, while tears started to form in the corners of her eyes.

"I'm so sorry, Sam. I think it's my fault. Before I switched phones, I texted him with my old phone and gave away his location."

"Why is this happening?" Sam said, shaking.

I grabbed both her hands and placed them in mine. "We'll find out. I promise."

We approached Rod's house. Robby and Rod were still on the porch.

"Are you okay, Sam?" Robby asked.

"I just told her about Jared," I said.

"Yeah, this thing is going from bad to worse. Samantha, this is my Uncle Rod. He was very helpful with the insurance information we used to double-check against your embalming records."

"Nice to meet you," Sam said, reaching out her hand.

Rod took her left hand, lowered his head, and kissed the back of her hand. "The pleasure is all mine, Samantha," Rod said.

"You can call me Sam."

Rod smiled. "I bet you all are pretty hungry. And sounds like it's going to be a long night." At that, Rod went through the porch door and into the house.

The three of us were huddled as if we were ready to break for the next play.

"Okay," Sam said. "Now. What's the plan?"

We spent the next five minutes going through the timeline. The meeting with Jared. The matching of the embalming records with the life settlement deals. Dad's cancer. Alan and the FBI. What was left with Dad's video footage.

"You're sure it was Jared that was found dead?" Sam asked.

"Positive," I said. "Alan confirmed it was a tall, dark-skinned man. Probably Indian. Dots, not feathers."

"That's racist. You should use other words," Sam said.

"You know what's racist? Killing minorities for a shit ton of money. And it seems they don't have any concern about killing us as well."

"Now just because they killed Jared doesn't mean they're going to kill us," Robby said.

Sam and I just looked at him.

"Okay, they're probably trying to kill us. What do we do now?" Robby asked.

The top of my head was sweating, partly due to the situation and also that it was still about eighty degrees. Probably close to a record for May around here. Rod came out holding a paper plate with three Hot Pockets on it.

"I live by myself and I don't cook much. It was either Hot Pockets or Bagel Bites."

"Good call, Uncle Rod," Robby said, and we each grabbed a Hot Pocket. Rod stood close to us.

"Uncle Rod? Can you give us a second in private? I don't want you to know any more than you already do. For your own protection, you know."

"Shit, boy. You ever been chased by the cops before? You ever had a warrant out for your arrest? You ever been wrongly accused of a crime?

We all stood there looking at him.

"Well, you're in luck. I have. Multiple times. I think you need a seasoned veteran to assist in your planning. And anyway, I've lived a good life. Rounding third and heading home, you might say. If someone offs me while I'm helping you kids, I have a feeling God will show favor to it."

Robby looked at me, and I shrugged. "I don't think we're in a position to turn down help," I said. "But if those cars are bugged, I'm not sure how much time we have left. They seem to be one step ahead of us. Probably more."

Rod started walking into the house. "It's hotter out here than a double-peckered frog in the middle of mating season. I got the window unit running inside. Let's at least sit down for five minutes, cool you off, and weigh the options." The man was smiling as he walked in. He seemed to be reveling in the situation.

The porch led directly to the kitchen, which had a square wood table in the middle surrounded by four chairs. The stove was older and probably hadn't been used in years. There was a half pot of coffee in the Mr. Coffee machine next to the sink. I picked up the scent as soon as I walked in.

"Rod, is that fresh coffee?"

"Depends on what you consider fresh. It's fresh enough that I'm still drinking it."

"Do you mind?"

"Shit, no. Let's finish this one off, and I'll make another pot," Rod said as he grabbed three coffee cups out of the cupboard. I looked at my watch. Just past ten p.m. *I haven't drank coffee this late since college.* I was praying for full strength. The adrenaline was wearing off, and I needed a pick-me-up.

We sat at the table in silence. Almost like the calm before the storm.

"Before we do this," I said, "my biggest concern right now, outside of the pulses in this room, are Denise and Jess. If things come to a boil tonight or tomorrow or whenever, we need to make sure they're safe."

"I agree," Robby said. "Denise I'm not worried about. She can kick the shit out of you ten times over," he said, looking at me. "But Jess. What do you think, Sam?"

Sam took a sip of coffee and crinkled her mouth and nose simultaneously. The coffee was terrible, but probably worth it. "I think if we're right and this thing is what it seems to be, that Jess could be in serious trouble. Being with her friend is not enough."

I took out my burner phone and put it on speaker. I found Alan in the recent calls and hit dial.

"Will. What's the situation?"

"We're in Elyria at Robby's uncle's house. Sam met us here. We're working on a plan and changing cars. That's as far as we've got. You?"

"The good news is that the bureau believes you. We grabbed some imagery around the assault of the Indian guy. Couldn't get a clear shot of who did it. Definitely a pro. Nothing was taken except the man's driver's license. And the samples, of course," Alan said, clearing his throat.

"But before we went all in with this, my superior wanted to make sure your story was legit. So our tech guys went to find imagery of your meeting with Xena Anthony. Our lead tech guy hacked into Sandusky's network and said he's never seen a city wired up like that. They have over two thousand cameras with views in every direction, and that's just a four-block radius downtown. We're bringing in the Columbus team to help us go through all the tech to see what else we can find."

"So my story checked out?" I asked.

"Oh, yes, we watched it a couple times here. One of the guys made some popcorn. How you walked away after she grabbed your junk? You're a better man than I," Alan said, chuckling. I looked away from Sam. "But, yes, your story checks. You left her at 12:08 a.m., got in your car, and drove off. The last shot of Ms. Anthony showed no facial bruising. If anything, she assaulted you." Alan was cracking himself up. "The guys are monitoring the video from the rest of that night to see what happened after you left."

Sam was looking at me. I wanted to say something but decided listening would work just fine for now. I didn't know if she was happy, proud, or disgusted.

"Thanks for that scintillating update, Alan. Look, we're all big boys and girls here, but we're concerned about our daughter Jess at Penn State. If this thing is really happening, which it seems to be, we feel she's in danger."

"I hear you. We've got small teams in Altoona and Harrisburg, not too far from State College. I'll put in a few calls and see what I can do."

"That would be fantastic. Thank you," Sam said.

"Keep checking in. Looks like we're pulling an all-nighter here, so I'll be around." The call went dead.

"Sure would like to get my hands on that video footage of you and that Xena," Uncle Rod said. "That's like *Xena: Warrior Princess*, right?" Robby and Rod bumped fists.

"You guys should take it on the road," I said. "Now let's do this."

Chapter 30 – The Plan

I'd been in hundreds of strategy sessions in my day, but nothing like this before. Regardless, I was thinking about it in the same way. What's the ultimate goal? What's standing in the way of that goal? How do we remove the barriers in our way?

"Who's the enemy here?" I asked.

"The Sandusky Alliance, right?" Sam asked.

"We think. Probably our best bet right now, assuming what Warrior Princess said was correct," Robby said.

"I think the fact they used her face for a punching bag means she was right," I said. "So it's us against SA. They're not only protecting a financial scheme, but they have some warped mission against people who are not white or not straight. They're smart. They have a lot of technology. I think we should assume they know someone hacked into their system. Once they realize that, whether they know it's the bureau or not, shit is going to hit the fan any second now."

"The question is, what do they want from us?" Sam asked. "I mean, do they want us quiet or dead or do they think we have something?"

"That's what bothers me about this whole thing," I said. "No one has come to us with demands. No one has directly threatened us. And I can't put a face on this, and it bothers the hell out of me."

"Right now, the only thing we know is that they didn't want you going to the Cleveland Police," Sam said.

"Well, yes," I said.

"I mean that's why they set you up," Sam said. "They found out about Jared and the samples, and they could have killed you both right there. There was probably a car right outside watching you. But they didn't. Instead, they killed Jared and beat up Xena. So they need you alive for some reason, we just don't know why yet. They just couldn't have you running off to the cops, and putting out the APB on you pretty much assures that you wouldn't."

"Jack!" Robby said.

"What about Jack?" I said.

"Jack was looking in the closet, most likely for the missing journals. If they exist. Your dad was leaving pockets of evidence. That camera, which we aren't done with yet. The samples, which we assume they stole. The last piece are the journals. They must think you have them."

"And I'm almost positive that Jack and Dan did not know about the journals before Dad passed away," I said. "Dad kept them to himself and locked in the closet. Very secretive. Now they know the journals exist and they're exposed."

"*John Wick*," Robby said.

"Not another *John Wick* story," Sam said.

"Seriously, guys, listen," Robby said. "In the beginning of the first *John Wick*, they come to John's house to kill him, and he of course takes them all out. Then he goes on the offensive. But before he kills everyone and walks away with the dog, he blows up all the money and assets from the Russians, and they come out of their hole. Then he starts to take them *all* out."

"Like in *Indiana Jones*," I said. "The one with Sean Connery. Where the Jewish guys set fire to the sewer and all the rats go running."

"Are you guys, like, twelve years old?" Sam asked.

"I like it," Rod said. "You want to flush them out of their holes. Get them in the open so you know what you're dealing with."

"Exactly," Robby said.

"The journals," Sam said. "We just deduced that they think we may have them. At least as of last night, they were hunting for them. Or at least Jack was. What if we play the game like we have the journals?"

"Holy shit," Robby said. "Like *Jerry Maguire*."

"Are you serious with the movie references, Robby?" Sam asked.

"No, not *Jerry Maguire*. Tom Cruise's character in—what was it?—*The Firm*. They make copies of all the illegal documents and put them on a boat that never docks at port. That was the leverage he needed so the Mafia couldn't touch him or his wife. We could do that with the journals."

"That's fucking brilliant," Rod said.

"Yes," I said. "It would be if we actually had the journals. But we don't."

"You got a better idea?" Robby asked. "Anyway, you're in marketing. You lie for a living."

"What do you think, Sam?"

"It's worth a shot," she said.

I MADE THE CALL. "ALAN!"

"Will, glad you called. I got two guys from Altoona on their way to Jess. I need her location."

"Sam's texting everything to you now." I looked at Sam, who quickly pulled out her phone.

"Roger that," Alan said.

"Question. How much farther have your tech guys got on tapping into the downtown cameras?"

"Not exactly sure. Hold, please." There was muffled talking in the background. While I waited, I gave Sam Alan's number, and she relayed Jess's information to him. Two minutes later, Alan came back on the line.

"Good news. We're seeing what they're seeing. The Columbus tech team has it set up that anything with movement bubbles to the top of the icon set."

"That's exactly what we wanted to hear. Is there any possibility that they know you hacked in?"

"Well, it's possible, but not likely at this point. We have a guy here that's smarter than Snowden and more conniving than the Chinese. I think he's in undetected."

"Great. We have an idea."

Chapter 31 – The Message

The four of us stood in front of Rod's kitchen table for inventory check. Two guns. Robby's.

A .357 Magnum. Rod's.

A Mossberg 500 12-gauge pump. Also Rod's. He said he keeps the Mossberg by the bed just in case Whitey ever came to take him from his house. "Or aliens," he said.

Right of the guns, we had three Redpoint folding knives Rod bought off of QVC. "Got a hell of a deal on those. Perfect when you're fighting a larger man." We also had three oversized firecrackers that Rod said would "blow the nuts off an elephant."

Left of the guns was the computer we purchased at the Sandusky Mall. Next to that, our three original iPhones, all currently turned off, and the three burner phones.

"As soon as we make this call, we roll out," I said. "I figure they've got someone fewer than ten minutes away, and this thing will light us up like the Fourth of July. Are we ready?"

Everyone nodded, including Rod.

"Okay," I said. "Here goes nothing."

I grabbed my iPhone and waited for it to turn on. Then I made the call.

It rang twice. Then again. By the fourth ring, he picked up.

"William. It's awfully late. What's going on?"

"You can stop playing stupid. We know you're involved in all this."

There was silence. "I'm not sure what you're talking about, son."

"Give it up, Dan. I'm not recording this, so you don't have to worry. We have Dad's journals. We know what's been going on with the Alliance. I can't believe you're involved in this shit show. But none of that matters now. I need you to do something for me."

"There's a warrant out for your arrest. Lily and I saw it on the news. You're having a breakdown. You need to get help. We understand, with your dad passing. Come to the house, and we can figure out a plan."

"Oh, yeah, that would be great. I'm sure I'd last all of five minutes before they shot me down. And then all you David-Duke-loving assholes would lynch up my buddy like it was Confederate Christmas." Sam gave me a stern look. "Shoot, you're distracting me. Dan, you need to tell the leadership of the Third Reich of Sandusky that I've made three copies of Dad's journals, all with a very nice note explaining what's been happening. If anyone I know and love even gets a haircut from you boys, that includes Denise and Jess and Sam and Robby and myself, those copies get automatically delivered to two local news outlets and one national outlet. I'm sure they'll take great interest in what's been going on. So tell them to call off the dogs. Now."

There was a long pause. "Son, it's not what you think. I need to explain things to you."

"Do it now. I'll be back in touch, calling from a different phone. Keep your phone on." I ended the call.

I was trembling all over. I started breathing hard and had trouble catching my breath.

Sam grabbed a plastic grocery bag from the kitchen counter and handed it to me.

"Breathe in and out in this bag. Slowly. You'll be fine" Sam said.

"You were magnificent," Rod said.

"I think Confederate Christmas was my favorite," Robby said.

I removed the bag from my mouth. "Let's go," I said. "Sam. You text Alan that the Eagle has landed, and he should be on the lookout for rats."

ROD INSISTED ON DRIVING. He asked me if I'd ever driven a Chevy Tahoe. I hadn't. Neither had Robby. Rod said it takes months of driving a Chevy Tahoe to really understand her.

Sam and Robby were planted in the second-row captain's chairs, and I was hanging over their shoulders, in the seat behind them. We all stared intently at the video screen as Sam maneuvered the seek function on the video player. Robby's portable Wi-Fi was cooking along, so the videos showed no buffering.

Sam was halfway through Thursday. Nothing of substance that we could see so far. And after this, three more days to go: Friday, Saturday, and half of Sunday. We felt like we were running out of time.

We drove west on Route 2 back toward Sandusky and hit the east side of Vermilion.

My burner phone rang. Alan.

"What did you see?"

"About five minutes after Sam texted us, we identified Daniel McGinty leaving his house. Five minutes after that, two gentlemen left from Traynor's crematory. One was in his thirties or forties, from what we could tell. The other was much older and needed assistance from the younger to walk."

"John and Alex Traynor," I said. "Anyone else?"

"Nothing of substance. It's pretty quiet."

"That's odd," I said. "I thought they'd bring out the entire Alliance. Well, at least it's something."

"We're monitoring them now. I'll keep you posted."

The call ended.

"I'm not sure this is working," I said. "Just Dan and the Traynors?"

"No, maybe it's working better than you thought," Robby said. "Maybe your Uncle Dan and the Traynors are like the big three. Jason Voorhees, Freddy Krueger, and Hannibal Lecter."

"I'm with you on the first two, but not Hannibal Lecter. Has to be Michael Myers," I said.

"Do you two ever stop?" Sam said. "Anyway, I think Leatherface from *Texas Chainsaw Massacre* would make the top three."

"Yes!" I said, and Robby and I bumped fists.

"Seriously, Robby could be right. On something like this, maybe just the main decision-makers would meet," Sam said.

Rod was driving in the right lane, while a Mazda CX-9 passed us on the left. Just like the one my mother used to drive. "Oh my God," I said.

"What?" Sam asked.

"What day was May 9th? When was it?"

"That was last Saturday. Your dad passed on May 10th, and that was a Sunday," Robby said.

"It's got to be it. And I never called him."

"Will, tell us," Sam said.

"May 9th was the anniversary of my mom's death. They transported her from the scene of the accident to the hospital. She was too far gone at that point. Sam, you remember. They couldn't do surgery or anything. I arrived at Firelands Hospital around eight thirty or so. She passed on at 8:52 p.m. on May 9th. I'll never forget the time. How could I be so stupid? Sam, go to Saturday in the camera database and forward to just before 8:52."

Sam navigated back to the date list and clicked on May 9th. The video opened, and Sam clicked and dragged the play time to just before eight thirty p.m. The camera must not have detected any movement, because the time went straight to eight fifty p.m.

The camera was only picking up shadows. No people. About thirty seconds later, my dad walked in carrying a brown paper bag and a red Solo cup. He sat in his swivel chair and removed the bottle from the bag. Looked like a bottle of Johnny Walker Black Label. My mother's favorite drink. He poured two fingers into the Solo cup and looked at his watch. Then he sat there, waiting.

He checked his watch again at 8:52. He closed his eyes for three, four seconds, toasted the air, and drank down the entire cup, tipping it upside down into his mouth. He set down the cup and looked directly at the overhead camera.

He started to move his hands.

"What is he doing?" Robby asked.

"He's signing. It's ASL. American Sign Language," Sam said.

"He knew I didn't know sign language," I said.

"Yes, but he knew that I did," Sam said. "Now shut up, and I'll translate. Shoot. I missed the first part. I need to go back." She rewound the video a few seconds. "Okay, here goes."

Hi, William. I'm assuming in one way or another Sam is with you. I'm so sorry that I couldn't just tell you what's been going on. I don't know how long it's been. Probably more than two years now they've been tracking me. The Traynor clan. They've been tracking all of us. The entire city.

I believe this room is bugged for sound, but there's no video. With my limited knowledge of technology, this is all I could do with the time I had left. Knowing how smart you all are, I'm assuming you found it with no problem and found all my clues. Colavito was a good one, huh?

A few weeks ago, my doctor told me I could drop any minute. I have inoperable cancer. Your Uncle Dan and I, with some help from Jack, have been collecting evidence against the Traynors as best we could. But it's been nearly impossible since they see and hear everything. Including emails and texts. And the post office too. Best to my knowledge, Alex has thousands of cameras and mics set up all over town. And all our loved ones have been threatened if we try to do anything.

This whole situation is partly my fault. About seven years ago, the wise men at Sandusky Alliance voted to build Sandusky into the city of the future. Alex Traynor, who is some kind of IT genius, gave us a great discount on all the tech so we could afford to fiber up the city. Now, Big Brother is always watching. Soon Alex knew the behavioral patterns of every person in this city. He had photos and videos and our passwords.

I was horrified, but at the same time, business was booming. Money was flowing into the downtown area like never before. It didn't take us long to realize why.

With his power, leverage, and blackmail, Alex was unanimously voted in as CEO of SA. Shortly after, John and Alex presented their new mission to transform the city. At first, it was about hiding minorities to encourage tourism. That was bad enough, but every day it escalated. Then they started to kill off what they called the unclean. Minorities of all types, homosexuals, even those people that supported diversity, you name it.

Much of that business, I'm sad to say, came through my funeral home. We were part of it. So was your Uncle Dan on the insurance side. When I started speaking out about it to others, I was punished. The business dried up, and then your mother died in the car accident. About a week after she died, I received a note in the mail. It contained your mother's obituary and pictures of you and Denise with the question, Who'll be next?

You'd be sad to know that I became complacent with the situation. Like there was nothing I could do. But then I was diagnosed with cancer. A few days later, I received a photo of Jess in the mail. On the back, it said, Always watching. *I received these notes all the time, but with Jess I just snapped. I'd already lost your mother to them, and I couldn't risk losing anyone else, especially your Jess. Not this way.*

I'm sorry to leave you with the burden of cleaning all this shit up. You don't deserve it. No one does. But I didn't know what else to do, and you might be the only one that could save the city of Sandusky and all the wonderful people in it.

The last piece of the puzzle is at Carol's. Sam has the keys. That location contains my journals with as much evidence as I could gather. I'm sure you'll know what to do with it.

I love you both very much. Please forgive me.

Dad wiped the tears from his eyes, grabbed the bottle and the red Solo cup, and left.

"That's it," Sam said.

"Oh my God," Robby said. "Dude, I'm so sorry."

"Guys, I'm fine. I'll go to counseling later. For now, let's figure the rest of this out, find the rest of the evidence, kill those racist bastards who killed my mother, and save the city."

"*Carpe* motherfucking *diem*," Rod yelled from the front seat, raising his hand in the air.

"Carol's? The restaurant by the funeral home?" Robby asked.

"Yes," Sam said. "But it could be anywhere inside. There are a lot of nooks and crannies at Carol's."

I asked Sam, "Why do you have keys to Carol's?"

"Last year, Carol had bouts of forgetting her keys to open up, so she gave me an extra set just in case."

"I think I know exactly where the journals are," I said.

I looked down at my phone. It was Alan.

"Alan. Any good news?"

"No. McGinty and the two Traynors had their meeting. They were inside for ten minutes. The old man came out first, then the young man pulling what looked to be a body on a cart. The younger one lifted the body into the trunk of their car and headed back in the direction of their funeral home and crematory."

"Shit!" I said.

"What happened?" Robby asked.

My heart sank. "He thinks the Traynors killed my Uncle Dan," I said.

"Shit!" Sam said.

"Shit!" Robby said.

"Fuck!" Rod said.

Alan cleared his throat. "We don't know about the state of the body, so don't say he was killed until we confirm that to be the case. But please, do not take this into your own hands. We're sending the cavalry in now. Normally we'd have the locals there in three minutes, but we all agree that there is a high likelihood they've been compromised. I'm in the car now and on my way. We should have the first crew there in twenty-five minutes. I'll be there in forty-five."

"You better hurry," I said. "Someone else could be dead in that time."

"Stand down, Will. You'll do no good heading into town. Just stop the car where you are and wait for further instructions."

"I'm sorry. The phone is breaking up. I'll call back when I get a better signal."

I ended the call.

Rod pulled the Tahoe into the back parking lot of the old post office, which was just to the west of Carol's Café and two lots away from Pollitt Funeral Home.

"You sure that's the key?" I asked Sam.

"I'm pretty sure. It's one of these two. I'm almost positive."

I pointed. "Rod, why don't you pull in that back corner under the mulberry tree? If someone happens to take a quick look, you'll be hard to see."

"Roger that," Rod said, making a slight right and pulling into the back corner of the lot.

Robby, Sam, and I got out of the Tahoe and closed the doors. "Keep it running, Uncle Rod," Robby said. "Hopefully no need for any action, but just in case we need to make a break for it or you need to run someone over."

"I hope it's the second option. Been years since I ran someone over," he said without emotion.

"Give me your phone, Rod," I said. I typed numbers into it, hit call, then immediately ended the call. "If we're not back in fifteen minutes, call Alan and tell him where we are. It's the most recent number dialed on your phone."

Chapter 32 – The Parking Lot

It was pitch black. I led the way since I knew the terrain between the post office and Carol's back parking lot. They were connected by a twelve-foot patch of grass from the street that led all the way to the back. I was worried about the small bushes in between, but we managed to find a gap and easily made our way to Carol's back door.

"Okay, Sam. Work your magic," I whispered.

She inserted the key while I lit up the lock with my phone. Sam twisted the key around twice and the lock released. Then she pushed open the door, and we made our way inside, with Robby closing the door behind us.

"Oh. What's that smell?" Robby asked.

"I think it's liver and onions. Must have been the special tonight," I said.

"God. The things white people eat."

"I could say the same about black people. Pickled pigs' feet. Need I say more?"

"That's a totally different category from liver and onions."

"How the hell do you two work with each other?" Sam said in a loud whisper. "Now focus." She moved to the side, letting me through. "Where are the journals?" she asked.

I pointed the phone camera toward the floor and avoided the windows. We scurried through the kitchen and opened the swinging door that led to the seating area. Off to the side was the breakfast bar. I made a right.

Shining the light on the area next to the bar sink, I said, "This is where one of the waitresses used to leave out Life Savers for me to steal. Dad knew about it. So I figure whatever Dad left should be around here."

"Look!" Robby exclaimed. "The plumber's door right under the sink."

I crouched down and opened the plumber's door. I waved the phone to the left and then to the right. There were cleaning wipes, a liter of bleach,

195

and a small pile of rags. I pushed the rags aside and brought the phone to the right side of the bottom of the sink bowl. Something was red and blue, but I couldn't make it out. I grabbed the side and pulled. It was sticky on one side like it was sealed with duct tape.

I pulled the end of the tape and something dropped under the sink bowl. The tape stuck to my hand. "Look," I said, "Cleveland Indians brand duct tape. That's my father all right."

I reached back in, pulled out a plastic bag, and lifted it up for Sam and Robby to see.

"A large Ziplock bag?" Robby asked.

"With two black notebooks inside. Just like the ones your dad used," Sam said.

"Let's get out of here," I said.

ROBBY WENT FIRST OUT the door, then Sam, then me. I pulled the door tightly shut, and Sam came over and relocked it. We started back toward the Tahoe.

"Damn, Will, you have mad puzzle-breaking skills, man. We found that quicker than I thought," Robby said.

"The three of us make a good team," I said.

We navigated our way back through the grass and avoided tripping on the larger bushes.

Sam and I saw it first. The Tahoe's passenger-side window, the one facing us, was black as night. We looked at each other. She mouthed "Rod?"

Suddenly there was a popping sound to our left, like a large balloon exploding, but muffled.

Robby dropped to the ground. "Oh my God! Oh God! My leg!" he screamed. I could barely make him out in the darkness, but his outline was curled into a ball, rocking quickly back and forth.

"Don't move an inch." The voice came from the direction of the pop. I could hear the sound of footsteps. Dress shoes. I took my left arm and pushed Sam behind me.

"That was a warning shot," the voice said. "I need the package."

"What are you talking about, and who the hell are you?" I said. I was hopeful he couldn't see what I was holding.

"My boss says you're smart. I'll have to tell him he was mistaken because I can see the package I want, in your tiny little hands."

"How bad is it, Robby?" I whispered.

"It's bad, man. This dickwad shot a hole in my leg. And what did you do to my uncle?" he screamed.

"I had to shoot your uncle," the voice said. "I quite enjoyed that actually. It's sort of like killing a raccoon." The voice laughed.

"What the hell is wrong with you?" I said.

"Look, I would have shot you by now, but I need that package and I'd rather not get blood all over it. If you pass it over like a good little boy, I'll give you and the bitch a head start before I shoot you in the back."

I turned to look at Sam. I couldn't see her eyes, but I knew she was looking at me, too. I reached out and clasped her hand. We were both shaking.

"I'm going to do a three-count, and then I'm gonna have to shoot you, package or not. One ..."

Before he reached two, a bright fireball of light came from behind the Tahoe, followed by what sounded like a small bomb. I wasn't sure how it happened, but Sam and I were already on the ground, side by side, still holding hands.

There was a squealing sound, which started softly and grew in intensity. Four steps. No, five steps running toward the squeal. Then the sound of metal sliding against blacktop.

"William, my boy. Are you okay?" a different voice called out. Lower, with a Texas accent.

"Jack?"

"It's me, boy," Jack said. He reached down and lifted both Sam and me off the ground, then went to attend to Robby.

"Get me some light over here," Jack ordered.

With trembling hands, I reached into my right front pocket and pulled out the burner phone. After a few seconds of fumbling, I found the light and pointed it at Robby.

There was indeed a quarter-size hole in Robby's leg. Robby just stared at me, gripping his leg.

"He's losing a lot of blood," Jack said. "Sam, get over here."

For the first time, I noticed that Jack was carrying a rifle. He set it down on the ground and crouched to Robby's level. Then Jack ripped off his white button-down shirt, exposing a white undershirt. "Use this, Sam. Just tie it around tight to stop the bleeding. We need to get him to a hospital yesterday." Sam took the shirt. Jack looked into Robby's eyes. "You take this light here and point it at your wound so Sam can tie you up." Robby did as he was told.

"How did you find us, Jack?" Sam asked while she was working on Robby.

Jack didn't answer. Then he stood up. "Do one of you have another phone with a light on it?"

Sam took hers and tossed it to me. I turned on the light and gave it to Jack.

"Come on, son. Let's see what we have over here," Jack said. I followed him.

Jack used the light to show about three feet in front of us. We walked about ten feet, and I could see a pool of liquid. No doubt it was blood. It was starting to stream down the parking lot into tributaries. Jack lifted up the phone to follow the trail of blood. A man was lying on his side reaching down for a leg that wasn't there anymore. What was left of the leg was splattered in a collection of debris to his left.

"I think you got him," I said to Jack.

"You know, that's the first time I've used that SKS since Vietnam. I forgot how much damage it can do," Jack said. He handed me the phone and walked over to a gun four feet from the man. He picked it up and put it in his pocket. I noticed the attached silencer.

"Who's the guy?

"Last name's Jones," Jack said. "One of Traynor's men. He's done a lot of bad to a lot of good people in this town."

I paused, looking at Jones's mangled leg. "Look, Jack, I know you just saved our lives, but I thought you were working with the Traynors."

Jack stood in front of me. "Boy, I served your father for over thirty years, and I continue to serve him after his death. We have a lot to catch up on. Right now, I'm glad you're okay." He gave me a huge bear hug.

"Ah, that hurts," Robby said ten feet away. Jack and I walked back. Sam was continuing to tighten Jack's shirt over Robby's wound.

"The gunshot missed the femoral artery, thank God," Sam said.

"Sam, my car is behind the funeral home. Go get it and bring it over here," Jack said, giving his key to Sam. I gave the phone back to her, and she used the light to find her way through the bushes.

I got on one side of Robby and Jack on the other as we prepared to lift him up. I heard the car behind the funeral home start.

"Jack, I saw you sneaking into Dad's closet last night," I said, and we shifted Robby into place.

Jack looked surprised. "The Traynors asked me to look for some missing journals of your father's. How he kept the journals hidden from the Traynors I'll never know. So last night I went through all the rooms, including the closet, because they can see and hear everything. I actually read a story or two from one of them journals while I was in there. Your father was a good writer. I'm actually supposed to be out at your father's house now searching for them. I just needed it to look like I was on their side until you found your way. And here you are. You did good, kid."

Sam pulled the car to the side of Robby. Jack opened the back door of his Buick. Sam got out to help.

"This is going to hurt a little, but we'll do it fast, get you in there, and Sam will take you to the hospital," Jack said.

"No," Robby screamed. "You can't take me to a hospital in this area. It's filled with white doctors and nurses. I'll never make it out alive."

"Don't worry," I said. "Sam will be with you the entire time." I looked at Sam. She was about to speak, but I said, "Jack and I are right behind you. Get Robby to the hospital. Keep the phone with you at all times. Don't leave him alone."

We lifted Robby into the back of the car, shut the door, and Sam took the car up to the turnaround and brought the Buick back the other direction toward the exit. Jack and I walked over to grab Dad's package, which was on the ground behind where Robby was shot.

Before Sam exited the parking lot, we heard a *thump-thump*.

I looked at Jack. "What was that?"

"She ran over what's left of Jones," Jack said. "Remind me never to mess with that little lady."

Chapter 33 – Boat Storage

I pulled out the burner phone and dialed Alan. I noticed the time had just turned midnight.

He answered after one ring. "What's your status?"

"Robby was shot, and Sam is taking him to the hospital. There is one, possibly two, dead in the parking lot of the old post office, two doors down from the funeral home."

"Dammit, Will. I told you to stand down. For Christ's sake." He started talking to someone else. "We are literally less than ten minutes from your location. Do not move!"

"Jack Miller and I will be in the parking lot of the funeral home when you arrive. I promise."

Alan hung up the phone. I knew I was in over my head, but at this point I didn't care. I started walking to Rod's car.

"Where are you going?" Jack asked.

I didn't answer. I opened up the driver's side door and used my phone light to see inside. Rod's body was there, but the entire passenger's side of the car was covered with blood, brain, and skull. I didn't examine the situation any closer. I grabbed the bag containing the guns and fireworks from the back seat and shut the door.

"Who was that?" Jack asked.

"That was Rod. Robby's uncle. He was trying to help us."

Jack and I both heard them at the same time. Sirens. Coming our way.

I started running back through Carol's parking lot and made it directly behind the funeral home. I heard Jack chase after me.

"Where are you going now?" Jack yelled.

"We have to get out of here now," I said. Another twenty seconds, and I reached the old garage in the back. It was locked and I had no idea where the keys were. Jack finally caught up to me, breathing hard, then bending over. "Do you have the key for this?" I asked, pointing at the lock.

"The funeral home. Janet's office," he said between breaths.

I stood staring at the front of the doors. Two large barn doors protected by a hinge and a Master Lock. The sirens were getting closer, less than a few blocks away. "No time," I said. I took three steps back and ran at the middle of the doors as fast as I could.

I hit the doors and fell to the ground. The pain was immediate. I did more damage to my shoulder than to the doors or the lock.

"Son, get out of the way," Jack said, pushing me aside, still breathing hard.

He stood to the side and raised his SKS, pointing the rifle at the lock, but at an angle. *So he doesn't damage the cars on the inside.* "Cover your ears," he said. One second later, he fired the SKS multiple times and lit up the backyard like it was a night baseball game. When the smoke cleared, the right side of the garage door was gone.

Without a word, we ran into the garage. The 1917 wagon was trapped in the back, but the hearse was facing out. The 1971 lime-green Cadillac Funeral Coach, the same exact one they used in the show *Six Feet Under*. I ran to the driver's side and threw Dad's package and the bag of guns in the back. Jack opened up the passenger door and slid in. I pulled down the sun visor. The keys dropped in my lap and fell between my legs. I grabbed them, threw them into the ignition, and turned forward.

The car squelched and choked but didn't turn over. I tried it again. Same result.

"Come on!" I said, pushing the ignition forward and stepping on the gas simultaneously. The car coughed itself to life. I went to put it in drive but there was no gearshift to the right of my leg. I looked up and it was right in front of me, sticking out about a foot to the right of the steering wheel. After a couple fumbles from reverse to neutral, I found the D and punched the gas pedal.

The left front of the Cadillac cleared the garage nicely, but I hit the right side and smashed it on impact with what remained of the door. I looked left and could see the cruiser lights entering the post office parking lot. I took a hard left turn and came around the other direction, rumbling over a patch of grass, through another parking lot, and into the back of a 7-Eleven. I found the light switch on the lower left side by my knee and pulled it toward me. Only the left beam of the hearse came on.

I passed two dumpsters on the right and took a back driveway that led north, away from the sirens and followed the same road north for three blocks.

"Where do we go now? The hospital?" I asked, half talking to myself and half asking Jack. I wanted to get to Robby and Sam as quickly as possible.

"Turn right at the next stop sign," Jack said. "We need to collect ourselves a bit and figure out the next move." I did as he said. "Make a left here." I did.

It looked like some kind of large storage facility for boats. There was a twenty-five-foot Bayliner on a hitch to our right. "Go straight for a few. Okay, now pull down this narrow row to your right." I turned off the Cadillac's remaining headlight.

There wasn't much more clearing than two feet on either side of the Cadillac. I pulled forward, going about ten miles an hour. We reached a set of doors on the right. "Okay, stop here," Jack said.

"Where are we?"

"This is my boat storage."

"I didn't know you had a boat."

"I don't. I decided to buy the storage first and the boat second," he said, slithering out the door. I did the same on my side. He closed the door and looked at me from over the Cadillac. "That was fifteen years ago. Still no boat. Go figure. Now I use this place when I don't want to go home or have exceeded my time at the funeral home. So I'm here most of the time."

There were two doors on the right side. Jack approached the first, put a code into the keypad, and it opened. He flipped on the light switch. I followed him in and went to close the door behind me.

"No, no" he said. "The front door is manual. You take the hearse around to the front, and I'll let you in."

I walked back out to the car and restarted the Cadillac. Before I moved, I texted Sam and told her we'd be delayed and to send me updates.

I shifted into drive and slowly pulled forward. About twenty feet up, there was an opening. I took it right. Another forty feet up was a larger drive and I turned again. Jack was pulling down on chains as I approached. The door was rising. Jack must have wanted a small yacht because his storage unit was huge. Easily fifteen feet wide and another forty feet deep. I made a right, and Jack directed me in. I pulled the hearse forward about ten feet, and Jack put up both his hands to stop me. I turned off the ignition, and Jack pulled the chains in the opposite direction to close the storage door.

The left side of the facility housed a desk and chair, a small refrigerator, multiple standing lights, and a secondhand couch with an ottoman. "Nice digs," I said. Jack leaned over to start the coffee machine. The burner phone rang.

It was Alan.

"Where the fuck are you?"

"Had to go. Couldn't be avoided. We heard the sirens and left as fast as possible."

"I'm standing in front of the shed behind the funeral home. Someone blew the doors off."

"Yeah," I said. "Did you just call to yell at me?"

"Look, Will, my team doesn't even think you exist right now. We need to sit down right now and talk this over."

"I'm happy to chat with your team now over the phone. Tell them we're in the process of trying not to die at the moment. The dead guy in the parking lot is one of Traynor's men. His name is Jones. The dead guy in the car was Robby's uncle." I was still breathing heavily and couldn't get my heart to slow down. "What's the update on your end?"

"The tech team is trying to follow the money from the insurance companies you gave us. Whoever it is, they're very savvy. The money seems to be in five places at once. But the Columbus guys are good. They'll find something."

"What about the two agents in Pennsylvania? Are they protecting my daughter?"

"I haven't heard back yet. They're supposed to check in shortly."

"I don't feel good about any of this, Alan. Get ahold of them now!"

"You're not in position to give me orders. I understand you're under a bit of stress, but we don't just jump into situations like these without all the details."

"That's great to know. While you're looking for details, my entire family is going to be killed." I paused. "Call me back when you have something good to tell me." I ended the call.

Jack had two cups of coffee in his hands. He gave one to me and sat on the couch, seemingly without a care in the world. I sat on the ottoman in front of him.

"Look, Jack. You've always been like family to me, but right now I don't know who to trust, and it's been a little crazy today. I need to know what you know, and I need it now."

Jack took in a deep breath and then breathed out. "You don't have any cigarettes on you, do you?"

"You quit smoking."

"Feels like a most appropriate time to start back up actually," Jack said, scratching the side of his face. He took a sip of coffee and leaned back. "Give me the short version of what you know about the Traynors, and I'll fill in the gaps best I can."

So I went through the details again. Jack had a feeling my father committed suicide but wasn't sure until I told him. Jack knew he was up to something that night. He confirmed the life settlements scheme and the targeting of minorities. He was unaware of the samples Dad was collecting and, of course, didn't know about Jared or that the poor guy was killed a few hours ago.

"The Traynors control the town through surveillance, but not just in this city. I'm not sure how sophisticated it is, but it's advanced enough that they have pictures of my son, his wife, and his family in places around Dallas, where they live. Last year, I was sent a care package warning me to stay in line or else, and it included a picture of them with red X's over their faces. They did the same with your father, as well as everyone else in SA."

I asked him about Janet and her involvement. My heart sank while listening to him. Apparently, Janet had been seeing the elder Traynor, in the romantic sense, since SA began. As the minority eradication plan started to take root, it was Janet's plants that provided the poison, with Janet herself taking the lead on the poisoning itself.

"Your Uncle Dan and I called her the Grim Reaper, believe it or not," Jack said. "She volunteers at all the nursing homes in the area, especially Blessings."

My thoughts went to Mr. Davies.

Then I told him about Uncle Dan. He didn't know.

We sat for a few minutes. It was all so horrible.

Then I stood and picked up Dad's evidence bag from Jack's desk. I pulled back the tab and removed the contents, taking inventory on the desk. Two black journals, just like all his other ones from the funeral home, and an orange folder. "Okay, Jack. Let's see what Dad got me for Christmas."

Chapter 34 – Deepfake

The first journal looked like the Grail Diary. It was filled with scribbles and notes and inserted pages from magazines and newspapers. I didn't know exactly what I was holding, so I kept everything like it was.

The second journal was dated, neat, and clean, just like my father's other journals. I flipped to the last few pages. The journal covered two years of activity. There were some numbers on the last page. I flipped back to the front. The first date was just before my mom's car accident.

Dad was extremely thorough. He noted SA board meetings and personal conversations in great detail, especially with the Traynors. Most especially Alex Traynor.

I set the second journal on the floor and moved on to the orange folder. Inside the right pocket was a map that showed Pennsylvania to Indiana and Michigan down to Kentucky. Sandusky was highlighted with a star. There were ten circles on the map, which all looked to be about an hour from a major city. There was one outside Detroit. One outside Chicago. One outside Indianapolis. One outside Pittsburgh. They were all connected to Sandusky.

I kept the map out and pulled a document from the left side pocket. It was stapled and had typing on both sides. The first page was some detail on the technology deal Alex Traynor set up with the city of Sandusky. The second page was about a city called Fenton, Michigan, which I assumed was the one on the map an hour from Detroit. The date was from six months ago. It was the same kind of deal Alex struck with Sandusky. After Fenton, there were eight more occurrences. Same details, just a different small city. The last page of the document was another map, this time with Sandusky, Wooster to the south of Cleveland, and Warren to the east all bolded. Sandusky, Wooster, and Warren were about one hour from Cleveland.

Jack was standing over my shoulder watching me without saying anything. I pulled out Dad's scribbled journal and flipped through it again.

"Jack, did Dad take any major trips over the past few months?"

"He was gone a lot more, that's for sure. But it's curious now that you mention it. With very little business coming in, there was no need for any trips."

I set the journal on the desk and approached the hearse. I stuck my head through the open driver's side window to take a look at the mileage gauge.

"This says over forty-two thousand miles. Dad never liked putting unnecessary miles on this thing, and the last I remember this had about twenty-two thousand miles on it. Do you remember him driving it?"

"Sure. At least a few times. Why do you ask?"

"If Dad thought he was being monitored, let's say through the flower van or his everyday car, but really wanted to get away for a while without being monitored, what car would he take?" I paused. "Don't answer that. He must have taken the hearse. It was all locked away in that back garage. The Traynors or whoever probably didn't even know it was in there. Or didn't care. He could pretty easily drive out of that garage and head out the back of the 7-Eleven, just like we just did, without being detected by the cameras. If he was seen out driving with it, he could say he was headed to a car show. I remember him doing that a few times in the past."

"What's your point?"

"The point is that Dad took this hearse to all these cities over the past six months to collect information about whatever the Traynors were doing. And it looks like he did a pretty damn good job of it."

"So is there a conclusion?"

I paused for a second. "I'd like to really go through these documents, but this is telling me that Sandusky was a test run for the Traynors and whatever cult is behind them. Looks like they've been pretty successful here, getting Sandusky set up for surveillance under the 'city of the future' moniker that all these other cities want. So these other locations want in and will most likely fall the way Sandusky fell."

I started to circle the hearse as I was thinking. "Looks like two phases. A test city. A smaller town that can more easily be manipulated, and probably more conservative with less diversity, gets turned. Then they add a few smaller cities around a larger metro area. Once these 'unclean,' as my dad calls it in his notes here, were killed off around the big cities, then they'd move in to tackle the urban areas. And the cake topper is that the whole thing is funded through these life settlement deals, financing the entire Nazi effort."

"Sounds like a science fiction book."

"It does," I said. "It's sick, perverted, and ingenious. The way they are moving so methodically, this is a fifty-year effort to drive everyone who's not straight and white out of the Midwest, either by killing them or making it such a horrible living environment that they'll voluntarily leave. What's the population change in minorities been in Sandusky the past five years?"

"I don't have a clue," Jack said.

I quickly pulled out the burner phone and did some quick Google searches. After a couple minutes, I found a site that compared the last two census numbers from any city in the United States. Five years ago, Caucasians were approximately sixty-five percent of the city's population. The current estimate was seventy-five percent, a huge jump in just four years. Their plan was working well.

I showed Jack. "Like father, like son," he said and slapped his hand on my back. "But what do we do with all this?"

I checked the time. It had been thirty minutes since I last saw Sam and Robby. I double-checked the phone. No word from either of them. I called Sam. I let it ring eight times before hanging up.

I dialed Robby. Same thing. No response. They could be back in emergency and not able to pick up.

I searched for the Firelands Hospital emergency number and dialed it.

"Firelands Hospital. How can I direct your call?" the woman said.

"Emergency, please," I said, and the phone immediately started ringing.

"Emergency room," a woman's voice answered.

"Yes," I said. "I'm trying to find out the status of Robby Thompson please."

I heard some papers shuffling. "We haven't admitted anyone by that name," she said.

"He's African-American. He was shot in the leg, accompanied by a Caucasian woman in her forties named Samantha Pollitt. About a half hour ago."

There was a pause. "I'm sorry, sir. There's been no one here by that description."

"Is there another emergency room in the area they might have gone to?"

"The closest one to us is Port Clinton. Or perhaps Vermilion."

"Okay, thanks," I said, ending the call. "Something's wrong, Jack. They never made it to Firelands."

I STOOD THERE MOTIONLESS for a while.

"Will?" Jack said. He was right in front of me. "Where's Jess?"

I dialed Jess. Three rings. Four rings. Five rings.

"It went to voice mail," I said. I texted her.

Jess, making sure you are getting this. It's Dad from a different phone.

The green text message sat there, waiting to deliver.

Text message not delivered, it said after thirty seconds. I forgot. Sam said she didn't take her phone with her. How could I get ahold of her? I didn't know her friend's number. Or even who the friend was.

I tried Denise's phone. No answer from her either. I tried a text. It didn't go through.

I called Alan.

"Will. I need you to come in."

"Okay, but have you had contact with the two agents protecting my daughter?"

He paused. "I'm sorry, Will. We've been trying to contact them but haven't received a response. We're sending another two agents from the Harrisburg office now."

"Oh God," I said, "Alan, Sam, and Robby were supposed to be at Firelands Hospital. Robby was shot in the leg, and it looked pretty bad. But no one has seen them there. And I've tried to get in touch with Jess, but I can't. Same with my sister."

He paused. "It's going to be okay. The good news is that my team is here, and we can help find out what happened to Sam and Robby. And we'll get to the bottom of Jess's situation as well. I'm sure there's a logical explanation."

Another call was coming in. I looked at the phone. Sandusky number.

"Alan, this might be Sam calling. I'll call you back."

"This is Will," I answered in a hurry.

"Hi, William. You sound a bit panicked. Are you all right?" a voice said. The disappointment from it not being Jess or Sam or Denise was weighing me down like I was under water.

"Who is this?" I asked.

"I thought you were more intuitive than that. At least you were when we were high school chums."

"Alex? Alex Traynor?"

"There we go. I knew you could do it. We've been moving our chess pieces for the past few days without saying a word to each other. I thought now would be a good time to be more social. We have so much to catch up on."

His voice was different since the last time we talked. More measured. His words seemed well thought out. "What's going on, Alex?"

"Yes. What is going on, indeed? You've been a very busy boy over the past few days. It would have been a lot easier if you just took our offer to buy the funeral home and headed back to Cleveland. You could have paid back all the debt and started a fresh life. But, oh well." He mumbled like he was talking to himself and then continued.

"At first, I was disappointed because you didn't look to be catching on to things. It seemed you'd lost the old Billy in you. But you're getting sharper, which means the William I knew is still in there somewhere."

"I have no idea what you're talking about right now." I could feel my heart beating inside my chest. I tried to slow it down. I needed to concentrate. I breathed in and out.

"Remember your junior year. You were concerned that you didn't have the grades to get a scholarship for college. And your dad's business wasn't doing as well as, say, my dad's business? Your high school guidance counselor told you that if you scored a 30 or higher on your ACT, you'd have a good chance at a partial college scholarship. And you really wanted out of Sandusky.

"The test was multiple-choice. Open-ended questions would have been a problem for you. You would have had to actually know the answer. But with multiple-choice, you only had to prove that some were wrong. You were always great at that William. Most people strain themselves looking for the truth in something. It's much easier to identify the lie. You could do that. Apparently, you still can.

"Now, granted, this method does take a bit more time than normal. You finished one minute before noon, with just a few of us left in the gymnasium.

"Three weeks later, the scores came in the mail. You scored a thirty-six. A perfect score. A few weeks after that, the full scholarship offers started to come in."

By my junior year I'd stopped talking to Alex. "How did you know about this? Please tell me what's going on."

I heard him chuckle. "I can only show you a small piece at a time. You'll understand soon enough. But for right now, I'd like you to turn your other phone on. Now," he lowered his voice, "you're going to say you can't do that because it will give away your location. But we already know you're in Jack's dusty old storage unit so, you see, it doesn't really matter. I need you to turn the phone on so I can show you something."

"What if I don't have it?"

"Of course you have it. I can see it in that pile next to the gift your father left for you. Thank you for that, by the way. I couldn't figure out where your father's notes were, but you led me right to them."

I froze for a second. I looked at Jack. Then I started to look around, up toward the storage room ceiling and down to the floor.

"Ah, William, don't bother looking for it now. It will take you quite a while to find it. The new cameras we have are almost undetectable to the naked eye. Technology sure has come a long way since we played Super Mario Brothers together, hasn't it? Good times, those were."

"Okay, Alex," I said. "I'll play along." I went over to the desk and grabbed my iPhone, pressing down on the side to boot it up. The Apple symbol appeared and held on the main screen.

I waited and said nothing while the phone regained connection. I was desperately trying to figure out my next move. Nothing came.

"Remember our sophomore year? We used to hang out playing video games all the time. Of course, I was better than you, but you always dominated Dungeons and Dragons. Anything with strategy. You were so good at strategy. But if it was on a computer, well, that was my specialty. Marketing,

William? I would have thought you'd join the CIA or something. They'd hire you to break puzzles like that movie starring Russell Crowe. What was that? *A Beautiful Mind,* right? Maybe you have a beautiful mind. Okay, I see you're connected now. You're going to receive a text message in a second. When you do, I need you to click on it."

A text message with a link popped up on the phone. "What if I choose not to?"

"Oh, William, it's not anything bad. Yet. And you might want to let Mr. Jack see this as well. He's a costar, after all."

Jack had been standing in front of the couch watching me the entire time. I waved him over to the desk and set my iPhone down. I clicked the link.

An image of a building popped up. I turned the iPhone on its side so Jack and I could see it clearly. The screen showed Uncle Dan's office building, but it wasn't an image, it was a live shot. The current time was showing in the lower left-hand corner. I looked at the watch on my wrist to double-check. It was 12:45 a.m., same as the video on the phone.

"Is it coming in?" Alex asked.

"We're seeing what looks to be a live feed of Dan McGinty's office. It's showing the side entrance."

"Oh, goody." Alex giggled. "I'm going to drop off the call now, but I promise to call you back in just a bit. I think you'll want this phone available for conversations with other people."

He ended the call, and I set the phone down.

"Do you want to fill me in on what's going on?" Jack asked.

"The short version is that Alex can see everything in this room, so he's been monitoring you for quite some time, which means he probably knows you've been working both sides of this. Other than watching this video, he said to keep the burner phone open for a call." I paused, looking around again. "Whatever's coming next, Jack, it's not going to be good."

We both watched the screen. The building was still. A passing car on the street once in a while, but no major activity. Then, two figures approached from the right, heading for the side entrance.

"Oh, shit," I said.

"What?" Jack said.

"That's you and me. You're carrying your rifle. I look like I have a pistol in my hand."

"How is this possible?"

I didn't answer, focused on the screen. The two figures, presumably Jack and I, made it to the side entrance. We both looked around. You could clearly see our faces. The image was grainy, but the likenesses were spot-on. Then it looked like I fiddled with the lock and opened the door, and the two figures went inside.

My burner phone rang. It was Alan.

I answered. "What the fuck, Will? My tech guys just watched a live image of you and the big guy breaking into McGinty & Associates."

"That's not us, Alan. We're being set up. It's a deepfake. They obviously know your tech guys tapped into the network and can see it."

"You expect me to believe that? Whatever your plans are, you better stand down and come out of that building right now. I shouldn't even be telling you this, but my team and the Sandusky police will be there in two minutes. After seeing that mess at the post office, everyone is on shoot-to-kill orders. We found a guy down there with his leg obliterated by a rifle shot, then he was run over by a car."

"Listen to me. Jack and I are not in that building. We're being set up."

"I'm sorry, Will. I know the stress really piled up this week, but the phone you are talking on right now is located inside the McGinty building. For your own good, come out of the building with your hands up."

"Please, Alan, don't go near that building. Something bad is going to happen," I said. Alan ended the call.

Chapter 35 – The Appetizer

As I watched Uncle Dan's building on my phone, I couldn't help thinking of how proud he was of the structure. Originally, it was the Sandusky Glass Company. While there were many updates over the years, the building fell into disrepair in the '80s and was nearly torn down. In fact, the wrecker was already in place to start knocking the building to the ground when Uncle Dan filed an injunction and was able to stop the destruction with just minutes to spare.

It took years of investment, including private donations and revolving loans, all led by Uncle Dan, to bring the building back to life. By the mid-1990s, the building was the talking point for a possible resurrection of the downtown Sandusky area. By 2010, the eight floor structure was the tallest downtown building, as well as a technological marvel.

At the present time, Jack and I were watching the Sandusky police barricade both the southbound and westbound streets heading toward the building. My phone rang. Alan.

I picked up. "Alan, do not go into that building."

"We just picked up a live feed inside the third floor of the building. It looks like you've taken two people hostage. They're bound and tied back-to-back just outside the southwest corner office."

"I'm telling you, I'm sitting inside Jack's boat storage. You have to believe me. Do not go in the building."

"I'm sorry, Will. I really am. But if you don't come out of there in sixty seconds, starting right now, we are coming in after you." He ended the call.

My iPhone screen changed to two images: one of the building and one showing a group of FBI agents in full protective gear. A minute later, six agents ran to the side entrance and six more toward the front entrance. Alan stayed back and was holding a walkie-talkie up to his mouth.

Then Alan signaled something with his hands, and all twelve agents disappeared into the building. Then nothing. Minutes went by.

Without warning, an explosion blew out all the windows on the top floor, while multiple smaller explosions cascaded from floor seven down to the first floor. Ten seconds later, the top floor was engulfed in flames. Jack and I huddled even closer to my phone, continuing to watch the devastation.

The combined FBI task force moved all team members and the cooperating Sandusky Police Department out of the debris area from the McGinty building. Five minutes later, just about the time the fire department was arriving, the first-floor bearing wall collapsed. The second floor became the first floor. Another ten seconds later, nothing could be seen except for a tornado of smoke heading skyward and gray snowflakes floating down from the sky.

JACK AND I STOOD OVER the desk watching Uncle Dan's building burn to the ground. There was no doubt we would be implicated in the bombing and the killing of the agents who entered the building and God knows how many more people.

My burner phone rang. It looked like Alex's number. I clicked to answer. I held the phone to my ear but didn't say anything.

"What's wrong?" Alex said. "Cat got your tongue?"

"Why are you doing this?"

"Oh you think this is bad? That was just the appetizer. Perhaps the soup or salad as well. The main course hasn't even started yet."

"Outside of our families competing in the same business for thirty years, I've done nothing to you personally."

"First of all, you have. But second, you're acting like this is a bad thing," Alex said. "I just gave you a new life. Lord knows how you've screwed up your current one. The feds most likely believe you died in that explosion. You could leave the city now and never come back. Maybe get a new identity and live in peace somewhere, perhaps. A nice spot in Mexico? Brazil is wonderful this time of year. Or you could stick around, show that you're still alive, and be hunted down by your college buddy. I have a feeling they don't take too kindly to someone killing their own. Tsk, tsk."

"It sounds like you are having a good time with all this, and whatever I did to you I'm sorry, but where's my family?"

"Careful, William. You're on my timetable now. But, okay, I can speed things along a bit. It's the least I can do since you've been such a capable character in my little play this week." Alex cleared his throat. "Be a dear and put me on speaker. I'm going to give you some directions."

I put the phone on speaker and set it on the desk.

"Hi, Jackson. It's Alex. How's your day been?" Alex said from the speakerphone.

"I'm looking forward to seeing you soon so I can shove my SKS up your ass."

"Well, I can't believe *you're* mad at *me*. After all, you were the one who's been playing turncoat."

I put my hands out to Jack and motioned for him to stop talking.

"That's a good boy, William. You were always so smart," Alex said. "Now, I need you to gather up all the papers and folders that your father left for you and put it in that tiny trash can to the right of the desk. And please do it quickly."

I took the journal, the orange folder and the map and placed them into the trash bin.

"Good. Now, Jackson, go grab that lighter fluid you have in the corner and squeeze some into the trash bin." Jack looked at me, and I nodded. Jack did as Alex asked.

"Good boys. William, now you light it with that lighter by the wall." I just stood there. Then I looked at Jack.

"I'd rather not do that."

"I was wondering when you'd say no to me. In high school, you were always so obstinate. Always had to have your way. Never listened to anyone. Actually, now that I think about it, you were very similar to your father in that respect. Oh, we tried all kinds of things to keep him in line, but nothing seemed to work. I thought we had him for good when I killed your mother."

He paused.

"You already knew that, didn't you?" he said. "I thought that would be a dramatic reveal. You're spoiling all my fun."

I felt completely helpless. It's the same feeling I had when I couldn't stop day-trading. The same feeling I had right after the divorce. But worse. I had an idea what was coming next and didn't know if I should delay the inevitable or get right to it and figure it out.

I'd studied conflict resolution for years and used it actively in our marketing strategy sessions and when selling a project. In a situation such as this, the best course of action was usually to keep the decision-maker talking as long as possible. Keep asking questions in the hope of gaining some insight that can be used as leverage. The more the decision-maker talks, the more they feel in control. But actually the opposite happens because they're giving up valuable information and are generally unaware of it. At the same time, the person asking the questions has to show no emotion. Any kind of an emotional reaction could set off a person in an unpredictable direction.

"What if I burn these documents? Then what?"

"Then I will tell you where your loved ones are."

"And who would that be exactly?"

"Oh, goody. You finally asked." Alex giggled. "I bet if I tell you how many I have, you can figure out who it is."

Everything in me wanted to shout at Alex, but I kept as calm as possible. "How many people do you have?"

"A-one, a-two, a-three, and a-four licks to the center of a Tootsie Pop."

My heart sank. How did he get Jess here so fast?

"Will you tell me where they are, Alex?"

"Tsk, tsk, William. This is very upsetting. I told you I would tell you after you set the documents ablaze."

I turned to Jack. "Where's your lighter?"

"There's a grill lighter over on the shelf in the corner."

I walked over, grabbed the lighter, and stood over the trash bin. I clicked the grip on the lighter, and the flame appeared.

"Don't do it," Jack whispered, now standing next to me.

"It's okay," I said to Jack.

"Okay, Alex, I'm going to light this as you've instructed, and then in return you're going to tell me where they are. Correct?"

"That's exactly what will happen. If you would, please move the bin out to the space in the middle so I can get a good look."

"How can I know you'll keep your word and won't hurt them?"

There was three seconds of silence. "You can't, William."

I moved the can out to the middle of the room and touched the tip of the orange folder, which was sitting just above the top of the trash bin. With the help of the lighter fluid, the documents were consumed by flame immediately. There was nothing spared.

"Can you confirm that I did what you asked?"

"You have. Thank you. And I will stick to my side of the bargain." There was some rustling over the phone. Switches? Buttons? I couldn't tell for sure.

"Sorry about that, William. Sometimes technology takes a human touch, which always wastes precious time. I sent you a link to your other phone. If you would click on it, please."

I clicked on the link and a video appeared with two camera views. The left view was of four bodies, mummy-like, wrapped head to toe with some kind of tape or wrapping gauze. Only the eyes were visible. It was clear who they were. Robby was on the far left. There was a blood stain that looked to be seeping through the gauze on his left leg. Next was Denise, whose eyes were darting back and forth. Clearly having some kind of panic attack. The other two were looking at each other. I could see the tears. Sam and Jess.

The right view was from behind the bodies, set further back. On the left was Jess, her hair almost touching the ground as she lay flat on what looked like a casket lift. Robby was all the way to the right. In front of them about ten or so feet were four large openings, just large enough to fit a human being. All bursting with flame. I could see the heat distortion on the screen. The crematory.

Chapter 36 – Chocolate Triumph

"What a dilemma?" Alex asked himself. "Which one should go first?"

It took a few seconds for my brain to start working, especially after seeing the real-life horror movie in front of me. Then the answers started coming. Different scenarios. Different possibilities. But I had to choose quickly.

"Wow, Alex," I said. "You are certainly a genius with technology. That almost looks real."

"Well, thank you, but I assure you this is real."

"If I'm not mistaken, I just watched myself and Jack here sneak into the McGinty building. Now that looked as real as," I paused, "as real as what I'm looking at now. Bravo!"

There was a pause. He wasn't anticipating this. The problem was there were a few scenarios where he could prove it was real without me being present. And for any of my plans to work, I needed to get to him.

"Let me run this by you," I said. "I'm assuming I'm the cake topper to your plan, so let me come to you. If I'm a good boy and do what you say, maybe you'll let one of them go, and I can take their place."

Alex laughed. "Cunning, William. I see exactly what you are doing."

"Of course you do. I'm not hiding anything right now. You're holding all the cards. Jack and I are all alone. You have the entire city on your side. And the FBI probably has us on shoot-to-kill orders, so making it to you is going to be a challenge in and of itself. But if we can, it would make for better theater, wouldn't it?"

Growing up, Alex and I would hang out at the mall and watch people fighting or kissing and all kinds of other human interactions. After each situation, Alex would grade what he saw as either good theater or bad theater or "could-have-been-better theater." I was betting he still used the terminology, and I could get on his good side, if just for a few seconds.

Alex's tone changed. The jovial nature was gone. This was serious now.

"Every thirty minutes, I'll be pushing one in. Starting right," he paused, "now."

I looked at the time on the burner phone. It was 1:02 a.m.

"Remember where we used to hide from our parental units, drinking and smoking, sophomore year?" he asked.

It took a second to register. "I remember."

"I'll call off the dogs so they won't shoot you. Take that entrance and follow it all the way. If you don't dillydally, you'll be here in time. It works out better this way anyway."

"Got it. What about, Jack?" I asked.

"Jackson can come. But if he tries anything at all, tell him I'd be happy to throw poor little Jess to my guys for a full physical examination before she's toasted. And they aren't gentle. She'll be praying for death."

The call ended.

"DO YOU HAVE A PLAN?" Jack asked.

"I don't know yet," I said, winking at him. "Come here. Let's see if there's anything left." I put my hand on Jack's shoulder and moved him over to the burning trash bin. We stood over it, with the desk to our left. "Let's get a bit closer," I said, pushing Jack's shoulder down until we were both crouching.

"Son, there's nothing left, it's just a bunch of ..." Jack paused for a second, finally realizing what I was doing. From the conversation with Alex about moving the trash can, I knew that his camera couldn't see under the desk, which meant the camera was located behind where Jack currently was. If my calculations were right, he couldn't see the lower half of my body.

Jack and I were now crouched facing each other, with the smoking trash bin to his right and my left. Jack continued talking, "I'm not sure we can do anything with this." He continued to inspect and groan and inspect some more while I reached between my legs, grabbed Dad's remaining journal from the floor, and slid it in the back of my pants. Then I stood up.

"We don't have much time, Jack. Let's go," I said, heading for the hearse. Jack quickly pulled down the chains that opened the storage door while I started the hearse. When the door was high enough, Jack got in and I took off, leaving the door open as I made a sharp right turn down the alley.

"Nice move," Jack said as I weaved in and out of the small storage paths and bolted out the exit.

"I don't know what kind of evidence the remaining journal has," I said. "But I saw something in there we're going to need." I made a left and headed onto Route 6. "Without stopping, we're fifteen minutes from where we need to be, but we need to make a stop first."

"For what?"

"I'll tell you in a second," I said, quickly making a left turn across the road, pulling into a 24/7 Convenient Food Mart. "I'll be right back."

I ran inside and stopped just beyond the door. A dark-skinned man stood up quickly as if I'd startled him. "Where's your frozen treat section?" I asked. He pointed toward the back corner. I took a quick right down an alley of corn chips and Hostess snacks and made a left at the Gatorade. There was one window dedicated to frozen snacks. It was foggy, so I suspected someone had recently opened it.

I grabbed the bar and pulled it open, scanning from top to bottom. *Thank God,* I said to myself, grabbing two PopC popsicle packages from the bottom shelf. I quickly reviewed both packages, then threw one back and picked up another one. Perfect!

I jogged back to the counter to pay, throwing down the last of what I had in my wallet. "Keep the change," I said. As I walked out the door, I noticed a small television in the corner near the ceiling. It was showing my picture with the subtitle *Fugitive At Large.* I looked back and saw the clerk pick up the phone, and I bolted out the door.

I jumped in the hearse, tossed the frozen treats in Jack's lap, put it in gear, and made a U-turn, heading back west on Route 6.

Jack said, "I have no idea what you're doing right now."

"No time." I blew through a stop sign. "Those are six-pack treats. Each one opens at the top, like a box. I need you to take the six from the fudge blister flavor and put it in the chocolate triumph package. Got it?"

"Yes, sir. I'm taking the six here from fudge blister and putting them in the other package, chocolate triumph."

"That's correct," I said. Jack began making the switch. "Will, why is he doing this to you and your family?"

I ignored his question. Taking Old Route 6 another two miles I turned and made a left onto Bardshar Road, passing Dorn Park on my right.

"How long?"

"Three minutes," I said, pulling my iPhone from my pocket. I looked at the time: 1:18 a.m. I tossed both the burner phone and the iPhone to Jack. "Pull up my recent calls on the burner phone. Find the one phone number ending in seventeen. Then call that number on the iPhone and put it on speaker."

Jack fumbled a bit but found the number, dialed it into the iPhone and quickly found the speaker button. While the phone rang, I took a left on Heywood, then another immediate left down a dirt road with no sign.

The call picked up. "Shit, Will. I was hoping you were dead. Well, you will be in about five minutes," Alan said.

"I'm sorry all that happened. It wasn't us, but you won't believe me right now anyway. I'm keeping this phone on. You can track our location and bring us in. We'll come in voluntarily," I said. "End the call, Jack."

Jack did. I stopped at a dead end about a hundred yards from where we turned. "Okay, this is it," I said.

I grabbed the burner phone from Jack and pulled Dad's journal from the back of my pants. I flipped to the last page where I saw the phone number. I opened up the messages app, typed my message, and sent it to the phone number. I made sure to leave the iPhone in the car as I exited. It was on. I opened the back-seat door, took one of Robby's guns, and stuck the two fireworks in my front pocket.

"Jack, take the chocolate triumph container and leave the other. Make sure you have the right one."

Jack double-checked the ice-cold container and stepped out of the hearse. Popsicles in one hand, an SKS rifle in the other.

Chapter 37 – The Collage

Remembering this place thirty years ago, there was only dirt. Now weeds had taken over the once-barren field like a cancer, butting up to newer apartment complexes to the west and to the south.

I started circling the ground looking for the marker.

"What are we looking for?" Jack asked.

"It looks like a manhole cover. It should be a couple inches off the ground." As soon as I finished my sentence, Jack fell.

"I think I found it," Jack said, his head barely popping above the weeds.

"Perfect," I said. The area around the steel cover was clear of weeds, which meant it was still in use. There were two open holes in the middle of the cover. I reached down and pulled up with everything I had, almost dislocating my right shoulder. Without a word, Jack came over and put his hand through one of the open holes. I grabbed the other with two hands.

"On three," Jack said. "One, two, three." We lifted and pulled the cover just off center by a few inches. But it was enough. I knelt down low to the ground and pushed the cover aside, revealing the entire opening.

"There should be a ladder dug into the side. It goes down about ten feet. I'll meet you down there," I said. I brought my left leg into the hole, followed by the right, made sure my footing was sound, and descended down the shaft.

There wasn't the faintest sign of light. I pulled the burner phone out of my pocket. I moved to the side so Jack would have some room and when he hit the ground, I checked the time. It was 1:22 a.m. We had ten minutes. I turned on the phone flashlight.

There were cigarette butts everywhere. Some were white but most were brown and half disintegrated. I wondered which ones were mine. Alex and I spent half of one summer down in this hole.

I double-checked to make sure Jack had the popsicles and scanned for the passageway. I found it quickly, pointing due south toward the crematory. As I scanned the walls with the phone light, Jack and I noticed all the papers stuck to the walls, from about our knees up to the ceiling, as far as the light could stretch.

Each paper was the standard eight and a half by eleven. Something you'd take out of an inkjet printer. But there wasn't any text on the sheets. They were all color photos. Of me.

The first one I came to was my high school graduation photo. There were other pictures of me as a teenager. Some were in school. Some were me on my bike. Then there was a collage of ten or so of me making out with my high school sweetheart, Robin Kaufman. Further down was Robin and me with our shirts off in the back of my dad's old car.

Jack and I just looked at each other. I took the phone light to show the other side of the wall. More and more pictures of me from every stage of my life. As we moved down the hall, there were pictures of me at college. One from the first day I moved into my college dorm. One of me during my summer internship at the radio station. More of me working at Pollitt Funeral Home.

When we reached the pictures of Sam, things seemed to intensify. The number of pictures doubled, and they were pasted on top of each other. I found one from our first date. One of us at a Cleveland Indians game. Another with both of us naked in our first apartment.

I felt violated. The only thing that was holding back the regurgitation was the near-death situation of every person I loved. I said nothing to Jack. I started walking faster. I broke into a slow jog. Then I was running, until I finally reached the door, with Jack following a few feet behind. I shined the light on the door handle and briefly noticed a picture of me at Gamblers Anonymous, taken Wednesday.

I looked at the phone time. It was 1:28 a.m. We still had four minutes. I pushed down on the door handle and heard a click, then pushed forward to open the door.

Chapter 38 – The Truth

It took four strong pushes to open the door enough for Jack and me to slide through. The more the door opened, the more the incoming light blinded my eyes. I heard a voice.

"Leave the gun in the hall. The same goes for you, Jackson. Leave that big bad rifle in the hallway, and then you can come out. I have a gun pointed at your daughter, William, just in case you do something unplanned," Alex said. "Then you can come out of my little tribute room with your hands up."

I kept the door open with my right shoulder and raised my hands over my head. Jack followed behind me with one of his hands holding the PopC popsicle six-pack. We were both squinting from the brightness, and I couldn't immediately locate where the four were.

"What's that in your hand, Jackson? Tell me quickly or I'll shoot it off," boomed Alex's voice from somewhere.

"It's popsicles. For Robby, Denise, Sam, and Jess. For the dehydration," I said loudly.

Alex laughed. "Popsicles? Don't you think good old H2O would work better, William?"

"We didn't have time. It's the only thing I could grab," I said.

"Okay, okay. If it makes you feel better. Totally unnecessary though. Jackson, be a dear and hand those cold treats to William, would you?"

I breathed a sigh of relief.

Jack lowered his left arm a bit and placed the six-pack into my right hand. As soon as I grasped them, I heard a loud pop, and Jack dropped to the ground.

I looked down, and Jack was holding his leg.

"Jesus Christ," Jack said. "This is exactly what happened in 'Nam. You motherfucker, Traynor. When I get up I'm going to cut your goddamned head off and stick it up your deranged ass."

"You do know how to talk dirty, don't you?" Alex said, laughing.

I looked at Jack's leg. The amount of blood startled me. He must have seen the look in my eyes. "It's okay, son," he said.

My eyes were beginning to focus. There were two levels. Jack and I were on the upper one. It almost looked like a running track of some sort, with stairs on two sides to get down to the main level. Alex was on my right, down a level and about thirty feet away. Behind him was a massive array of screens and technology. If you didn't know better, you'd think it was the IT department for Apple or Facebook.

Around the turn, another thirty feet away or so, were the four mummified bodies. Their eyes were looking my direction. Another five feet away from them were four open retorts. Even from this distance, I could feel the heat. Traynor's old crematory, the one that I knew about, was in a different location on the east side. This one must have been added in the last twenty years. I've never seen one large enough to cremate up to four bodies at one time.

The side opposite was cluttered with cardboard containers, most likely for body disposal into the crematory, which led to a door on the far side. There were large boxes, for humans, and smaller ones, like the size of a gift box. For pets? *Against the law to mix humans and animals.* Not that it mattered now.

"Before you come down the stairs to me," Alex said, "I want you to close that door tight. I wouldn't want anyone else getting in. Or Jackson getting any crazy ideas."

I pushed the door shut tight and knelt down in front of Jack. "How bad?" I asked.

"I've had worse," he whispered. "Go do what you came here to do."

The popsicles were cold in my hand, but they were thawing a bit in the humidity of the room. Not bad though. The PopC advertisements were true—the six-pack box did act like a portable cooler.

"Can I bring these down with me?" I asked Alex, raising up both my hands, one holding the six-pack.

"Come on down nice and slow."

I kept my hands raised and balanced down the steps one at a time. As I reached the bottom, I took a good look at the four, especially Robby. His left leg was sopping in blood. I could no longer tell if he was conscious or not. Then I looked at Sam. Ever since I've known Sam, her eyes were always those of hope, even in the worst of times. At this moment, I only saw despair. I used it as motivation.

Alex was close-by, pointing a small gun in my direction, watching my every move as I set the popsicles on a double stack of cardboard boxes.

"Now keep your hands as high as possible," he said, walking in my direction. As he approached, he strolled behind me, lightly grazing a gun along my shoulders. Then he thoroughly patted me down, starting at my hips and moving down to my ankles. "Good boy, William," he whispered and grazed my back with his shoulder as he passed, picked up the popsicles, and headed back to his monitor station.

"Do you want to explain the 'This Is Your Life' walk down memory lane I just saw?" I asked.

"I've so wanted to show you that over the years," Alex said. "Yes, I must confess that I had a boy crush on you so many years ago. When that," he paused, "faded, I decided to keep a living journal of your escapades. I must say, I'm awfully disappointed with you."

"Why's that?"

"You don't know? Why, William, that may be the saddest thing I've ever heard. Well, you were given everything on a silver platter. In high school, you were so smart. You could have been anything. But you went to an average college, barely challenging yourself, and came out with a marketing degree," he said with distaste. "Then you seemed to make up for it a bit by finding an intelligent woman to marry. You had a daughter. I thought you were making a comeback. But then you showed your true self."

Alex started walking toward the four, waving his gun back and forth. "I'm wondering if you really told her everything," he said, now standing over Sam. "I bet your daughter certainly doesn't know."

Alex walked over, lifted up a portion of Jess's hair, rubbing it together. Then he smelled it.

"Jessica," he said, looking down at her. "Did you know your daddy had to take a second mortgage on your house because he gambled away a half million in the stock market? I bet you didn't. And did you know that when he went to the bank to take out the second mortgage, he forged your mother's signature? Did you also know that your father had thirty-six—that's three-six—credit cards at one time? My favorite was the Farmer's Bank of Iowa card. Was that your favorite, William? Or maybe it was the one from HongLeong Bank where your name was Jack Loh?" he said, looking back at me.

He walked around Jess and stood to the right side of Sam. "And dear, sweet Samantha," he said looking down at her. He placed his hand on her forehead. "I'm sure you think you know everything by now, even after all of William's lies and cover-ups. Well, I bet you didn't know he has yet to pay for your sweet daughter's tuition. It was due in full more than thirty days ago. Tsk, tsk. Both a lying husband and a deadbeat dad. Not a worthy combination."

While I didn't want Sam and Jess to know those things, it didn't matter at the moment. The only thing I cared about was making sure we all made it out alive.

Alex was out of range of the monitors, but I could see them clearly. There was activity around town. People were moving. Little by little there were more and more cars. Maybe the message was received. I needed to create more time.

"Let me ask you, Alex," I said. "You were always such a gentle, kind person. Remember that time we found the toad by the side of the road. You picked it up, and we walked it about a mile and took it to the marsh. So why all this killing of minorities? How could you hurt innocent people?"

Alex dropped the smile from his face. "Why, we just hit fast-forward on the inevitable. These bodies were going to die regardless. We gave them a little push in the right direction and made some money in the process to fund something greater. All this technology is expensive. You should know that. The end does justify the means. Some people don't believe that you know, but it's most definitely true."

"But African-Americans, Latinos, Asian-Americans, even homosexuals. Why? Because they're different in some way?"

"That is my father's vision. And his band of merry white men. To rid the world of the unclean. I have a higher calling, a different calling, but as they say, two birds with one stone. They get their perfect world, and I get to have my tech toys. It's actually quite brilliant." His eyes lit up. "These far right-wingers will do practically anything to turn the clock back on America. Back to the good old days. They believe anyone not white and straight is to blame for their lot in life. Always looking for someone to blame," Alex said, lowering his voice.

"In high school, we had black friends, we had gay friends. How can you turn your back on them, murder them?"

"They were never my friends. I only had one friend ..."

"Are you talking about me, Alex? Yes, we were great friends. We were best friends. And then something happened after sophomore year. What happened?" I asked. This was where I was hoping to go. "When junior year came around, you were a different person. You were angry at the world. You stopped talking to me."

Alex was pacing, moving around Robby, then Denise, then Sam, seemingly talking to himself. Whatever he was saying, I couldn't hear it.

"Tell me, Alex!" I said. I looked again at Robby. He was definitely unconscious.

Alex started walking back over to the monitors with his head down. "I was unclean," he said. "My father fixed me."

"How did he fix you?"

He frowned. "He tied me up to a chair and ran electric current through my body."

"What did he say was wrong with you? How were you unclean?"

"Because I liked boys," he paused. "Because I liked you. My father helped me get rid of my sickness."

"But if you liked me so much, why are you doing this to my family? First my mother, and now everyone I love in my life. If I've done something wrong, that's fine. Take it out on me. But not them. They've done nothing."

"That's not true," Alex said, suddenly angered. "They are a part of you, William. It's partially their fault that you've failed so much. They've been way too lenient on you, just watching you make mistake after mistake. That's the opposite of love. Now you need to be punished, and they need to be punished with you. There is no other way."

"Why do I need to be punished?"

Alex hesitated, then lifted his head to meet my eyes. "I'm unclean because of you. If you don't exist," he paused, "I can be free. That's the only way."

Chapter 39 – A Disappointment

The entrance at the back opened. A short, round woman came through and held the door, followed by an older man with a cane. It took me a second to see that it was John Traynor with Janet. My Janet. The same Janet that practically raised me while my parents were busy running the funeral home. Just when I thought it couldn't get any worse.

"Alex," the old man said. His voice was strong and carried. "What the hell is going on?"

"What are you doing here, Father? You should be napping. And where's your wheelchair?"

Janet helped the old man reach a section of boxes. They were about twenty feet to my left, and Alex was twenty to my right. I stepped back.

"Janet just ended her volunteer shift, and I wanted to stay up for her. And how could we not notice that half the city of Sandusky is headed this way, led by the feds. And now I see this?"

"Our best men are guarding the entrances," Alex said. "Nothing will happen. No one will find their way down here. This is all part of the plan."

"You are assuming again, Alex. We live in a world of fact. And the facts are that whatever this little pet project you have here is distracting you from the truth."

Part of me wanted to let this play out to see what would happen, but Robby was in real trouble. The blood was beginning to pool, and he was losing time. I peeked back up at Jack. No movement. So I decided to take a risk.

I blurted out, "Alex, we could have been together if it wasn't for him."

Alex turned his head. "What did you say?"

"I liked you in high school as well. We could have been together." I pointed at Alex's father. "But he took it all away from us."

"I don't believe you," Alex said. "I don't believe you."

"Is that what this is?" the old man asked. "Some kind of sick homo fantasy."

"I knew it," Janet said. "He was never cured of his sickness," she whispered to the old man, but both Alex and I could hear her.

"Are you having sex with this unclean piece of trash?" the old man asked. "Have you lost your way again, Alex?"

Alex's eyes started to tear up. His arms hung straight to the ground. I could see his hands starting to tremble. I had seen him like this a few times in high school, but every time I asked him about it, he snapped out of it and changed the subject.

"Listen, Alex," I said. "You are not unclean. There is nothing wrong with you. Being gay is not wrong. Your father is trying to take all that away from us."

"Oh my God," Janet said. "I should have known Abe's boy was like this when he started hanging around with the black boy. How did we even think for a second that he could be useful? We could have taken care of this problem days ago."

I was almost caught off guard listening to this from the wonderful woman I grew up knowing. I quickly cut her off.

I turned toward Alex. "Your father shocked you and made you hurt all over because he has the problem. He's the one that's unclean. He's been lying to you your entire life."

There was something coming from Janet. Almost like a huffing and puffing. I turned to look at her. Her face was the color of an apple. Then she said, "Are you going to do something about him, Alex, or do I need to teach you both a lesson? This is such a disappointment. Alex...you are such a disappointment."

She was already falling backward before I even heard the popping sound. The bullet pierced the center of Janet's forehead, traveled through her skull, and lodged itself into the back wall of the room. There was blood everywhere. I looked back at Alex. The gun was shaking in his hand. He was staring at the ground.

The old man screamed out. "Oh my God. My love. My love." He dropped down beside her and went to caress her face, but there was little left. He held her hand tight in both of his and began to wail. Then he wiped his eyes with his forearm and tried to compose himself. He picked up his cane off the floor and pushed himself upright.

I looked back at Alex. The gun was now pointed toward the floor. He'd stopped trembling, but had begun mumbling something over and over. I finally made it out. "You are not my mother. You are not my mother. You are not my mother." His chanting was the only sound in the room.

John Traynor stomped his foot. "Boy, you have sinned. You must repent and do penance. Now." The old man pointed to the back door. "Now leave the gun, go to the special room, and wait for me. I'll clean up this mess you started, and I'll be back for you shortly."

I hadn't foreseen this. If Alex left John Traynor to *clean up this mess*, the old man would waste no time and kill us all. I had no leverage with the older Traynor. At the moment, I could only think of one thing.

"Alex, please let me take the popsicles down to them. They're severely dehydrated. You're still in control, and I have no weapon. Please let me do this."

I wasn't sure if he heard me. Alex just stood staring at Janet's dead body. "Father, Janet served her purpose. She wasn't needed anymore. Can't you see that?" Alex was talking to the old man but wasn't. He seemed to be talking through him.

Then he snapped out of whatever trance he was in. He turned his head my way. "Oh, the popsicles, did you say, William? As a child, my favorite thing in the world to eat was popsicles. Couldn't get enough of them."

With his right hand still clutching the gun, he took the top off the six-pack and seemed to read the cover. "Chocolate triumph," he said. "What a wonderful flavor and a fitting name for the best of all flavors. I can't believe they haven't melted entirely. It's a bit toasty down here, isn't it?"

I didn't answer.

He tore the multicolor wrapper from one of the popsicles, grabbed the stick, and brought the popsicle close to his lips. It had already started melting down his hand.

He turned his left hand to the side and took a bite of the popsicle like he was eating ribs. "Such an odd version of chocolate," he said. He took another bite, trying to figure out the taste. His face quickly turned red. His hands convulsed. He dropped the popsicle and the gun to the ground and tried to grab his throat with his hands. Then he collapsed, heaving in short breaths.

I ran over to him. He was on his stomach convulsing. I felt for his two back pockets. Nothing inside. I reached around to feel his front pockets and found what I was looking for—a small black container. I unzipped it to expose the epinephrine injector that looked like a large Magic Marker. I removed the black tip, exposing the needle, and jammed it into the back of Alex's neck.

I pulled back the injector from his neck and breathed a sigh of relief. I looked over at Sam. I could see her eyes. She tilted her head. The warning was too late.

I was knocked forward. Something hit the back of my head. Almost in slow motion I could see the shards of splintered wood falling past me to the ground. It had to be the old man's cane. I fell on top of Alex. I tried to move my arms. Nothing happened. I couldn't feel my legs.

I was beginning to lose consciousness. I looked up to find Sam but couldn't see her. I couldn't hang on. *Please hold on.*

The last thing going through my mind, before I blacked out, was the sound of a rifle shot.

Chapter 40 – Win One for the Gipper

I woke up in what looked to be a hospital room but different. The same in that I was in a hospital bed and had machines to my left and right that played the part. A tube stuck out of the top of my right hand and led to a bag above my shoulder.

Different in that there was no outside-looking window, no pictures, and nothing around that projected comfort. There was a small glass square at the top of the door and I could see what looked to be a large man standing outside. Keeping guard, I supposed. Somewhere off in the distance I could hear an instrumental version of Bowie's "Let's Dance."

My mind was still on Jess and Sam. Robby and Denise. I pushed the covers back and sat up straight. Then I brought my legs over slowly so they were hanging off the bed. My head started pounding. I tried to grab on to something to keep balance but only managed to grab a blanket with my right hand and a pillow with my left.

The door opened, and I started to panic. There was pressure on my chest. A hand pushed me back into the bed. Someone picked my legs up and set them back in bed.

I looked up. It was Sam.

"Will, can you hear me?" Sam asked. She sat down on the bed, to my left.

"Yes," I said.

"Do no try to get out of this bed again. Everything's all right. I promise. You're at Firelands Hospital."

I breathed in.

"What's the last thing you remember?" she asked.

"Someone hit me."

"Good. Someone did hit you."

I breathed out. "Where's Jess?"

"Jess is fine. She's down the hall. I called Zoe, and she's with her. They have Denise two floors up. She's pretty shaken but will be fine. They put her on a morphine drip. Robby is in intensive care. He lost a lot of blood and has some kind of infection in his leg, but the doctor said he's going to be fine in a week or so. They pumped all kinds of blood into him. He requested a black doctor," she said, smiling.

"And Jack?"

Sam chuckled. "Jack's been trying to bust himself out of here for the past two hours. They patched up his leg. He's fine and wants to go, but he killed someone tonight and they're being fussy about it. He's on the other side of the building, and his wife is with him."

"His wife?"

"I know, right? She's actually a really sweet person. They're very affectionate with one another. Go figure."

I breathed in and out again. "Did you say two hours? How long have I been out?"

She looked at her watch. "It's almost seven a.m., so you've been unconscious for what, four, five hours? Doctor said you have a concussion. And technically, I think you're under arrest, or you're going to be until they figure this mess out. None of us are allowed to leave the hospital until Alan gives us the all clear. He was here a couple hours ago and filled me in on what I missed."

I looked up at Sam. "Are you okay? Did he ... hurt you?"

"You mean Alex? No. His guys roughed me up a little, and I can't say I was that happy to be naked in front of so many guys while they wrapped me in Ace bandages, but yes, I'm fine. And before you ask, the same with Jess and Denise. Robby got the worst of it, with his leg and all. Alex's crew has no love for black people, I can tell you that. He looks like Apollo Creed after *Rocky II*."

Thank God. I leaned back into the pillow and closed my eyes. I listened to my breathing, the silence around the room, and I began to cry. I covered my eyes with my right hand, trying to hold the tears back. Sam put my left hand in both of hers. "It's okay, Will. It's over. Just let it go."

And I did. At least as much as I could for now. I wiped the tears from my eyes and looked at Sam. She pulled two crumpled tissues from her pocket and handed them to me. "Here," she said.

"Are these used?" I asked.

"Does it matter?"

"Not really." I wiped the tears away, blew my nose, and wadded the tissues in my right hand. I looked back at Sam. "Do you have to go, or can you fill me in on what happened?"

"I can stay as long as you want," she said. "There's a lot I don't know, especially after I talked to Alan. As soon as the old man cracked your skull, Jack literally blew his head off from the other side of the room."

"Jack?"

"You couldn't see it because you and Alex and his dad were talking, but Jack was sliding across the floor, as slow as I've ever seen him move. He opened the door you came out of and reached for his gun. Then he just lay there, waiting for the right moment. When you ran at Alex, the old man ran after you. By the way, he can walk just fine. He made it over to you in record time. He slammed down his cane on you and as soon as he stood upright over you to do it again, his head just disappeared. I looked over, and Jack was leaning against the wall holding his rifle."

"God, I love that man."

"And then all hell broke loose. There must have been twenty feds that busted through the door you came through. Actually knocked Jack to the ground, which was a good thing or they probably would have shot him. They cuffed Jack, and a few agents attended to us. The old man's body fell on top of you, so they pulled him off, then pulled you off of Alex. I really hope they took a picture of that." Sam smiled.

"You are a sick, twisted woman."

"I know." She smiled. "Anyway, they rushed Alex out on a stretcher, from where the old man came in. He's in recovery, and they're guarding him. By the way, how did you know about the peanut allergy? The popsicle thing was ingenious, but as it was happening, I thought you'd lost your marbles."

"Sophomore year, Alex and I went for ice cream. We both ordered sundaes. After we started eating, he began to suffocate. His throat was closing. I called 911, but he had an epinephrine injector in his pocket. I just didn't know it at the time. He almost died. Apparently, the person making the sundaes used a spoon that was in the peanuts. That's the day I found out he was severely allergic to them. But the man loves popsicles. At least he used to. We devoured them together when we were friends. I was betting both the allergy and his love for popsicles were still in play."

"Why didn't he know better? I saw him look at the box."

"I had Jack switch the contents before we entered the room. He thought he was eating chocolate triumph but ended up eating fudge blister, which has a shit ton of peanuts in it. In preparing for the PopC pitch, I learned every ingredient in every single kind of PopC popsicle." I started to chuckle, but it hurt all over. "Sorry. Please continue."

"When we made it outside, you would have thought it was World War III. There were bodies everywhere. I guess hundreds of residents responded to your little text message and took out Alex's guys. Alan said they found over twenty dead guards around the crematory. A couple of the guys from the Sandusky Alliance were injured really bad in the fighting. Barry White didn't make it at all. Last I heard more than fifty residents of Sandusky lost their lives tonight." She paused. "But hey, your girlfriend fought back as well. She's here actually. She took a shot to the shoulder but she's going to make it. What Alan didn't know is how you sounded the alarm."

"Dad's notebook. The one we found at Carol's. It took me a second, but I figured it out when I saw the bible passage."

"What bible passage?"

"The last page of the notebook said Joel 2:1, and then there was a phone number. Four-one-nine area code. Sandusky. I can't believe I almost forgot, but my dad would sometimes leave me little notes before a sporting event or a math competition, and he would include that bible verse. It says, 'Sound the alarm in Jerusalem. Raise the battle cry on my holy mountain. Let everyone tremble in fear because the day of the Lord is upon us.'"

I wiped a tear from my eye. "He used that as a little motivation piece when I was growing up. He wanted me to know that as long as I had the Lord everyone else better watch out. Well, when I saw the bible verse and the phone number, I put two and two together. I didn't know how many people the message went out to, I was just hoping it was the cavalry."

"What did the message say?" she asked.

"Something like, 'This is Abe Pollitt's son, Will. Now is the time. I'm on my way to take Alex down tonight and need your help. We're at the crematory. Today is the last day Sandusky is held hostage by the Traynors.' I was trying to do a 'win one for the Gipper' speech." I chuckled. "It's a lot harder to do in a text message."

Sam looked away for a moment. "Will, I know this isn't the best time, but what Alex said about the tuition bill?" She turned back toward me.

I shook my head. "Alex wasn't lying. I have the invoice. I should say invoices. But I didn't have the money to cover the tuition bill."

"Why didn't you just tell me? We could have figured it out."

"I've messed up so badly over the past few years. I was trying to take care of it myself." I started to tear up again. "I thought I had it covered, but I need help. I don't think I can do this on my own."

"We can discuss it later." She paused. "Well, you did good, kid." She leaned over and kissed my forehead. "I'm going to make the rounds, but I'll come right back."

She opened the door and, just before she closed it, looked back and smiled.

Epilogue

The city had never seen anything like it. Half the downtown streets were closed for what was called a "death parade" in the newspaper. Thousands of residents came out to line the streets in honor of a woman they never knew. There were floats and costumes and clowns dressed in black, riding Segways. The casket was painted black and white in some kind of tribute to Beetlejuice, and the pallbearers were all made out as movie characters. There were Freddy and Mike Myers, that guy from *Krampus,* and a woman dressed up like Sandra Bullock in *Bird Box.* She kept bumping into the crowd, but Jack kept pushing her back to the center and kept her safe.

To date, it is our most profitable funeral ever. Probably the most profitable funeral in history. In all, we took in over sixty thousand for the three-day event, including all the special orders and coordinating with city officials for the parade.

The call came in last week. Another blog subscriber. The woman who passed on was a nut for horror movies, and the family apparently had some money to burn.

It's been this way for the past couple of months. Well, ever since Robby started publishing Dad's crazy stories. I fought him at first, but he told me to trust him, and I did. Every Tuesday and Thursday, Robby publishes one of Abe's stories of the past, with gentle editing by both Robby and Jess. He called the blog *On Death's Door*, and it links directly to the Pollitt Funeral Home site.

Jess needed an internship as part of her major, so she's been a paid intern at the funeral home since she finished spring semester. The first month of Robby publishing was met with little fanfare. Whatever attention we did receive was negative. I mean, how many funeral homes publish weird stories about death? Plus, most Sandusky folk thought it worsened the reputation of the battered city. But once Jess got involved, everything changed.

Not only does the blog come up in many death-related search engine inquiries, but she recruited a couple of YouTube influencers who were super interested in the topic. Of course, they did videos on it. Then someone created a subreddit, and there's a small yet growing following of over fifty thousand people who dissect every one of Dad's stories. A short time after, someone from the *New York Times* did a story on the crazy funeral home from Death City, a.k.a. Sandusky, who started a "Death Blog." It was a rather negative article, but it ended up driving so much traffic the site crashed seven times that day. We now have over one hundred thousand subscribers to the blog and add a couple thousand every few days. Last week, a book publisher called and wondered if we'd like to put Dad's stories in a book. I have a feeling Dad wouldn't mind at all.

While this would all be great in and of itself, it blew the doors off the business. As Robby predicted, Pollitt Funeral Home is now in the event business. We just happen to cater to extremely weird events around death and dying. One guy requested to drop his mother's ashes from a hot air balloon over Lake Erie. We made that happen. Another woman wanted to hold a Barenaked Ladies concert as part of her son's wake. BNL was his favorite band. The band was so intrigued with the offer that they cut their rate to almost nothing and flew down from Toronto in economy seats. I love Canadians.

A few weeks ago, I sold my share of PT Marketing to Robby, using the proceeds to pay for Jess's next two years of tuition at Penn State. Of course, Robby agreed to keep me on as a special consultant, especially since he wanted me to continue working with him on the PopC account. PT Marketing signed a two-year agreement with PopC to create a network of media sites, which happened to increase the notoriety of PT Marketing substantially. Robby is bringing in new business like crazy and has rehired a few employees we'd had to get rid of just a year earlier.

With Denise's permission, I moved into Dad's house on the water full-time. I'm still getting used to it, but Jess is staying with me over the summer, so that makes it easier. Dad would have loved it. We drive to work together every morning, and she learned to fall in love with coffee just like her dad.

We've become regulars at Coasters coffee shop. I have the loyalty card to prove it.

A combination of our new marketing plan with the simultaneous closing of Traynor Funeral Home meant we could barely keep up with all the business. We were actually cash positive, and I was able to start paying down my massive debt. But funeral home staffing was now a concern. Denise has been studying under Sam to become our second embalmer. Jess suggested hiring Zoe on to run our marketing. We think she'll ultimately do a fantastic job, but she's still a bit too emotional about everything that happened three months back. A few weeks after old man Traynor took me out with his cane, we found out that Zoe's dad was on the list to be poisoned and killed. She, of course, thinks I'm her savior, but for now, I'm not going to spoil her with the truth.

Sandusky, the city, has had a rough go of it. The events hit national news the next morning after the old man lost his head. The explosion killing a dozen FBI agents was the first to unravel, followed quickly by the Traynor's plot to remove anyone who was not straight and white from the earth. The life settlement plan, the poisonings, the Big Brother technology scam—all of it was covered by every major media outlet in the world.

Up to this point, Alan and the FBI have uncovered more than eighty million dollars in illegal life settlement deals. The bureau thinks that's not even a quarter of what's really out there. In the wake of the Sandusky disaster, Alan became an FBI celebrity and moved off WMD full-time to investigate the Sandusky aftermath. I think he's considering an offer for a DC post. His investigation into Traynor's plans also continues to uncover new players, although he doesn't think John Traynor was the main architect. Alan's team just identified funding to Traynor from a group of white nationalists, one of whom has ties to the White House.

The papers are giving me, Sam and Robby some much-deserved love about our detective skills. But whenever possible, I deflect it to my father. The FBI would have very little to go on without his notebook of times, places, and transactions. And thanks to Sam, we had enough of the tissue samples left over to link the poisonings, the deaths, and the insurance transactions together.

As of now, Alex Traynor is keeping his mouth shut, spending all of his time in provisional detention awaiting trial. I don't know the final numbers, but they have him on multiple counts of murder, extortion, and laundering. His trial date isn't for another three months, but they'll be pushing hard for the death penalty, especially with the killing of twelve federal agents on his hands. Word on the street is that he's going to plead insanity, and judging by the little thirty-year wall of fame he built for me, he could win the case.

But most Sandusky residents just want to go back to their normal lives, at least as much as possible. Almost all the technology installed around the city is in the process of being dismantled, with the parts being split up between local high schools and colleges to their computer programming and engineering courses, as well as to up-and-coming YouTubers and podcasters.

The Sandusky Alliance decided to disband. Although the city elders still believed in the core cause, they also believed a radical leader could come in and take it over again, like John and Alex Traynor did. Plus, the remaining SA board members, minus Uncle Dan, my dad, and Barry White, will be serving time once their court dates hit next month. I'm told deals have been worked out, and each one will be serving six months in minimum-security prison plus a hefty cash penalty. Even Uncle Dan's coroner nephew got a deal.

For right now, SA is not needed. The business owners and leaders in Sandusky are all working together to create a new Sandusky we can all be proud of.

And that includes me. I'm a Sandusky resident again. I'm proud to help lead Sandusky back to something better than the living hell this community has seen for the past few years. Robby decided to buy a place here as well, sharing time between both Cleveland and Sandusky. He's on a mission to, in his words, "bring the brothers back to Sandusky." Xena actually gave him a great deal on the condominium above Tony's, and he moved in a few weeks ago. They celebrated their one-month dating anniversary last month. I knew he liked her.

When Uncle Dan's funeral took place, most people still didn't know which side he was on. The evidence isn't conclusive either way. I like to think he was working with my father to free the city, and I'll continue to search for the *truth*. Regardless, his good name has taken more than one roll in the mud. Denise and I have been taking donations to claim the property of

the former McGinty building, currently a pile of rubble, as a park. We nearly have enough funds, and once we do, McGinty Park will be born. Robby
had the idea of showcasing the diversity of Sandusky in different locations
around the park, and Sam and I agreed that even though most of Robby's
ideas are terrible, this one actually has merit.

I MISSED MY FIRST GA meeting in nine months the Wednesday after
"the incident," but I've made every one since then. Roger and I continue to
be friends and support each other. Our little GA group has become one of
the largest in the state now. I'm somewhat of a cult hero in the community,
so gamblers from all over Northern Ohio tend to visit Sandusky on Wednesdays.

It's fifteen minutes from the GA meeting to Sam's condominium. I pull
in her driveway with the old Econoline and exit the van.

Sam is at the door. She's wearing a black skirt, not too short, not too long,
and a white blouse showing just enough cleavage.

She approaches, tilting her head. "Where are you taking me?"

"I've been asking you out on a date for almost three months now, and
you finally agreed. I've got something truly special in mind, and you'll have
to wait," I say, kissing her on the cheek. "You look fantastic."

"Slow down, Mario," she says, smiling. "You look nice too."

I walk over to the passenger door and open it for her, helping her into the
raised cab.

The drive takes us past the crematory, beyond Traynor Funeral Home,
and through the downtown area. Although things are getting more normal
every day, I don't think I'll ever know normal again. I'm not sure if that's a
good or bad thing. Yet.

"I have some good news," I say.

"Go on."

"The foundation was approved today for Jared's son. Whenever he de-
cides to go to mortuary school, he won't have to pay a cent for it."

"That's amazing. Did you tell Jared's family yet?"

"Absolutely not. It was your idea. I thought you should tell them the next time you're in Cleveland. I'd be happy to take you."

I make the right turn onto Perkins Avenue and then turn left at the second light. The parking lot is on the right. We can see the shiny red and black sign from the entrance, and I park just below the sign.

"I thought they closed at nine p.m. on Wednesdays?" Sam asks.

"Not sure you heard, but I'm a pretty big deal in this city."

The warm August air hits me like a blanket as I open the van door. We meet at the back of the van. I hold out my hand. She places hers in it.

Emily, the night manager, is there waiting at the side door, twisting a series of locks. She opens the door.

"Hello, Mr. Pollitt. Hello, Ms. Pollitt," Emily says.

"Thanks, Emily. We really appreciate it," I say.

"For you two? Anything." She escorts us to a table in the back. "I took the liberty of making these myself, Ms. Pollitt. Yours has extra Horsey Sauce, as requested."

She winks at me and excuses herself.

Sam sits. I sit across from her. We unwrap the sandwiches, look each other in the eyes, and touch the sandwiches together.

"To Abe," she says.

"Agreed," I say. "To Abraham Pollitt. The man who saved Sandusky."

"How did you know? Beef 'n Cheddar. This is going to be hard to top," Sam says.

I take a bite and set the sandwich down. There is a mixture of cheese and red sauce smeared at the corner of her mouth.

Right now, I'm not thinking about what's coming later tonight. Or what happens tomorrow or the next day. Or even next year. There are no distractions. No fleeting thoughts. There are no plans to trade a stock or make a bet. No plans for any upcoming presentations.

I look at Sam. At this moment, and maybe for the first time in the last few years, I'm just happy to be present.

Continue the Journey

Thank you so much for reading *The Will to Die*. If you'd like to continue the journey, go to TheWilltoDie.com, sign up for Joe Pulizzi's newsletter (delivered two times per month), and get a bonus chapter from Abe's diary absolutely free. Joe includes book and series updates in every newsletter. You can easily unsubscribe anytime if you don't like it.

For any additional information about *The Will to Die* or the Will Pollitt Series, go to TheWilltoDie.com. For more about Joe Pulizzi's other books or hiring Joe to speak at your next event, go to JoePulizzi.com.

If you enjoyed the book and would like to do more, Joe would love a review on Amazon or Goodreads (and tell your friends about it).

Thanks again. Now go out and be epic!

Acknowledgements

I've written nonfiction my entire career. *The Will to Die* is my first novel. The only reason it exists is because I wanted the love of my life and best friend, Pam, to read one of my books (my other five published books are business marketing books, which she doesn't care for). Thankfully, she thoroughly enjoyed this book.

Thanks to Wendy Wood and Sarah Mitchell for making the final version sing. Thanks to my initial editors Antionette DeJohn and Chris Rhatigan, as well as my early review team of Pam Pulizzi, Laura Kozak, Marc Maxhimer, Ann Handley, Robert Rose and the Riley/Kozak & Friends Book Club. Thanks to Kyle Tait and Elephant Audiobooks for an amazing audio production of the book. To Joseph Kalinowski for the cover design and Michelle Martello, David Gengler and Penny Sansevieri for the promotional help. Also thanks to my RANDOM newsletter subscribers who have been so encouraging along this journey.

To my parents, Tony and Terry Pulizzi, who have always been so supportive, even when they didn't have a clue what I was doing with my career. Also to Joshua and Adam, my two wonderful sons, who cheered me along every step of this novel's creation. And to my Coolio framily, a truly amazing group of people who always manage to keep it real. *#NFTG*

Special thanks to Jim McDermott, the entire Content Marketing Institute team and the board of The Orange Effect Foundation.

Finally, to my grandfather, F. Leo Groff, who was born in Cleveland and became an entrepreneur in Sandusky, Ohio. He was a truly great man.

Phil 4:13

AVAILABLE BY JOE PULIZZI

The Will to Die (fiction)
Killing Marketing (nonfiction)
Content Inc. (nonfiction)
Epic Content Marketing (nonfiction)
Managing Content Marketing (nonfiction)
Get Content Get Customers (nonfiction)